I0609511

CAPTURING HER

THE MURPHY BROTHERS
BOOK TWO

DANICA FLYNN

CAPTURING Her

Book Two

The Murphy Brothers

DANICA FLYNN

CAPTURING HER

ebook ISBN: 978-1-957494-17-3
Print ISBN: 978-1-957494-18-0
Alternate Paperback: 978-1-957494-20-3

Cover Photography: HayDmitriy/DepositPhotos
Cover Design: Emily's World Of Design
Editor: Charlie Knight

For all my LGBTQA+ people fighting to be yourselves.

PLAYLIST

"Pictures of You" By The Cure
"Fireflies" By Owl City
"Ode To My Family" By The Cranberries
"Boy Bi" By Mad Tsai
"Somewhere Only We Know" By Keane
"Like Summer" By Kyan
"Phoenix (feat. Fleet Foxes & Anais Mitchell)" By Big Red
Machine, Anais Mitchell, & Fleet Foxes
"the lakes - original version" By Taylor Swift
"Happiness is Not a Place" By The Wind and The Wave
"1957" By Milo Greene
"Girls Like Girls" By Hayley Kiyoko
"Homesick" By Noah Kahan
"Breaking up My Bones" By Vinyl Theatre
"Pink Pony Club" By Chappell Roan
"Sweater Weather" By The Neighborhood
"Strawberry Wine" By Lemondrop
"Entropy" By Beach Bunny
"could this be love?" By Silverdeer

CHAPTER ONE

LACHLAN

JUNE

*T*his was either the smartest thing I'd ever done or the stupidest.

As I stood in the center of my apartment surrounded by moving boxes, I was gonna go with the latter. Who in their right mind upended their life and moved back home to their gossipy small town? Me. That's who. Hence, not being in my right mind.

What the fuck was I doing?

"You ready, bro?" Killian asked.

I shrugged.

I felt a meaty hand on my shoulder. I turned and found my other brother, Finn, giving me a concerned look. "You don't have to do this if you don't want to."

Yes, I did.

I could continue to commute to Drakesville, but now

that I owned my photography studio back home, it was much easier to move there rather than keep driving back and forth. I wouldn't admit to my brothers that opening the studio was an impulsive move. Or that I was moving home with my tail between my legs in an attempt to escape my ex-boyfriend. At least Mom was happy her baby was coming home.

My phone buzzed in my pocket, and I inwardly groaned.

I already knew who it was and what the message would entail. Another hollow promise that he wouldn't do it again.

I slid my phone out of my pocket and wished I hadn't.

> HENRY: Come on, babe. I promise it won't happen again.

I rolled my eyes.

That's what he said last time. And the time before that. And that time, I discovered him in *my* bed with another man. I probably would have believed his lies that time had Killian not been with me. It didn't help that my hothead brother calmly waited for the other man to leave and then sucker-punched Henry. He was such a meathead that he screamed at Henry to stay the fuck away from me.

Did that stop Henry from trying to get me back? Or from me giving in and getting back together with him? Of course not. Did I admit that to my brothers? Absolutely the fuck not. Especially not Killian.

I tried to move on, but Henry had this way of spinning me back into his web. He sabotaged my new relationships by pleading with them about wanting to win me back. They usually fell for it, like I did, because Henry was just that charismatic.

It was why I needed to get the fuck out of Philly for good.

I shoved my phone back into my pocket, and when I glanced up, I caught a disappointed look from Mindy. My best friend's bubblegum pink lips were pursed while she directed my brothers out the door. Then she spun on her stiletto heels and rounded on me.

Mindy was like Elle Woods personified. She was decked out head-to-toe in pink with tanned skin and perfectly sleek blonde hair. She was beauty and fierceness all rolled into one. I'd be attracted to her more if we hadn't been there already and realized we were better off as friends. Plus, we weren't sexually compatible. At all.

"Block him," she ordered. "Be done and over with that asshole."

"Min, stay out of it."

She arched an eyebrow at me. "You drive me up a frigging wall. You're lucky I love you so much that I'm following you to your boring ass hometown."

A grin tugged at my lips. There was that Philly attitude I loved.

She looked all sweet and innocent, but she'd cut a bitch if she had to. Her words, not mine. Also, why she was my assistant. I took great photos, but she was the one enforcing my contracts and telling clients where to shove it. All in a sugary-sweet tone that made them agree. It was her superpower.

The argument stopped short at the thunderous steps of my brothers returning. For once, I was grateful to the big lugs.

"What's next?" Finn asked.

Mindy looked around the nearly empty apartment. Last

3

weekend, we took most of my clothes to my new place. Today was about roping my brothers in to help with all the furniture. My other brothers Ronan and Brian had already taken the moving truck with my big furniture back to Drakesville and were putting things together. I needed Ronan's muscles to help with that the most.

"We still gotta clean the apartment," Mindy explained.

Finn nodded at Killian. "You owe Lachs. You're here with Mindy."

Killian opened his mouth, but I shot him an annoyed look. "You owe me for helping move Siobhan into your house. And then again, on Christmas Eve, when you had us help you decorate your house for the holidays to cheer her up. I'm cashing in."

"Fine, but then we're even. Mindy's a tough boss."

Mindy grinned. "Too bad you're not single, Kill. Then I could really show you."

"Hey, I am," Finn told her with a flirtatious smile.

Geez. Finn and Mindy had been flirting hard all day. I had to keep reminding Mindy that my brothers were off-limits. I wasn't losing my best friend over something stupid one of those meatheads might do. Especially Finn.

Mindy laughed. "I don't think you could handle me."

"Oh, I think I can," he teased with a wicked grin in his eye.

I shot him a warning look.

I also had to remind my brother, who changed partners weekly, that Mindy was off-limits. She might play it fast and loose, but I've dried her tears enough times to know she caught feelings fast. And Finn wasn't good at catching on to that.

"Can you two quit it?" I asked. "Let's get this done today."

"Relax, shrimp," Finn teased. "Lead the way."

All my brothers were towering men over six feet tall, while I somehow got Mom's short stature. Five-foot-ten was a shrimp to these assholes, and they had called me that pretty much my whole life. Sometimes, I really hated being the baby of the family.

I headed out of the apartment down to my car with Finn hot on my heels. I somewhat felt bad that Killian was stuck with Mindy ordering him around like a drill sergeant, but he still owed me.

I got into the driver's seat of my car and started the engine, but I felt Finn's gaze on me. "What?"

"You gonna explain why we're moving you now when your lease isn't up for another couple of months?"

"What are you talking about?"

How did he know when my lease was up?

"You told us that a couple of weekends ago. When the band crashed on your floor after a gig in the city."

Shit. I remembered now. That night Finn wouldn't get off my back about when I was moving home, so I finally told him my lease wasn't up yet. Which wasn't exactly a lie. But that hadn't quite been my plan.

At Christmas, I told everyone I was moving back home. I started packing up my life here in the city, ready for a new start far away from my ex-boyfriend. But then he came crawling back on his knees, begging me for another shot. Stupid me believed him again and renewed my lease. I tried to make the commute work, but the only person it worked for was Henry. That was how he cheated again so easily and in my own damn apartment just because he could.

"You got back with that fucking asshole, didn't you?" Finn accused. "That's why you renewed your lease again."

"It's none of your business," I snapped.

I flicked on my blinker and gunned it out of the city.

"That's why I asked in private, not when those knuckle-heads have something to say about it. You know how they stick their noses into everything."

He was full of shit. He also liked to stick his nose in other people's relationships. My brothers were these in-your-face tough guys, but also the biggest gossips I'd ever met. And I went to art school, so I knew all about drama and gossip.

"It's complicated," I explained.

"Little bro, he sucks and not in a good way."

I almost laughed at his attempt at a joke. "Stay out of it. It's my life."

"And that dickhead broke your heart, and you just let him. It's time to move on."

That was the last thing I needed right now. I had to get away from Henry and work on my business. That was why I decided to finally move. Living in town would get me immersed back into the community, grounding me to my roots. I wasn't ready for a new relationship. My wounds were still too fresh.

"I'm focusing on my business," I explained.

"Hmm."

I needed to distract him and fast. "Is the band doing another summer festival tour?"

Finn perked up at talking about his band, Celtic Kiss. He was a music teacher at the high school in our hometown, but playing the fiddle in his Celtic band was his passion. The turn in conversation distracted him so much, he filled me in on the band drama all the way back to Drakesville.

Driving into town, I felt a sense of calm come over me, like the universe was telling me this was the right call. Like I didn't blow up my whole life by moving my business to this small town. There was something magical about Drakesville, Pennsylvania. As much as I was a city boy, pulling my car into a spot in front of my studio made me feel like I was home.

"You sure you're ready for life back here?" Finn asked.

I nodded and cut the engine. "This is something I have to do."

"Alright. But don't say I didn't warn you when you moving home is all anyone whispers about. Now that Killian and Siobhan are officially together, they need something else to gossip about."

He wasn't wrong about that. This town did like to gossip, but my brothers' merciless teasing all my life had given me a thick skin. Plus, I was from here. This was my town. I could handle a little hometown razzing.

Finn got out of my car and glanced up at the second-floor unit above my studio storefront. "Why this place?"

I groaned. The apartment above the studio wasn't my first choice. After not being happy with my options and not wanting to live with Finn or crash in Brian's guest room, the tiny apartment would do.

"Not a lot of options," I explained.

"Dude, I have room."

The walls were too thin for my perpetually single musician brother. I needed quiet and my own space.

"I shared a room with you before—I'm good."

Finn shrugged, and his attention went to the coffee shop next door. More particularly at the doors that met in the middle of the two storefronts. "Which door's yours?"

But my gaze wasn't on them. It fell on the pretty brunette in the Drakesville Drip apron chatting with a customer sitting at one of the outdoor tables. She tossed her hair back, and I felt like I swallowed my tongue when she walked over to an empty table and bent over to clear it off.

That was the ass that set off every horny boy's fantasy when I was in high school, including mine. Willow freaking Rivers. The pretty yet kind cheerleader who was one of the few who stood up for me when the jocks called me a slur after I came out as bisexual. Some said you never quite got over your high school crush, and that was the truth for me.

"LACHLAN!" Finn screeched at me.

Willow's head jerked at the sound of my name, and I felt heat boil on my face at the prospect of getting caught staring. Willow was sweet and didn't deserve my ogling. Christ, I couldn't even form complete sentences around her, reverting to that shy kid again.

Finn pushed me. "Now that's who you need to get under and help you get over your ex."

I turned around abruptly and glared at him. "Stop it." I pointed at the door closest to my shop. "It's this one. We have a lot of work to do."

I keyed into the door, and we trudged up the steps. The apartment wasn't big, but it was perfect for me. The front door to my actual apartment was unlocked, and we walked inside to find Brian and Ronan in my bedroom putting together my bed.

"How's it coming along?" I asked.

"Almost there," Ronan explained while he tightened a screw on the headboard, locking it in place.

"What else needs to be done?" Brian asked.

"You two focus on putting my furniture together. Finn and I will bring in the rest of the boxes," I explained.

They nodded, and then Finn and I were back down at my car, breaking a sweat to bring all my stuff into my new home.

"Why are we doing this on a Friday?" he asked after we carried the last box in from my car.

"Because I have a wedding tomorrow."

"You got a date?" he asked. "Ask Willow!"

"Not a bad idea, kid," Brian agreed.

"It's for work. I'm not asking her out."

"Why not?" Ronan asked. "She's pretty."

"Christ! Of course she's pretty. She's so fucking pretty it makes me tongue-tied!"

The three of them shared a look, and I rubbed my hands down my face. "I need some air."

"Lachs..." Brian began.

"Drop it!" I seethed and then stormed off down the stairs before I lost my cool.

Was the universe trying to tell me my brothers were going to butt into my love life more now that I moved back? Was this a mistake?

I pulled out my phone and texted Mindy.

ME: HELP ME!

MINDY: Why?

ME: They keep encouraging me to ask someone out.

MINDY: Who? The pretty barista you always drool over?

Did everyone notice how I made a fool out of myself around her? Killian was right. I had zero game, and it showed.

9

MINDY: She's so hot. You SHOULD ask her out.

ME: Min. Not helping.

MINDY: You know what they say...

ME: NOT HELPING.

I groaned and shoved my phone into my pocket. What had I gotten myself into?

CHAPTER TWO

WILLOW

Okay, Willow, time to pull up your big girl panties and talk to him. You're going to be neighbors in more than one way, and he looks stressed out. Make your move!

I peered out the window of my coffee shop, spying on Lachlan Murphy standing outside the door to his apartment. He had a scowl on his face as he scrolled through his phone.

Bingo.

Now was my time to shine in the guise of being a friendly neighbor, and then I could pounce on him. Or finally find out whether the man was interested in me or not. If I cornered him, he couldn't stammer and run away like he normally did.

The shop wasn't that busy, and Siobhan had it handled. God, I wished I had her full-time, but she made more money at the pub. I maneuvered toward the drip coffee pots and poured a small cup of black coffee.

I eyed the espresso machine. Should I bring coffee for his brothers? I reached back into my brain, trying to recite all their orders. Lachlan was easy with a black coffee, but his brothers all had distinct orders. Finn liked cold brew, Brian was the Americano, Killian liked his lattes, and Ronan... Shoot, I forgot.

"What's wrong?" Siobhan asked.

"What's Ronan's coffee order?" I asked.

She squinted at me. "Why?"

I put a lid on the coffee for Lachlan. "Lachlan looks stressed, so I was going to be neighborly and bring him a coffee."

Her smile made her eyes sparkle. "That's really nice of you, Will."

"Mmmhmm."

"Why do you want the boys' order too? Ro likes a cappuccino."

"Just being nice," I explained.

She rubbed her pregnant belly. "Hmm. Is that what they call it these days?"

I laughed. "Look, not everyone gets to fall madly in love with their baby daddy."

Her grin got bigger. "I love that our story's unique."

"Then help me figure out if his brother likes me or not."

That wasn't fair to Siobhan. She had already asked Killian about his youngest brother for me, and what she came back with confused me. Killian told her Lachlan had 'no game' but was also still nursing a broken heart. I tried to be mindful of that, but I still shamelessly flirted with him on the rare occasion he popped into the shop. Now that it looked like he was officially moving to town, I had ample opportunity.

"I think you have the right idea," Siobhan admitted.

"Lachs is quiet. He's not like his brothers. He might need someone to lay down their cards."

I held up the coffee. "So, give it to him?"

She nodded enthusiastically. "Go get 'im, tiger. And ask him out. He needs a push."

She didn't have to tell me twice. I sprinted out of the shop as fast as I could while carrying a to-go cup of hot coffee.

Lachlan hadn't moved from his spot. He was still leaning against the door that led to the apartment above his studio. Where he was very obviously moving into.

"Hi, neighbor," I greeted.

His head jerked up at my voice, and his eyes got wide as he took me in. "Um...Willow...uh, hi."

Okay...not exactly excited to see me.

I took him in. His dark brown hair was tousled, not because he spent a long time on it but rather from running his fingers through it too much. Unlike his brothers, he didn't tower over everyone, and given that I was five foot nothing, I didn't look for a giant when I dated someone.

I held out the coffee toward him. "It looked like your brothers were stressing you out and, well...I make excellent coffee."

Not gonna mention it was a new roast I was testing out, and I wasn't sure what customers thought yet. My first foray into the much-desired dark roasts.

He took the coffee from me but dipped his head down, not looking me in the eye. "Um...thanks."

"I guess we're gonna be sharing two walls now."

"Huh?"

I pointed to the apartment above the coffee shop. "I live there too. Guess we both like to take our work home."

"Right."

Okay...

I shrugged off the nerves. "So...anyway, I was wondering—"

Lachlan launched away from the door, and I darted out of the way while I watched the door slam open, and his brother Finn bounded out of it.

Finn was a big guy who reminded me of a ginger version of Jack Black, but maybe that was because he was a charismatic, larger-than-life musician. His size and fiery red hair made him stand out in the crowd, but I wasn't interested in the fiddle player. Who was being a major cock block right now.

Lachlan rubbed his shoulder. "Ow. What the fuck?"

Finn ignored his brother's complaint. "Where do you want your camera equipment?"

The blood drained from Lachlan's face, and he sprinted up the steps, leaving Finn and me standing there confused.

And...the moment was lost. Yet again.

Every time I tried to talk to this man, someone either interrupted us or he ran away. Maybe this was the universe's way of telling me I was chasing a lost cause. If it was anyone but Lachlan, I'd move on. But you never quite got over your first crush.

Finn shrugged at me and yanked the door open again. I cringed at the sound of thunderous footsteps charging up the stairs. I hung my head and trudged back toward the shop.

Siobhan gave me a hopeful smile, but I shook my head slowly.

"I'll be in the office," I told her.

She gave me a sympathetic look but had known me well enough by now not to press it.

Siobhan's shift was almost over, and then Kelly and

Matteo would take over. That gave me time to forget about Lachlan and focus on my business.

I took off my apron and slung it on the back of my chair before slumping down and opening my work laptop. I kept it down here so I wasn't tempted to work upstairs. I had been joking with Lachlan about bringing my work home with me. Since I lived up top, I had to practice boundaries with myself.

My struggles with my shop didn't lie in my finances. I had made calculated moves, opening first as a coffee truck to gauge interest. Then, when the old coffee shop closed, I jumped at the vacant storefront for rent. After careful research and learning to roast coffee myself, I leased a second storefront two years ago with a staff of roasters I trusted with my life. Last year, I bought a grill and started offering breakfast sandwiches and bagels after years of customers asking for it. I never made any of these decisions without carefully weighing the options and running the numbers on ROI.

My problem at the shop was arguably much bigger: a lack of baristas.

I fully intended to pull up the three resumes I needed to investigate, but then I ended up paying bills and doing inventory. The job of a business owner was never quite done.

Siobhan walked into the office and slid off her apron. "You wanna talk about it?"

"Nah."

"What happened?"

I shook my head. "Same thing. He literally ran away."

She frowned. "I can talk to Killian again."

"Nah. I think he was busy, anyway."

"Sorry, Will. But with Lachlan moving back, maybe you'll get a chance."

I wasn't convinced. We had been circling each other for months, and I was starting to give up hope. Maybe he kept running away because he couldn't stand me.

"Don't work too hard, okay? You need a break," Siobhan told me.

I rubbed my temples. "I know. That's why Kacey broke up with me."

"I'm sorry, but maybe she had a point. You work twenty-four seven."

My ex-girlfriend wasn't wrong. I worked a lot, but this business was my baby, and sacrifices had to be made. We broke up last year, but her words still stung. Mostly because she was right; I didn't make time for her. I basically didn't even have friends anymore because the shop was my whole life.

"I'm taking off tomorrow," I told Siobhan.

She frowned. "For a wedding that you don't want to go to."

Damn. For someone who only worked with me a couple of days a week, Siobhan sure knew way too much about me. We were friends, but maybe I hadn't paid attention to how much she noticed.

It's not that I didn't want to go to my cousin Aspen's wedding. I just didn't want to deal with my family's questions. Especially when I showed up alone. Again. That was when they'd sink their teeth into me, peppering me with questions about when I'll settle down and have kids. Despite the fact I've told them repeatedly I was never having kids.

Siobhan put her hands on her hips. "You know I'm right."

"Will you get out of here?" I teased.

Siobhan grinned. "Killian's still stuck in Philly helping clean Lachlan's apartment, so I'm not in a rush. You okay?"

I nodded. "Good. It's all good."

"You sure?"

"Yup."

She gave me one last smile, and then she was out the door.

I went back to sifting through resumes. Why couldn't I find a decent barista that wanted to stick around?

The first resume was hard to even read. Who was teaching people how to format their resumes? I quickly deleted that one and went to the next one. This one was from a college freshman in the next town over who was looking for part-time work and could do mornings. Bingo. I flipped to the other resume, but they were looking for nights only. They clearly hadn't bothered to look up my hours.

My manager Kelly came into the office. "Someone wants to talk to you."

If they wanted to speak to the owner, it was bad. "How badly did you mess up an order?"

She shook her head, her short blonde curls bouncing wildly. "No! Sorry. It's one of the Murphy brothers...the redhead? He's a bigger guy. I forget which one he is."

Okay...could be Brian or Finn. They had similar husky builds and red hair, so that didn't narrow it down.

Kelly snapped her fingers. "The hot one."

Again, not helpful. They were all hot.

"The fiddle player?" I offered on a guess.

"Yes! Sorry, there's so many of them I forget who is who. I only remember Killian because he always lurks when Siobhan's on shift."

I grinned. Killian was so protective of Siobhan, but it was cute.

Finn asking for me was odd. The only time I ever spoke to him was regarding his coffee order.

I set my phone down and walked out to the front. Matteo was helping a customer with their order while the giant redheaded man stood waiting patiently. He nodded when he saw me.

"Is everything okay?" I asked.

He rubbed a hand across his scruffy jaw. "Did I interrupt something earlier? With my brother?"

I shook my head. "Oh...no."

He tilted his head at me as if he could tell I was lying. "If you're interested in Lachs, you should go for it."

I blinked at him.

"You're gonna need to chase him." Then he shrugged. "Anyway, can I get a cold brew?"

I got whiplash from the abrupt change in conversation.

"I got it!" Kelly chimed in.

I plodded back into the office with Finn's words playing back at me.

You're gonna need to chase him.

Maybe he was onto something. I've never been afraid of going after what I wanted, as evident by having a successful business by the time I was twenty-eight. I liked a challenge, and those shy boys always delivered once they opened up.

Okay, Lachlan Murphy. Challenge accepted.

CHAPTER THREE

LACHLAN

*I*n hindsight, moving the day before I was on an all-day shoot was a bad idea. Weddings were my bread and butter, but they were draining. Especially when you were slightly hungover because your brothers brought over a case of beer to christen your new apartment.

"You good?" Mindy asked.

I took a sip of my black coffee and nodded as I drove to the venue for today's wedding.

I made Mindy go over to the coffee shop before we left so I didn't have to run into Willow and stumble over my words again. Yesterday, Willow was trying to be neighborly, and again, I froze up, barely getting a word in. It was like I transformed back into that shy fifteen-year-old kid who was struck by her beauty.

Mindy frowned at me. "You sure?"

"Just hungover. My brothers are a-holes."

She laughed. "I love them. I thought you were exaggerating, but they really are that loud and in your face."

I snorted.

She didn't know the half of it. My brothers were extreme extroverts who liked to see who could yell the loudest to get their point across. Maybe it was because I was the baby and my parents were plain exhausted by the time they had me, but I've always been the opposite of them. Sometimes they didn't get that.

"So...Is Finn single? You weren't serious when you said your brothers were off-limits, right?"

"Absolutely the fuck not, Min. You're not fucking one of my brothers."

Her laughter rang out in the car. "Okay, okay, message received. You're so testy today. What's got you on edge?"

Everything. Willow. Henry. Gah. This fucking town. What was I doing here?

"Nothing," I muttered.

I felt her eyes on me, but she said nothing else as we pulled up to the venue. I was on autopilot by now, knowing exactly where to go. The last wedding I shot here, I was on my own, but with Mindy, we'd divide and conquer, especially this morning since the bride texted that they got a late start.

I cut the engine. "You got the book, right?"

She lifted the photo album the bride requested for her new husband. Once I got into boudoir sessions, brides started requesting them. Now, I had it in one of my bridal packages. It was extremely popular.

"Her photos were great," Mindy told me.

"I know."

"So humble!"

I grinned and got out of the car. We got our equipment out of my trunk, double-checking that everything was charged and that we had extra batteries if need be.

"You got the groom?" I asked.

She handed me the album. "Yup! I'll handle their prep while you work the bride. She's more important, so she'll want you to shoot her."

I put a comforting hand on her arm. "Don't sell yourself short; you're a talented photographer."

She gave me a grin. "No, I'm a great assistant, makeup artist, and hairstylist. This is all yours, babe."

I shook my head. "I would be a complete mess without you."

She knew I didn't just mean about the business. Mindy picked up my pieces after all my terrible breakups with Henry. She was not happy I got back with him again, especially when he did exactly what she said he would.

My phone buzzed in my pocket, and I checked it quickly, thinking it was the bride, but my face fell at the unwanted message.

> HENRY: I heard you moved back to your boring hometown. :(Come on babe, you love the city. Come back.

Why wouldn't he get the message? We were done.

I glanced up, and Mindy's pretty face was in a hard line. "BLOCK. HIM."

I shoved my phone back into my pocket. "Forget it. Let's get to work."

We lugged our equipment inside the venue, where we met the wedding planner, and she directed us to where the bride and groom rooms were.

"Lachlan!" a male voice called out.

The groom, Kai, waved a hand at me. Kai and I dated in high school when we were both figuring out our sexuality. He had reached out to me when he and Aspen got engaged.

I did those photos, and Aspen fawned over them so much that she hired me for their wedding, too.

"Hey, Kai. Ready for the big day?" I asked.

He was dressed in a t-shirt and jeans, so obviously not. "We'll see. I wanted to say thanks again for doing this."

"You're paying me," I joked.

He ran a hand through his inky black hair. "It's not awkward for you, right?"

"I used to date him, too, and now he's my boss," Mindy chimed in from beside me.

I cut her a glare, but she just grinned.

Kai nodded. "Right."

"Is it awkward for you?" I asked him.

He shook his head. "Oh, no! Of course not."

"We're cool, Kai. You know that. Congrats. Aspen seems great."

A smile spread across his face. "She is. She's different from high school, you know?"

Aspen was one of the popular girls in school and had a lot of growing up to do. But a lot of us were shit-head teenagers. Like her cousin, Willow, she had been one to push back on some jocks that said mean things about me and Kai. Not that I needed the help since Finn had been a senior then, and he fought everyone who had something to say about me. My brothers were way better with their fists than their words.

The realization dawned on me that I may run into Willow again, but I pushed the thought to the side. I was here for work, not to socialize.

"A lot of us had growing up to do," I said.

"True, true. Well, don't let me keep you. Take care of my girl and give her the wedding photos she wants."

I held up my camera. "That's why I'm here."

I waved to him and headed into the bridal suite, where I found the bride in tears. Oh shit. Here we go. Just another day as a wedding photographer.

My shutter clicked repeatedly as the couple took their first dance, and I went in for the best shots while Mindy took candids of the guests.

When I walked into a shit show this morning, I wasn't sure what to expect, but after helping dry Aspen's tears of nerves, everything went off without a hitch. I've been to worse weddings, and nothing ever prepared you for that. Even after years of doing this.

The audience clapped as Kai dipped Aspen low, her long blonde curls nearly touching the floor. They were a cute couple, and I thought they'd last. I've photographed a lot of weddings where I didn't want to hand over the photos because the couple looked like they didn't even want to be there. Not the case tonight.

I held in a laugh when I realized this was the same venue where my brother Killian and Siobhan connected and later found out they were expecting. It was a beautiful location, and tonight, the rustic barn sparkled under the summer sky.

The couple sauntered off the dance floor to the long table in the center of the room, and the toasts began. I focused on the speaker while Mindy got reactions from Kai and Aspen. My attention was on the light and angles, making sure I was getting the best shot possible. I didn't notice the pretty brunette at the table beside me.

Not until the first speaker got up and she walked around me toward the table, where she was handed a mic.

My brain malfunctioned as I drank her in. Gone was the cute girl next door with her hair pulled up in a ponytail and wearing a Drakesville Drip apron. Tonight, she wore a strappy blue dress with yellow flowers and a huge slit in the side, directing my eyes to the black stilettos on her tiny feet. Her chestnut locks were in loose waves, and it looked like the type of hair you wanted to wrap your fist around and...

FOCUS, LACHLAN! TAKE HER FUCKING PICTURE.

Across the room, Mindy glared at me, and I took that as my cue to get my shit together. I lifted my camera back to my face and clicked.

I didn't even pay attention to Willow's speech. I found the best angles while trying not to focus on the pink of her lips. Or imagining the taste of them. I couldn't even talk to the woman without being launched back into a bumbling fifteen-year-old again. I had to physically shake it away and focus on my work.

After her speech, she walked by and paused for a second, noticing me. Maybe it was the twinkling fairy lights, but I swore her eyes sparkled when she smiled at me. Then she returned to her table.

I went back to shooting away throughout the night until it was time for the cake cutting. I smiled as Kai let his wife shove it in his face. It was clear he was so smitten with Aspen.

Kai pulled me aside while guests were gathering around the cake.

"Is something wrong?" I asked.

He squeezed my shoulder. "Bro, those photos you took of my wife..."

I immediately tensed.

Mindy always attended my boudoir sessions because, as

a male photographer, I knew it made some of my women clients uncomfortable. Also, since I was a guy, I've had some men not happy about me taking photos of 'their woman.' Which always showed their insecurity over anything else.

Kai waved a hand in front of his face, fanning himself. "I didn't know she could be hotter. You got a good eye."

I sighed in relief. "She showed you already?"

A grin tugged at his lips. "She was too excited. She showed me right after the ceremony."

"So...good?"

He nodded enthusiastically. "I'm gonna hang some of those above our bed."

I laughed at his joke, and he gave me a sly grin.

"So how the hell are you, man? Did you move to town yet?"

I nodded. "My brothers moved me in yesterday. I'm living above my studio."

We shot the shit for a couple of minutes until I reminded myself that I was on the job. But it was nice to catch up with an old friend.

It made me proud to see the bi pride flag on his lapel. There were a lot of things I could say about Drakesville. It was gossipy. Everyone knew everyone's business. But over the years, it had become way more inclusive for people like Kai and me. In high school, assholes had some nasty shit to say, but I've always known who I was. I was never afraid to proudly show my queerness.

Kai's grandmother came up to him, speaking to him in Japanese, and I took that as my cue to get back to work. Catching up with him reminded me that maybe everything about moving back home wouldn't be so bad.

CHAPTER FOUR

WILLOW

I hated weddings. Not that I was opposed to love or anything. I was so happy my cousin Aspen found her beloved with Kai, but I could have lived without Mom-Mom's nagging about where my ex-girlfriend Kacey was. Or if I had a new partner. Or when I was going to settle down and have lots of babies. I'd give her credit for not batting an eye when I came out as bisexual, but her archaic idea that everyone wanted to have children made me want to scream.

"Hi, I'm here to rescue you," Aspen's voice whispered in my ear.

I spun around and pulled my cousin into a big hug. "Let's get a drink."

She pulled me out of my chair, and we walked over to the bar together. Props to them for having an open bar with local beer. But that was partly because Kai worked at the brewery. I honestly didn't even remember what he did there.

The bartender ignored the other guests when he saw Aspen. He immediately started making her a Moscow Mule and handed it to her. I was pretty sure she already had several by how loud she was talking.

I waited in line and then ordered a Mac Daddy—the hefeweizen from the brewery. Also one of my favorite beers.

I walked with Aspen and sipped on my drink.

"Thanks for coming. I know you hate weddings," she said.

"I hate our family hounding me."

Her lips twitched. "Well...Kacey was right. You do work too much."

"I know, but the shop's my baby."

"You need to get out there and find someone worthy of your time away from it."

I took another gulp of my beer and looked across the room. I spotted Kai chatting with Lachlan. "There might be someone, but I'm not sure he's interested."

Aspen forced me to look at her. "You still have the hots for Lachlan?"

"Yeah..." I admitted weakly.

In high school, I was a cheerleader and popular since I dated the star quarterback, but we only dated because we thought we were supposed to. In truth, I was more interested in the shy artist with the kind eyes in my math class. After my eventual split with Jack, Lachlan never quite got the hint that I had been asking him out. And after all these years, the man still intrigued me.

I glanced over at Lachlan again, but he was already back to work in the middle of the dance floor. How he made a simple button-down and dress pants look hot was beyond me. It was inappropriate to ask him out when he was working, but I couldn't help but hear his brother's words ring in my head.

You're gonna need to chase him.

"He just moved back," I told Aspen.

"For good?"

I nodded. At least I thought so. He wouldn't have opened the studio next door or moved in yesterday if that wasn't a permanent decision.

"His brother told me I needed to chase him."

Aspen laughed and then gave me a little push. "Then hop to it, cuz."

I shook my head and laughed at her. My cousin was definitely drunk. I drank more of my beer, sucking it down for the liquid courage I needed.

Out of the corner of my eye, I saw Kai sauntering over to us. My cousin's eyes lit up at the sight of her new husband. "Baby!"

Kai had an amused look on his face, and he took the Moscow Mule out of Aspen's hand. "How strong are these?"

I giggled behind my own drink.

"Babe!" Aspen cried. "Tell my cousin she needs to go for it."

He furrowed his brow. "What am I encouraging you to do?"

Aspen groaned. "To put on her big girl pants and FINALLY ask the guy she likes out."

"Who are we asking out?" Kai asked, amusement lacing through his voice.

I dipped my head down and pushed a strand of hair behind my ear. "Lachlan Murphy."

Kai raised an eyebrow. "Oh...then yes, please do that. That man will never get the hint. Trust me, I know."

We grinned together.

Aspen jumped up. "Go now. Mom-Mom's walking over, and she's gonna ask why you don't have eight billion babies yet!"

I jumped at her warning and sprinted off to the dance floor. I so didn't want to be stuck in another conversation with Mom-Mom as much as I loved that woman. She couldn't take a hint. Even Mom and Dad had given up on that front.

Speaking of which, as I weaved my way through the dance floor, trying to catch the attention of one hot photographer, I spotted my parents. How many people could say their parents were still so deeply in love? Both were so busy with their respective law and business careers, but they always made time for each other.

My dad was a portly, balding man in a well-fitted suit, while Mom was so glamorous in her slinky black dress, her hair in a sophisticated chignon. Mom saw me first and spun out of Dad's arms.

"Hi, hon!" she greeted me, a big smile on her face.

I gave her a side hug. "Hi. I think Aspen's already drunk."

Her smile crinkled around her eyes. "Good for her. Your speech was excellent."

I gave a slight nod in acknowledgment.

Dad squeezed my arm. "Good job, kiddo. As always."

"Thanks. Enjoy your dance."

I skittered away before they could ask me more questions.

I'd get the third degree the next time I was over at their house. Dad liked to go over my business plan and where I stood monthly. I didn't have to secure a loan since I used my trust fund for my business capital, but Dad was always there as my backup. I was extremely privileged that way, which was why my business couldn't fail. I wouldn't let it.

I ended up running into my other cousin, Rowan. Yes, we were all named after trees. My mom and her sister thought it was cute, not annoying like we did.

Rowan was drunker than Aspen, and we ended up dancing for a bit. I forgot the reason I came out on the dance floor. Then, my beer was empty, and when I walked over to the bar, the reason was standing there taking a water break.

Oh God, the way his forearms bulged when he held his camera was too much. I quickly got another beer and not so subtly sidled up next to him. His assistant glanced up with mild interest but then went back to adjusting something on her camera.

"Hey, neighbor. Fancy seeing you here," I said, my voice having gone all low and thick.

Oh, God. What was I doing? Maybe I was a little tipsy.

Lachlan's head jerked back suddenly, and the tips of his ears went red. "Oh...hi."

"So...how was moving?"

"Exhausting."

One-word answers. Cool.

"Are you ready to be town gossip?"

Why did I ask that? What was wrong with me?

He laughed. "I'm from Drakesville. I can handle this town."

I gave him a sultry smile and put a hand on my hip. His eyes dragged down my body at the action, and for a second, I wondered if he liked what he saw. But then he snapped his eyes back up to my face. "Can you now?"

He dipped his head back down and set his empty water cup on the bar behind him. "Mmmhmm."

I lifted my bottle of beer. "You like the brewery?"

"Mmmhmm."

What was with these answers?

His blonde assistant appeared interested in the conversation now, as it looked like she was shooting daggers behind Lachlan's head. Shit, did he have a girlfriend? Finn wouldn't have told me to go after him if he did.

I stepped closer to Lachlan and placed a hand on his arm. "Well... we could go together, and I'll buy you a welcome home beer."

He jolted away at my touch, his cheeks splattered with pink. "Great. Sure. Um...I...gotta go!"

I stared after him as he yet again ran away from me. I was aware I was a little drunk, so maybe I came on a little too strong. Shit. Was that over the line?

Then I heard laughter from beside me. I glanced over to find the blonde with tears in her eyes. "Oh God. Holy shit. It's worse than I thought."

"Excuse me? Oh, shit...are you his girlfriend?"

She shook her head, wiping at her eyes, but in that dainty way where she kept her makeup fully intact. She looked familiar, but she wasn't from Drakesville, so I couldn't place her.

"I'm confused," I admitted.

"So is that frustrating man." She held out her hand. "Sorry, where are my manners? I'm Mindy. I'm Lachlan's assistant at the studio."

I was gonna guess Barbie by her head-to-toe pink.

I shook her hand. "Willow. I own the coffee shop next door."

Mindy nodded. "Right."

"So...not his girlfriend?"

She snorted. "Not anymore."

"Anymore?"

"We dated in college. We're better as friends. That man's my best friend in the entire world, but he's also so oblivious and didn't realize you were asking him out."

I frowned.

"Don't feel bad. Lachlan went through a nasty breakup recently, and I don't think his head's on straight."

Oh. Well, shit. That explained why he had no interest.

"He's interested, but he doesn't know what he wants."

I pinned her with a confused look. "Um, he literally ran away. Like he always does."

"You didn't see how he stared at your ass when you got that beer. Or how he completely froze when you did your speech."

I tilted my head at her, drinking in her words. All of this was really confusing.

"Finn told me I have to chase him."

A mischievous smile spread across her pretty pink lips. "Oh, I agree. Lachlan needs to be hit over the head by a freaking two-by-four to understand you're interested."

"You got any ideas?"

Her wicked grin got even wider. "A few."

She was trying to help, but something about that mischievous smile made me terrified.

"What's your suggestion?"

She looked like the evil queen with that grin. "Seduce him."

"Seduce him?"

"SEDUCE him."

"Um...okay? How?"

Her eyes sparkled with delight. "I've got some tricks up my sleeve."

I should be afraid, very afraid, but something told me Photographer Barbie was my key to Lachlan Murphy, and I'd take all the help I could get.

CHAPTER FIVE

LACHLAN

*W*edding shoots were so exhausting that I always planned the day after to be an easy admin day, where I worked on postproduction. I rolled out of bed and rubbed a hand through my hair at the thought of unpacking the rest of my apartment. The only thing my brothers helped me unpack were my beer glasses. If my sister-in-law Kelsey wasn't pregnant, she might have come over to help, too.

I was still so tired from the wedding I couldn't be bothered to look for my coffee cups. Good thing there was a coffee shop downstairs. Maybe if I got in and out, I wouldn't have another weird encounter with Willow. God, she looked so pretty last night. Not just pretty, sexy, like a wet dream. It made my brain go haywire. And, of course, it made me revert to my awkward ways again.

I dug through a storage container of my clothes and threw on a pair of jeans and an old t-shirt. I left my apartment and walked the few steps to the coffee shop.

A blonde girl with short curly hair was behind the register, and I almost sighed in relief. I stepped up to the counter, but my eye caught on the basket of coffee cups in front of it. A chalkboard sign was above the basket, and in neat handwriting, it read: 'Recycled Mugs to take away. Please return if possible. Drop off unwanted mugs here.' Was that something new? I loved sustainability efforts like that.

I pulled out a cup that bore the coffee shop's logo, but then I saw one with a heart that looked like the bi flag. It looked handmade, and it immediately called to me. I set the cups on the counter.

The barista gave me a bright smile. "Hi. What can I get for you?"

"Black coffee in the bi mug and..." I had to think for a minute about Mindy's order because it was complicated. I pulled out my phone because I was sure I put it in my notes app. "Sorry, this is complicated. Oat milk latte with three shots of caramel."

"Not too complicated. Anything else?"

I scanned the menu. "An avocado toast and a breakfast burrito."

She gave me a smile as she punched in the order. I handed off my card, and she rang it through. She handed me the drip coffee in the bi heart mug seconds later and then spun around to work on Mindy's order.

I gazed around the shop, taking it all in. I never paid much attention when I was in here before. There were tables in front of the big window and on the other side of the room. I settled myself at a table while I waited for our food. The thing I loved about the shop was the local art for sale.

There was one painting that spoke to me. It was a

simple piece with a black background. In the center were moon phases depicting a right-facing crescent, a full moon, and then a left-facing crescent. The moon wasn't in white but in the same pink, purple, and blue of the bi flag. Below the moons were the words 'Not A Phase.'

I stood up and went over to the wall, but unlike the other paintings, there wasn't an artist name or price.

"Hi! Here's the rest of your order," Willow's voice pulled me away from the painting.

She handed me Mindy's coffee and a paper bag for our food.

"Thanks." I pointed to the painting. "Can I buy this?"

She shook her head. "That one's not for sale."

"It speaks to me."

She toyed with the beaded bracelets on her wrist, and I noticed for the first time the color scheme. Oh. The queer flag on the door and the coffee cup now made sense. How didn't I know that about her? And why did that make her even more interesting to me?

"It's important to me. To live my truth. And it's my shop, so I'm not selling it," Willow said firmly.

I nodded. "I get that. Compliments to the artist but I'd pay top dollar for it."

Her cheeks tinged pink. "She says thanks, but she's still not selling it."

Oh. Willow was the artist. Now that made even more sense.

There was a long, awkward silence between us. She looked tired after a night of drinking at her cousin's wedding, but even with her hair in a messy bun and wearing her work attire, she still made me clam up. Because this woman had been my high school crush, and I never got over her.

"I should go," I blurted out before she could say anything else. I darted out the door and over to my studio before I made a bigger fool of myself.

I was surprised to find Mindy already at the studio looking fresh-faced, like she didn't drive home to Philly in the dead of night after the wedding. I strolled into the studio and set down her cup of coffee.

"Oh, cute. They have their own cups." She eyed the bag. "What did you bring me?"

I slid into the chair next to her behind the check-in desk. "Avocado toast."

She wrinkled her nose. "What did you get?"

"Breakfast burrito."

She reached across the desk and grabbed the bag. "Yoink!"

"I thought you were on a health kick?"

"I need carbs and grease. I went home and drank with the hot drummer."

I waggled my eyebrows at her. "You bad girl."

She gave me a saucy grin. "You know it."

I laughed because I did, but another reason we didn't mesh. Our kinks didn't line up at all.

I opened my laptop and pulled up the files from the wedding. The studio wasn't open on the weekends, but that didn't mean I wasn't working. Especially during wedding season. Before Mindy left last night, we backed up our photos, but I'd spend today culling all the shitty ones and then retouching and color-correcting what was left.

I chewed on the avocado toast and sipped my coffee as I started going through the photos. There were a lot of ones in the beginning I wished I hadn't taken. I had thousands of photos to go through, so this would be a long process.

Mindy and I fell into a comfortable working silence as

she emailed back clients for me and confirmed appointments while I worked on the photos.

I took a sip of my coffee an hour later and frowned, glaring into the empty cup.

"I got more in the break room. Their coffee's so good," Mindy told me.

I took my cup and went into our tiny break room, where Mindy stocked the coffee bar. I hated those machines with the pods, so I insisted on a drip machine. There was a white coffee bag next to the pot with the Drakesville Drip logo on the front. Below the logo was a purple text box that gave details about the coffee.

Drakesville Morning

A medium roast with hints of caramel, apple, and chocolate.

Roasted here in Drakesville, PA

Huh. I didn't realize Willow was doing all of it. I thought she carried a local brew, not that she was roasting the beans herself. That was cool. Why did that make her hotter?

I grabbed a coffee filter and put it in the machine, spooning coffee into it. I poured water into the carafe and started the machine.

I took my phone out of my pocket and scrolled through my social media, ignoring a bunch of texts from my brothers reminding me to be at our parents' house for dinner later. A photo came across my feed of Henry. He looked impeccable in a tailored suit, his silver-grey hair styled to perfection. He had his arm around a bleach-blonde man who didn't even look old enough to drink.

Why the fuck did he keep bothering me if he already had a new boy toy? Was it merely a way to torment me? Why couldn't I get over this man?

I went to his profile and clicked unfollow. I hovered over the block button but stopped myself.

The coffee steamed to life, and I poured myself a fresh cup. I wasn't sure I tasted all the flavor notes, but it was tasty.

I walked toward the desk and got back to work.

"Who was that girl last night?" Mindy asked.

"What girl?"

Lie. I knew exactly who she was talking about.

She cut a glare at me. "The one who aggressively asked you out, but you were too busy trying to swallow your tongue."

"Willow?" I asked and then shook my head. "No. She was being neighborly."

The offer to get a beer at the brewery was something people said here. 'Hey, let's grab a drink sometime and catch up,' but then you never actually did. It was polite conversation to pass the time. She might have been a little too friendly last night, but I blamed that on the alcohol.

Mindy groaned. "I love you, but sometimes I want to wring your neck."

"Willow's a sweet girl. She was being nice."

Mindy pointed at the photo on my screen, which was of the woman in question dancing the night away. Under the fairy lights of the barn, she looked ethereal, like a brunette Tinkerbell. Her beauty sparkled under the lights, and I captured it at just the right second.

"You took the most amazing photo of her, and yet you ran away when she was obviously hitting on you."

"Min, drop it. She was only making conversation."

She peered at me. "Do you not like her? Is she an ex or something? Did she bully you in high school?"

I laughed. "No. None of that."

She dramatically shook my shoulders. "Then what's the problem?"

I set my cup of coffee down and crossed my arms over my chest. "You ever like someone so much you have this idea of them in your head, and you're not sure if they'll ever live up to that? Like you put them on a pedestal?"

"Sure."

"That's Willow for me. I spent high school, like everyone else, staring as she walked down the halls, trying to work up the courage to talk to her. And now I feel like that fifteen-year-old kid again every time I talk to her. It's like looking at the sun. She's so pretty it hurts."

Mindy's mouth fell open. "Oh."

"Yeah. Oh. So, drop it because every time I talk to her, I run away because I'm gonna say something completely fucking stupid. She makes me tongue-tied, and I make a complete ass out of myself."

"Lachs."

My phone buzzed on the desk, and I rolled my eyes at a reminder of why I shouldn't entertain the idea of Willow.

HENRY: Miss you :(

Yeah, missed me so much that he was already posting photos with another man.

Mindy grabbed my phone before I could stop her.

"Hey! What are you doing?"

She shot me an evil glare. "Blocking that asshole. Because that's your problem."

"What is?"

"You're too afraid of opening yourself to someone else because you're holding onto a man who only gives you the time of day so he can torment you. You're his plaything, and you let him hurt you over and over again. It's almost like you like the way he tears your heart out of your chest and stomps on it. Block this asshole and move on."

"Min..."

Her eyes were glassy. "I hate the way he makes you small. I want you to be happy."

I reached for her hand and squeezed it. "I know, hun. But I can fight my own battles."

"But you don't have to."

I sighed and pulled her into a hug. "I love you, you know that?"

"I love you too, but I still want to hit you over the head with a brick. You're holding onto someone when you could find someone to love you like you deserve."

"Min..."

She pulled back. "I don't mean me. God, been there and done that, and we're not compatible that way." She pointed at my computer screen. "But maybe there's a pretty brunette that could get your mind off Henry. If you decide to put your big boy pants on and take a shot."

"She melts my brain."

"Brain melting's good. I can think of ways you could melt her brain."

I shook my head. "You're ridiculous!"

"Think about it. She has."

"Can we stop talking about my non-existent love life and get back to work?"

"Ugh. Fine. You're no fun. But she was not being nice. You didn't notice the way she looked at you."

I shook my head and went back to my work. Mindy was trying to help, but she didn't know what she was talking about. Willow Rivers has not and would never look at me in desire. I was so far out of her league; it wasn't even funny. Mindy wasn't from Drakesville, so she'd never get that.

I rubbed my eyes hours later after spending most of it circling through all my photos. I wanted another cup of coffee, but Mindy said my heart might explode. This coffee was superb, and I didn't think that just because I was dead tired.

The front door of the shop opened, and I could kick myself for forgetting to lock it despite the CLOSED sign on the door.

"We're closed," I said, not even looking up from my work.

I was going through the photos from the speeches now, and the photo staring back at me was of the pretty coffee shop owner that kept running through my mind.

"Oh, hi, Willow," Mindy's cheery voice greeted.

I snapped my head up and felt like I was caught red-handed at seeing the petite woman in my studio. She wasn't in her casual work attire anymore; instead, she wore a pretty blue sundress that had tiny white flowers on it and those heels from last night.

My lustful brain flashed images of that dress scrunched up around her waist while her heels dug into my back as I made her come undone beneath me. Why did I turn into a horny mess of a man whenever she was near?

Blue was her color. It accented her ivory skin and dark chestnut hair. It also was my favorite color.

"Hey, Mindy," Willow greeted back.

My phone buzzed on the desk, but I had been ignoring it for the past hour. I looked at it for a second, and all the blood drained from my face, realizing it was way later than I thought.

Shit.

Mary Pat Murphy was not a woman to be trifled with, and I was in deep shit for being late to family dinner. But I felt frozen as Willow stood before me, looking like a vision.

"Um...what do you want?" I asked. I cringed as soon as I said it, realizing the harshness of my tone.

Mindy jabbed me with her elbow.

But Willow gave me a friendly smile. "Well, I was wondering if you wanted to get that drink I mentioned last night? You've been working all day. I figured you could use a break."

Wait...*was* she asking me out?

My phone buzzed again.

> MOM: LACHLAN JAMES MURPHY! Where are you?!?

Christ, I was so fucked.

I saved my work and shut down my computer. "I'm sorry. I gotta go."

I sprinted out of the studio and into my car, trying not to speed too much as I drove over to my parents' house in a rush.

I steeled myself and walked into the house. Mom would be pissed, but I also knew that I could use my baby of the family status to placate her. The only time I got away with not coming to family dinner was if I had a wedding to shoot. Which happened occasionally.

"Oh, look who decided to show up," Finn teased. "Can we eat now?"

I dropped into the seat beside Eilish, Finn's best friend

who usually came to dinner. She gave me a sympathetic smile.

"Yes, you can eat now, you heathens," Mom joked.

My brothers dug in, and I felt like I might have gotten a finger bitten off if I wasn't careful.

"Sorry," I offered to Mom. "Really busy doing the post-production from the wedding last night."

"How was it? Was that awkward seeing Kai?" my sister-in-law Kelsey asked.

I shook my head. "Nah. Him and Aspen are cute."

"When are you going to settle down?" Mom asked.

I nodded at my brother Killian, who sat next to Siobhan with a protective hand on her pregnant belly. "If anyone's next, it's that one."

Killian glared at me because that was something he wanted, but he hadn't asked Siobhan to marry him yet. Not sure why he was waiting since she'd say yes immediately.

"You should have told us you were running behind," Mom scolded.

"Sorry, I've been busy. It's a lot trying to finish unpacking while having a ton of work to do. Plus, trying to figure out how to live here again. Sorry, Mom."

That seemed to pacify her, but my brothers still gave me death glares. They could wait two minutes to eat. Neanderthals.

I piled spaghetti on my plate. "You didn't have to wait for me."

"Mom made us," Brian said. "It's okay."

"You make out okay with unpacking?" Ronan asked.

"Yeah," I lied.

If I told them everything was still in boxes, they'd barge in and try to help me. Which meant the big lugs would break half my shit.

"It's good to see you home, son," my dad said.

I nodded. I wasn't sure how I felt about that yet.

"Are you okay?" Brian asked.

"Just tired," I lied again.

I wasn't okay. I was pretty sure I made an ass out of myself in front of the girl of my dreams. Yet again. But I tried to forget about it as I shoveled Mom's delicious pasta into my mouth.

After dinner, my brothers and I sat around the TV in our parents' living room with a baseball game on while the girls helped Mom clean up.

Ronan handed me a beer. "Now tell us what's wrong."

I picked at the label. "I think Willow Rivers asked me out."

Ronan raised an eyebrow, but Finn shoved me. "You asshole. Of course she did. What did you say?"

"I was late for dinner."

"And?" Ronan asked.

I shrugged. "I said I had to go and booked it here. Mom was gonna have my ass for being late."

Brian hung his head. "Bro, are you for real? You ran away?"

I took a swig of my beer.

Killian cackled. "You have ZERO game!"

I glared at him.

I wished my brothers would stop telling me that, even though they were right. It took me a while to warm up to people. I was never the person to make the first move. Not until we were already comfortable, and then I showed my partners the me who lived behind closed doors.

Finn shoved me again. "Make the next move, then. Ask her out and get over your shithead ex already."

Three heads swiveled in my direction.

I stared daggers at Finn. "You told them, didn't you?"

He shrugged. "They needed to know so you'd stay the fuck away from him this time."

Killian rolled up his sleeves and jabbed a fist in the air. "Fuck that guy. I can show him where he can shove it again."

"You're all assholes. I'm going home."

I set my beer down on the coffee table and got up. I didn't need their noses in my business right now. I especially didn't need Killian trying to literally fight my battles.

"Get a grip and ask her out!" Ronan called after me, but I gave him the two-bird salute on the way out.

Mom would get mad at me for slipping out, but I didn't feel like dealing with my brothers tonight. I needed to get my head on straight. Because there was no way Willow asked me out. No freaking way. She was being nice and welcoming me back to town. No way a girl like her was interested in me.

CHAPTER SIX

WILLOW

S o much for leaving my work downstairs. After being rejected once again by Lachlan, I headed up to my apartment with my tail between my legs.

It was a slow day at the shop, and Kelly had it handled, so I went home to call those prospective employees. A much better use of my time than chasing after a man who wanted nothing to do with me.

I sat at my kitchen table and went through more resumes. I had three people lined up to call; all had barista experience and were looking for full-time work.

I spent the next hour calling and scheduling interviews with all three of them. After the calls, I had a good feeling about them, but we'd see how the formal interviews went.

I moved on to scheduling social posts and checked in with my roasters. We were on track with our next roast, and so far, customers liked the new brew. That made me happy that all the hard work I was putting into my business was worth it. If I got a couple more people on staff, I'd feel like I could breathe.

Summer specials were out, but I started working on fall ideas. Pumpkin pie latte was always popular, but maybe I'd do a hot apple cider topped with cinnamon as another option. And, of course, some fall-flavored specialty teas.

I saw an email from the brewery. I perked up as I read the email from the brewmaster, Nolan MacGregor. He wanted to use my dark roast for a new coffee beer. A way for both of our businesses to partner with each other. I didn't hesitate to email back that I was interested and for him to give me the details on what exactly he needed.

That was one of the best things about living in Drakesville. The local businesses liked partnering together and helping each other out. The brewery made an Irish Red beer and partnered with Sullivan's Irish Pub, so you could only get it at either establishment. I loved that local mentality. I suspected my friend Gemma might have had a hand in Nolan reaching out to me since she was the brewery's marketing director. Hey, sometimes it paid to have connections.

I saw another email from Bob at Drakesville's Bagels, but I ignored him. He kept trying to renegotiate my coffee purchase rates. I tried to be nice at first after his father died, but now he was being a dick. I had a contract in place with him, and I wasn't budging. He was trying to get me to roll over because I was a woman, and he thought screaming at me intimidated me.

I shut my computer lid. That was enough work. I could use a beer.

I craned my head to one side when I thought I heard knocking. And then the doorbell rang. I wasn't expecting anyone, so that was odd. I grabbed my key and walked out my front door and down the steps to the outer door.

I pulled back when Mindy stood there in her head-to-toe pink again. "Um. Hi?"

"You wanna get that beer?" she asked.

"Um..."

She looked me up and down. "You're dressed for it. Come on, let's go."

I stared down at my blue sundress but with pink bunny slippers on my feet. "Not exactly. Gimme a minute."

I ran up the steps and grabbed my purse off the back of my door. I looked down at my slippers and kicked them off, shoving my feet into my favorite heels. When you were a tiny thing, you wanted to get all the height you could. Hence the four-inch stilettos.

Mindy smiled at me when I stepped out onto the street. She threaded her arm through mine. "Lead me to the brewery. I need a drink."

I sighed. "Me too."

We walked together, me leading her the couple of blocks to the brewery. I loved the brewery. It was a highlight in town and growing so much, they probably needed to expand soon. The two brothers who owned it were a little older than me, so I only knew them in passing, but I had a couple of friends, like Gemma and Kai, who worked there.

I opened the door for Mindy, and she peered up at the high vaulted ceilings and the loft space on the second floor.

"Oh. I like this," she said with a smile.

"It's a cool space." I pointed up top. "Their brewmaster got married to his wife up there. They rent it out and host events there now."

The hostess sat us at a booth, and we scanned the menu for a minute before a bartender came over to our table.

Asher was a blonde pretty boy, and he knew it, but I could say that because we were friends.

"Hey, Will. How are you?" he asked.

"Good. You?"

Asher scanned Mindy up and down. "Good, now."

I rolled my eyes, but Mindy ate up the attention.

"What can I get you ladies?" he asked.

Mindy gave him a sultry smile, matching his flirty energy. "What do you recommend?"

"If you want something sweet like you, Radle my Cage is the perfect summer beer."

Way to lay it on thick, Ash. But Mindy surprised me with her response.

"I want something that punches me in the face with hops. You got something like that?"

Asher's eyes widened, and then he grinned. "Oh, hell yeah. You want Area 267."

He turned to go, and I stopped him. "Hey! What about me?"

"I know you want a Mac Daddy," he said with a grin and darted off behind the bar.

I had regulars at the coffee shop that I didn't need to ask for their order anymore, so I understood Asher's point. It was part of being in the service industry.

Mindy tilted her head and ran her tongue over her pink lips. "So, what's his deal?"

I waved my hand. "That's Asher. He's full of himself."

"I wouldn't mind taking him for a ride."

A laugh bubbled up inside me. At that moment, I decided Mindy was fucking hilarious, and I liked her a lot.

She gripped my hands. "Give me all the deets, and then we can discuss my captain oblivious bestie."

I grimaced at how crushed my spirit was from earlier.

Asher came back with our beers. "Enjoy, dollface," he said with a wink to Mindy.

What a ham.

Mindy laughed. "Oh. He knows how to play it. Maybe small town isn't so bad. I like a blue-collar man. Or a drummer. Or an artist. Maybe all three at once."

I choked on my beer.

This woman really said what she was thinking.

"Asher's actually a good guy," I admitted. "We went to high school together."

"Isn't that like everyone in this town?"

I lifted one shoulder. "Somewhat. He had to grow up a little, though, so don't let that flirty banter fool you. He's a single dad who had to get his shit together quick."

Her smile reached her eyes, and they sparkled in interest. "Oh, single dads are great. They're so good at taking my commands."

I felt my cheeks grow hot at her innuendo. Geez. I didn't consider myself a prude, but I wasn't sure I needed to know that about her.

She took a sip of her beer. "Oh, this beer's awesome. You should see your face. You're as shy as Lachlan. That's cute."

I stared up at the ceiling. "Can we not talk about him and how embarrassing that was?"

She reached over and directed my gaze back to her. "Yes, we need to talk about that. Because partly that was my fault."

"Huh?"

"I forgot Sunday's family dinner night. He was interested. He got the wild look in his eye when he saw you in that dress and those heels. Just bad timing."

"I don't want to keep pursuing him if he's not interested. It makes me feel like I'm harassing him."

She waved me away, my vision going to her perfect pink manicure. "I have an idea about how you can seduce him."

I sighed. "Mindy, I'm not sure that's a good idea."

She shushed me. "Listen! Book a boudoir shoot."

I felt my eyebrows go all the way to the ceiling. "What?"

"Lachlan's very talented at boudoir."

That was true. When I found out he rented the storefront next door, I checked out his portfolio on his website. He did it all. Weddings, engagements, maternity, newborn, headshots, and there, almost like it was hidden on his website, were his boudoir shoots. I had looked through hundreds of photos of brides, couples, and solo women looking fierce and sexy.

"How would that seduce him? Do I even want to seduce him? I want him to talk to me without running away."

She took another sip of her beer and was quiet for a moment, like she was contemplating something. "Can I be honest with you?"

I nodded.

"Lachs is intimidated by you."

"Me?" I squeaked.

"Mmmhmm."

The tone of her voice told me there was something she wasn't saying, but I didn't press her. Lachlan's photography was beautiful, and the idea of being on display for him appealed to me. I wanted him to want me, but it was brazen. Although, I needed to be bold if I was going to get this man to pay attention to me. Desperate times called for desperate measures.

"Wear blue. He likes blue," she told me with a smile.

I rested my cheek on my hand as my thoughts swirled around me. Mindy would know Lachlan better than anyone.

"Why are you helping me?" I asked.

"Because he's my best friend and I love him. Also, he needs to get over his ex, and you could help him with that. Why are you so interested in him?"

I sunk into the booth, startled by her throwing the question back at me. "He sat next to me in algebra freshman year and said he liked my bow."

She arched a blonde eyebrow.

"I was a cheerleader. You know, we put ribbons in our hair for pep rallies."

"You still got that outfit?"

I laughed. "Oh God, no!"

She gave me a sad little shrug. "Too bad. He might have liked that too."

"Lachlan's always been this quiet mystery. He gave me that compliment and then buried his face in his sketchbook, ignoring me for the rest of the year. There was just something about him that called to me."

There was a naughty light in Mindy's eyes. "Interesting."

"It's not that interesting."

She shook her head. "Oh, it is, trust me. Come to the studio tomorrow, and we'll do a consultation. I'll shuffle his schedule around to get you in ASAP."

"Mindy..."

She gave me a big smile. "You can thank me later."

I had a feeling I wasn't prepared for what was in store for me.

"Can you handle closing?" I asked Kelly.

She waved a hand at me. "Go, boss lady. I got this."

I took off my apron and smoothed down the Drakesville Drip t-shirt. It was just a consultation, but I was nervous.

Kelly eyed me suspiciously. "Where are you off to, anyway?"

"I have an appointment. Call me if you need anything."

Today had been a whirlwind of a day. I hoped to ease into the week, but the brewery got back to me on the order for the new beer, so I went across town to the roastery to start the batch myself. I was being a micromanager, and my head roaster called me out on it. But I wanted to give the brewery quality ingredients so they'd use us in the future.

Nolan wanted a more coffee-forward porter for this one, so I wanted to make sure we made this darker roast to perfection. Chatting with him this morning made me realize the similarities in how we approached brewing our respective products. He was a bit gruff but a master at his craft, and we came away from the conversation with mutual respect.

"Wait!" Kelly called after me as I opened the door.

"What's wrong?"

"Are you okay on your own for the farmer's market the next couple of weeks?"

Oh, right.

Drakesville was weird in that instead of in the morning on Saturday, like every other town, we had a night market. I made it a point to always have a presence there. Honestly, for any event nearby, I made sure we had a table. Fall Arts Fest? There. Farmer's Market? Of course. Christmas Tree

Lighting Ceremony? People want hot drinks in the dead of winter. Summer Fest was coming up too, and while it was in the next town over, I had a booth there too. It was important the community knew the shop would always be there.

But right then, I didn't care about that.

"I've got it," I told Kelly and then shuffled off next door.

Mindy gave me a smile when I walked in, but Lachlan was still busy with a client. I sat in his waiting room and watched him at his work. He was entertaining an unruly toddler whose parents gave Lachlan apologetic smiles. But Lachlan worked his magic and had that baby smiling in no time. It was honestly impressive.

I waited patiently, and then Lachlan sat opposite me in one of his comfy chairs. He ran a hand through his hair, and his mouth dropped open when he finally glanced up and noticed it was me. "Um. Hi."

"Hi."

"So, Min said you're interested in booking a Boudoir session. Is that right?"

"Mmmhmm."

He nodded, but his jaw was tight, as if he was clenching his teeth too hard. "What are you looking to get out of it?"

"What do you mean?"

"How much skin do you want to show? I want you to be comfortable. Most of my clients like to wear something..."

"Sexy?" I answered.

Redness blossomed across his face. "Yeah. Or partially nude. I have a package for Min to handle your hair and makeup if you want. But bring whatever you're comfortable with. We can make you shine with whatever you want. Lingerie, comfy sweaters, a hockey jersey, whatever."

I couldn't hide the amusement from my voice. "A hockey jersey?"

"You'd be surprised. I did a shoot for a Bulldogs hockey player."

"Interesting."

"They were a cute couple and matched each other's energies. That was fun to shoot and bring to life in my art. So, what are your thoughts on this?"

"I have some ideas," I admitted.

I saw a flash of heat in his eyes, but then it disappeared. "Do you have a theme?"

"Sexy. On display," I answered, my voice thick.

He cleared his throat and cast his gaze down to the floor. "Okay...we can work with that. I like to ask my clients to know what we're looking for. Is this for you to empower yourself? Or are you doing this as a gift for someone special in your life? It helps so I can figure out the best angles and the vibe you want out of it."

'It's for you,' I wanted to scream, but I gave him a flirty look instead. "There's one person in particular I'd like to see it."

He gave me a strained smile, trying hard to be polite. "Okay, cool. I have to look at—"

"We had a cancellation!" Mindy called out. "We could squeeze you in next week."

"Wow, what luck," I said with a smile, but that luck was Mindy shuffling appointments. I hoped I didn't get her in trouble because of that.

"Great," Lachlan said.

"Awesome. I'll see you then."

I knew exactly what theme I wanted. To be a gift for the photographer himself.

CHAPTER SEVEN

LACHLAN

*T*his was going to be the hardest shoot I ever did. Mindy should do this one. She needed the practice anyway.

Be professional.

She's fucking hot and your crush from high school, but don't be a creepy photographer trying to get it on with your client. Do your job and pretend she's not the woman who has been invading your fantasies since you were a teenager.

Whoever this session was for was a lucky person, but it was proof she hadn't been asking me out if she had a partner. Willow was a sweet girl trying to welcome me back to Drakesville. That was all.

I've seen tons of women like this and photographed them in their best light. Showing them the beauty they've never seen before. Today, I'd do the same for Willow. She was my subject, a client, and nothing more. I'd forget that she was my high school crush and bury myself in being a professional.

She'd been in the bathroom for the last thirty minutes with Mindy, doing her hair and makeup for the shoot. I didn't rush Mindy's process. I was supposed to be going over the shot list, but I kept switching out my 35mm lens for my 85mm while debating where we should start. Or should I use a 50mm for all the shots?

I stopped myself from changing lenses again. I never second-guessed myself like this because I was good at my job, and I had an eye for detail. Willow being my client had my nerves running miles.

The bathroom door opened, and Mindy came out with a big grin on her face. "She's all set for you."

I narrowed my eyes as she sauntered back to the front of the studio. "Aren't you sticking around?"

The wicked grin on her face told me I should have been more suspicious of her. "I gotta run some errands."

She had an innocent look on her face, and I studied her with intense scrutiny.

Mindy always attended my boudoir sessions. I wanted my clients to be comfortable with a male photographer, and Mindy's presence always helped them relax.

"I trust you," Willow spoke up. "Min doesn't need to stay."

I raised an eyebrow at my best friend. Willow was already calling her by her nickname? Why did I get the feeling these two were up to something?

Mindy gave me an apathetic shrug and hurried out of the studio like she was running late for something.

I turned around and swallowed hard at the vision in front of me. Willow's dark hair was curled into loose waves, and she had natural-looking makeup on. She wore a baby blue sweater that fell below her waist, but the knee-high socks really put the sweet girl next door look together.

Fuck me.

I led Willow over to the bedroom set Mindy and I had assembled this morning.

"We'll start with you on the bed to get you comfortable. We can do some full body shots and then get into close-ups as we progress," I explained.

She climbed onto the bed, sinking onto her knees with her feet behind her. She looked like such a good girl, ready to be told what to do.

Christ on a bike. This shoot wasn't for me. I had to stop viewing her as an object of my desire and do my damn job.

"Can I fix your poses? Or would you rather me demonstrate throughout?" I asked.

Consent was so important during my sessions. My subjects needed to know they were safe in my studio.

She gave me a demure smile. "You can touch me as you please."

Well, I knew where all the blood in my body just rushed to.

I adjusted her position and stepped back, putting the camera to my eye. I began clicking away and directed her with subtle movements, having her play with the ends of her sweater and then her hair. Her body moved with my directions, and then, without me asking, she clung to the bottom of her sweater and bit her lip as if she was about to tear it off.

Fucking beautiful. If her plan was to look like that sweet girl you wanted to be naughty with, these photos would show that.

She got into it, her body naturally progressing into each new position I coached her into. She took direction well. A little too well.

BE A FUCKING PROFESSIONAL, LACHLAN!

I took shots of her lying on the bed with her arms shyly over her head, smiling like she was happy to see me. My favorites were the close-ups I did of her face and those knee socks. Until I got a good silhouette of her against the window with the sunlight shining through, making her look like a goddess.

I switched out my lens, giving her a second to take a breath. "Need a break?"

"Costume change."

But she looked flushed and needed to hydrate so her skin looked good in these next photos. I set my camera down and grabbed a bottle of water Mindy had left out for her. I handed it to her. "Drink your water."

Her body froze, and I realized at the last second the edge of sternness that had come into my voice. I didn't ask; I commanded. "Um... Okay."

She took the bottle and drank a few sips before darting back to the bathroom to change.

I rubbed my hands down my face. I can't believe I used my bedroom voice on her. This woman melted my brain so much that I was either a fumbling mess or the beast inside was ready to mount her. What the fuck was wrong with me?

I heard the click of her heels against the wood floor before I saw her. When I glanced up, I had to pick my jaw up off the floor.

She stood in front of me in a royal blue lacy lingerie set. Complete with what looked like a collar around her neck that led to a chain. The chain connected down past her breasts to a lace midsection and went down to garters attached to fishnet stockings. On her feet, she had matching blue stilettos. We were definitely incorporating that into a close-up.

My horny brain imagined my hand wrapped around her pretty neck instead of that collar while I crashed inside her, and she screamed my name.

I pretended to adjust my camera settings and counted back from ten in my head.

She tilted her head at me, but I kept staring at her, at this goddess-like creature standing before me. She stepped forward and pressed a hand against my chest, the warmth of her skin seeping into my thin t-shirt.

"Lachlan? You okay?" she asked.

My tongue was so thick for my mouth that all I could do was nod.

Her hand slid down my chest until she landed on my belt. "Are you sure?"

Her voice was husky, and if I didn't move right now, I'd do something I'd regret.

I stepped back from her, knowing if she moved that hand, she'd find out how hard this session had been for me all afternoon. "Let's start with you on the floor with your legs up on the bed."

She did as she was told. So fucking well.

We moved through more shots, and once behind the camera again, I could focus on the work and not on who the subject was. That collar made for a great close-up of her fingers spread out across her mouth. It was suggestive and sexy.

We moved to the chair, moving on to different poses, getting the best out of her now that she was feeling herself. These shots, she was confident in, like she had something to prove.

"Did you have another outfit you wanted to try?" I asked.

Her gaze landed on the photo of me behind the desk. "Do you still have that flag?"

"I think so. Why?"

"Can we use it?"

My eyes widened when I realized what she meant. "Uh... yeah... let me see if I can find it."

I set my camera down and went into the office where I knew the bi pride flag hung.

When I came back to the set, she had a sheet over her breasts, but I knew she wasn't wearing anything under it. It was very sensual and the perfect shot for this type of shoot.

"I didn't know if you'd be comfortable with any nudity," I admitted.

"Subtle, I like. Give them a taste of what they could have."

Whoever she was doing this for was lucky indeed.

I took a few shots of her with the sheet and then grabbed the bi pride flag. I looked her in the eye and nowhere else when I handed her the flag. She wrapped herself in it, and I stepped back to take more shots. Her petite frame was gorgeous, and the curve of her breasts peeking out gave that tasteful tease.

"Do you think you got enough?" she asked.

"Plenty," I nearly shouted at her.

She dropped the flag, but I still didn't let my eyes wander to her body. "Lachlan."

Her voice was thick with want. But I wasn't about to violate my integrity. If I looked at her body, I wouldn't see the beauty of the naked form. Nor the art I could create in capturing it. I'd see the woman I wanted, and I'd take her.

"This was great. I hope you got what you wanted out of this," I said.

Then, I promptly walked away when the girl of my

dreams was naked in front of me. My brothers would tell me I was a fucking idiot, but I had a business to take care of. I didn't fuck my clients after I took sexy photos of them. No matter how hot they were.

I slammed back another beer, and Killian gave me a curious glance as he made a drink for someone else at the other end of the bar.

He whirled around the bar, handing off the drink to his customer, and then came back to me. Instead of refilling my beer, he set a lowball glass on the bar and poured whiskey into the glass. He pushed it over to me, and I took it, nodding at him in thanks. Killian spoke in the language of fists and alcohol. It was how he cared, even when he pretended he didn't.

After I ran out on Willow today, I had been on edge. What was even worse was that I hid in my office and didn't say goodbye to her when she left. That was a dick move, but I was trying to be a professional. I wasn't a sleazy photographer that asked out my clients.

I hadn't even been able to bring myself to back up the photos yet. If I looked, it would only spell trouble for me. I begged Mindy to do it, but she left me on read. I needed to have a talk with her about how she bailed on me today. That was unlike her.

I lifted the whiskey glass to my lips and took a big gulp.

Siobhan walked over to the bar, mostly to sneak my brother a kiss. She did that every time she had to punch something into the computer. Killian pretended to hide a smile every time. I didn't want to know how she enchanted my hoe of a brother, but I was glad for it.

She peered at me and then turned to Killian. "What's with him?"

Killian rolled his eyes. "Waiting for him to spit it out."

"You okay?" Siobhan asked.

I gave her a curt nod, hoping one of her customers would wave her over so I didn't have to explain that I spent today pretending my dick wasn't a steel beam in my pants when I photographed the sexiest woman on the planet. Maybe even the universe.

She shared a look with Killian.

I took another swig of my whiskey. "I'm fine."

"You don't look fine," Brian said. He wiped down the bar and scanned the serving floor of Sullivan's Irish Pub.

Why did I come here when two of my brothers worked here, and the other one was playing the fiddle in the corner of the room? I should have gone to the brewery.

"I'm fine," I repeated.

I downed the rest of my drink. I needed to get Willow out of my head, but every time I closed my eyes, my brain flashed images of every photo I took. It was tattooed on the back of my eyelids.

Killian poured me another drink, and I clenched my teeth as the last note on Finn's fiddle sounded. That was Celtic Kiss' ending song, which meant yet another brother would be up in my business.

Why the fuck did I move back here?

I took another drink, and seconds later, a sweaty Finn slid into the seat beside me. I glanced back and noticed his bestie, Eilish, was already making out with her new boyfriend in the corner. Yeah, Finn didn't like that.

Killian poured Finn a beer and handed it over.

"Hey, did you ask her out yet?" Finn asked me.

"No," I growled.

"Sheesh. What crawled up your ass?" he asked.

"Just ask her out!" Brian urged me.

"Who?" Siobhan asked.

"Nobody," I muttered.

Killian nudged her, and her eyes got big. "Oh! Willow? Yeah. You should do that."

"She's seeing someone."

Sure, some people did boudoir shoots for themselves, but Willow said it was for someone special.

"I have it on good authority she isn't," Siobhan told me. "There might be a shy guy she's interested in, but he's not getting the hint."

My brothers gave me knowing looks, but I shook my head again.

Siobhan nodded, but she couldn't elaborate as one of her tables must have gestured for her attention, and she sprinted across the pub floor.

Killian blatantly stared at her ass. "Goddamn is that woman smoking."

I rolled my eyes at him.

Brian shoved him playfully. "When you gonna make her a Murphy?"

Killian pushed him back. "Get off my ass. I'm working on it."

Finn nudged me. "Hey. So, the farmer's market?"

I swirled my glass around. "Yeah? What about it?"

"They do a summer concert series, and the band's going to play the next couple of weeks."

"And you need me to photograph it," I finished his unasked question.

"You know it. You available?"

"Yup. I'm on it."

Finn pushed his sweaty hair off his forehead and then

wiped it with the back of his t-shirt sleeve. Ew. What an oaf. "Cool. Alright, I gotta chat with the band. But ask that girl out already."

"He's right," Killian agreed.

"Mmmhmm," Brian added.

"Fuck this, youse are annoying as fuck. I'm outta here," I told them.

Killian waved my receipt at me. "Not until you cash out."

I took it from him and pulled my card out of my wallet, sliding it back to him. I angrily signed my receipt, much to the amusement of my brothers, and then high-tailed it out of there.

Walking back to my apartment, I realized those drinks were way stronger than I thought. Killian had a heavy hand, and I knew he slid me a family discount. Usually, he didn't do that, but he knew I was fucked in the head.

Drakesville being walkable was why I had entertained the idea of leasing the storefront. Otherwise, I would have continued to work out of rented spaces in the city. It felt like I was putting down roots here. Or coming home. And I wasn't sure I wanted that. Or maybe I did. Conflict swirled inside me of what I really wanted. Now that I was here, I hoped I figured it out.

I pulled my key out and struggled to get it into my lock. Until I realized that it was Willow's door. Those last two drinks had me fucked up.

After finding my door and unlocking it, I stumbled up the steps and into my apartment, careful not to trip over boxes until I crashed onto my bed.

I needed to get my shit together and order the chaos of my life. And I had to stay clear of Willow. She'd only bring out the wild man in me, and that was strictly for the bedroom with my chosen partner. Not a client. Never, ever that.

I pulled out my phone and texted Mindy again.

> ME: Do I have appointments tomorrow?

> MIN: Look at your damn calendar.

> ME: Help me, obi-wan Mindy.

> MIN: Editing day. Working on photo selections for the art show.

Thank God. I could sleep in and maybe dig through some of these boxes. I saw a message from one of my social media apps pop up. It was on my business profile, so I checked it, thinking it was a client. I groaned at who it was.

> HENRY: Baby don't block me. Come back to the city and play with me.

God, he was getting desperate. Didn't he get the hint? We were fucking done.

I blocked him and threw my phone down.

As much as I was apprehensive about this move and what I was doing in Drakesville, it was messages from Henry that were the universe's way of telling me I was doing the right thing.

CHAPTER EIGHT

WILLOW

"*A*nd this is our new espresso machine," I announced with a flourish to my new hires.

Did I want to be doing training on the morning shift today? Nope, but I needed to get everyone in place and fill out staffing so I could finally relax. Plus, being busy kept my thoughts from being too loud in my head.

Like the ones about how I made a fool out of myself the other day. I shouldn't have listened to Mindy's advice to seduce Lachlan. I stripped myself down and made myself vulnerable, only for him to yet again run away. I needed a few days to recuperate from it.

"Any questions so far?" I asked.

All three of them shook their heads.

My gaze traveled over to Siobhan, who had walked over to the door and flipped the sign to 'OPEN.' She gave me a nod, indicating she felt good about the new hires. They all had great experience, and I needed that in the shop. More hires out front meant I had more time for the business and marketing.

It wasn't long before we had our first customer of the day. I smiled at the balding man in a tailored dress shirt and dark dress pants. I bought him those last year for his birthday.

"I'll handle this one," I said

"New hires?" Dad asked.

"Breaking them in today," Siobhan added.

Dad grinned. "Well, in that case, let me test one of them and give them something complicated."

I crossed my arms over my chest. "Don't listen to him. He just wants a small black coffee."

Siobhan already had it ready and slid it over to my dad. He was our best customer.

Dad usually stopped by most days before he drove to Philly for work. I couldn't imagine doing that. I loved that my commute consisted of merely walking down my steps and unlocking the door to the shop.

Siobhan took over training as I led my dad over to the table by the window. I sat with him as he took a couple of sips of his coffee.

"This is good. New roast?" he asked.

I nodded. "Trying a dark roast."

"That's great, pumpkin. How's business?"

"Good. Three new hires. Oh! The brewery's gonna make a coffee beer and use my beans. The brewmaster reached out to me himself. I'm about to head over to the roastery to make sure my guys got it covered."

Dad couldn't help the smile that broke out on his face. "I'm so proud of you. Look at all you accomplished. Now if you could find someone to settle down with, your mother would be happy."

I gritted my teeth. "I'm too busy with the shop."

"Your mother worries you work too much."

She wasn't wrong about that. That was why half the time they wanted me to come visit, I couldn't get away.

"I had a lot of turnover and had to pick up the slack," I explained.

Dad nodded. "I get that, honey. When you have a free night, we'd love for you to come over for dinner. We barely saw you at Aspen's wedding."

"Okay," I agreed.

He took another sip of his coffee and then stood. He gave me a kiss on the forehead and was out the door. I walked into the office to prepare myself for the day.

I wanted to get over to the roastery, but I had some other things to deal with before I did. Like telling Bob once again that no, he couldn't get a discount outside our agreed-upon terms. The guy was seriously pissing me off. I wanted to sic my cold-blooded lawyer mother on him. Abigail Rivers wasn't a woman to be played with, especially with contracts. Since she wrote most of mine, if I emailed her for help, she might try to throw hands. But in the politest lawyering way possible.

I dealt with Bob again, made sure our inventory order was set, and then worked on the schedule. By the time I was finished, I still hadn't made it over to the roastery, and the opening shift had flown by.

Siobhan stopped by the office. "I'm gonna head out. Matteo will finish training."

I nodded. "Okay, good. What do you think about the new hires?"

"They picked it up quickly. I'm glad you can fill in the space for when I go out on leave."

That was why I hired all of them. Siobhan was the best,

and I needed talent to fill her shoes. I couldn't do it all by myself.

She reached out and squeezed my hand. "You okay? You haven't seemed yourself in the last couple of days."

Leave it to Siobhan to notice that. She was already an insightful mom, and her baby wasn't even born yet.

"Yeah, I'm good," I lied. "Just stressed out, as normal."

"Can I help?"

I shook my head. "No. I'm not having your baby daddy come in guns blazing because I had you working more toward the end of your pregnancy."

She let out a light laugh. "He does that, huh?"

As jealous as I was of what they had, a small smile crept across my lips. "Because he loves you."

"If it's about Lachlan, he'll come around. The boys have been working on him. He's in a weird place right now. He might not be ready to date yet."

"It's not about him," I lied again.

She knew I was lying through my teeth, but instead of calling me on it, she squeezed my hand again and then left.

I walked out to the shop floor and found one of my managers, Matteo, finishing training the new hires.

"Hey, boss lady," he teased.

"You good if I head out for a bit? I need to check on the beans."

He waved me off. "We're solid."

"Text me if you need anything. I'll just be on the other side of town."

I didn't wait for his reply and headed out the door, grabbing my purse and searching for my keys. My car was parked out on the street in front of the shop, like always. Street parking was one major downside to living above the shop, but you got used to it after a while.

71

I unlocked my car and slid into the driver's seat. The light sounds of an indie rock band blared out of the stereo, and I welcomed the noise.

When the space next door went up for lease, I considered it. I thought long and hard about renting that space, too. We could have moved the roastery next door and done tours to show people how we made our coffee beans. But when I finally felt like it was a sound business decision, someone already leased it. So, while the roastery was on the other side of town, it was still in Drakesville. It was a sense of pride to say my shop and its products were all local.

To be honest, sometimes it was nice to get into my car and leave the shop behind me. Even if it was only a five-minute drive.

I found a spot in front of the roastery and parked. My team of roasters were great. Some of them were my original baristas who got interested in the craft when I first started roasting on a grill in my parents' backyard.

I got out of my car and walked into the storefront we used. I shelled out the money this year for two new Loring Smart Roasters to up production. I was still waiting to see if that was a good business investment. The brewery calling to use our beans told me it was. As long as I saw the growth in our bottom line.

The smell of toasted bread and hay hit my senses as I stepped into the room where our machines were chugging along. The current batch was still in the browning stage, and I loved the smell of the process.

"Hey, boss lady," Jack called out. "Here to micromanage me some more?"

I grinned. When you lived in a town as small as Drakesville, it wasn't unusual to be friends with your ex. It was hard to avoid them. But it may be a little odd for them to be your first-ever employee who now headed up your roastery.

"Wanna make sure we're all good for the order from the brewery," I explained.

Jack waved me off. "Me and my guys got it. Relax."

I took a deep breath. "I want this partnership to be a success. The brewery's wildly popular. It could really increase sales."

"Making our own roasts increased sales—that's how they noticed. Right?"

I nodded.

My business was successful. There were still the trials of making sure I stayed out of the red, but my cautious nature had ensured that.

"Then go home and let us take care of it."

I glared at him. "You're annoying."

"I got it covered."

"I know."

He eyed me suspiciously. "Or is it because something else is on your mind?"

I felt my face grow hot. "Um, no."

A salacious smile spread across his face. "No? Not because Lachlan Murphy moved back to town?"

"Uh..."

He burst out into a big belly laugh. "Man, you've been carrying that torch for a long time."

I fidgeted with the hem of my t-shirt. "Is there something wrong with me?"

"Huh?"

I looked down at my feet. "Like a reason he wouldn't be interested in me?"

"Will, he'd be the dumbass of the century to reject you."

I nodded. "Right. Thanks."

Jack gave me a hard look. "I mean it. We were shithead teenagers who weren't right for each other, but maybe now Lachlan can see the real you."

"Maybe," I said with a shrug. "Now get back to work."

He grinned at me but did as I asked.

Before I left, I double-checked everything was, in fact, okay. Checking on the machines and listening for the pop of the beans cracking, making sure they didn't burn. I triple-checked inventory and placed a new order for our supplier. Jack had to kick me out before I'd leave.

The life of a business owner was never over.

I drove back over to my shop and squinted at two figures standing on the sidewalk in front of my door. Not at my shop, but in front of my apartment.

I checked my phone and rubbed my temples at all the texts I had ignored while I was busy working. A lot from Mindy asking to regroup re: Lachlan, and then one from my cousin asking if we were still on for takeout and wine tonight.

Crap. I forgot about that.

I got out of my car, locked it, and walked up to the two women.

"You're a hard woman to find," Mindy said.

Aspen gave me an annoyed look. "You were at the roastery and forgot we had plans."

"Sorry. I'll explain later."

Aspen held up the boxes. "I got food from the pub. You're lucky I love you."

I keyed into the door and led them up the flight of stairs and then keyed open my inner apartment door, letting them into my space.

Mindy glanced around my apartment, taking in my

paintings and colorful furniture. "Oh, this is cute. Who's the artist? I love the moons and fairies."

"She is," Aspen answered for me.

"Oh. That explains the paintings in your shop."

Aspen went into my tiny kitchen to find plates and put out the food. Usually, when we got dinner to drink and gossip, we ate like trash by getting a bunch of appetizers. We hadn't done this since before the wedding, and she needed a break now that it was over.

I poured glasses of wine and brought them out to my living room, handing one off to Mindy, who had made herself comfy in my armchair. Aspen and I sat on my velvet blue couch.

"So, how was your honeymoon?" I asked my cousin.

She shook her head at me. "Oh, no you don't. Tell me what's going on."

I sighed and gestured to Mindy. "Have you met Mindy?"

"Yes! One of the photographers at my wedding. Now tell me, what has you all a mess?"

"This is my fault," Mindy admitted, giving me a sheepish look.

"Explain," Aspen demanded.

I reluctantly told her everything that had been going on, including Mindy's idea to seduce Lachlan. Heat rose on my neck as I went into detail about the boudoir shoot. I had made a complete fool out of myself.

Mindy sipped on her wine pensively. "You read that wrong."

"Huh?"

"Lachlan's boudoir shoots are hot," Aspen said. "But he was a complete professional when he did mine. Maybe that's why he ran out. He was trying to keep that air of respect there."

Mindy gave a tilt of her head in agreement. "This is my fault. I forgot he guards himself. But I know it affected him."

I leaned down to take a piece of pita bread and dip it in hummus. "How?"

She gave me a saucy grin. "Because he passed the post-production job off on me."

I took a bite of my bread, trying to comprehend her words. She was Lachlan's assistant, so that didn't seem that outlandish.

"He's a control freak about his photography. He lets me do the admin work he hates doing, but the real work — doing the art is where he shines," Mindy explained.

"I still don't think he's interested," I said.

"He so is," Aspen argued. "Kai said he couldn't stop staring at you at the wedding. He thought it was hilarious that he was still hung up on you."

I paused as I went to grab a mozzarella stick.

Hang on, what?

I cocked my head at her, and Aspen slapped a hand over her mouth, realizing what she said. I shifted my gaze to Mindy, and she had a knowing look on her face.

"Either of you wanna explain that one?" I asked.

Mindy waggled her eyebrows, but Aspen mimed zipping her lips.

"Explain!" I demanded.

"Will, Lachlan had a crush on you in high school," Aspen told me gently. "You knew that, right?"

I slowly shook my head.

"Really? It was so obvious. But then again, you were the hot cheerleader, and everyone was in love with you."

That wasn't true.

Lachlan had a crush on me that whole time? And yet, after Jack and I broke up, he never took me up on my offers to hang out. I thought I annoyed him.

Mindy put a hand on my leg. "Let me see if I can work my magic tomorrow. I'm helping Lachs finish unpacking his place."

I took a bite of my mozzarella stick, reveling in the crunch of the fried outer part. "Don't bother."

Aspen set down her wine. "Why not? Will, you've never been one to back down from a challenge. Why now?"

"Lachs needs someone pushy," Mindy agreed.

I swallowed my food, thinking hard about why I was so ready to give up on the elusive Murphy Brother. "Because I can't keep taking this rejection. Besides, I'm so busy with the shop anyway."

"Bullshit!" Aspen called me out. "You just hired three new people. THREE! Girl, make time for someone that matters."

I frowned at her. "What's that mean?"

My cousin rolled her eyes. "Kacey wasn't good for you."

"I thought you liked Kacey."

Aspen shoved a mozzarella stick in her mouth so she didn't have to answer.

Mindy's eyes got big. "Oooh. Tell me more about that."

"My ex," I explained. "She said I didn't have time for her. Which was true."

"Also, she was mean," Aspen added.

"No, she wasn't," I argued.

Aspen gave a slow shake of her head. "Girl, you were too in love to notice all the teasing she did to you wasn't light-hearted. It was mean girl shit."

I tried to remember what Kacey would have done to make my cousin think that. I remembered how she said blue made me look washed out. I thought she was being helpful, and I stopped wearing that color, even though it was my favorite.

Oh no. When she met my other cousin Rowan, she asked how far along she was. Rowan was a voluptuous, plus-sized woman who had laughed it off. But she shouldn't have.

I put a hand on my mouth. "Oh no. She asked if Rowan was pregnant."

Aspen nodded. "And you know I don't fuck with people who hate on my sister."

Mindy swirled her wine in her glass. "Lachlan would never say anything like that."

"Of course not," Aspen agreed. "He's always been a sweetie."

"He is. Most of the time..." Mindy agreed. "So, what's our plan?"

I took a gulp of my wine before answering. "I'm going after what I want."

"Atta girl," Mindy cheered.

"I like this girl," Aspen said, pointing at Mindy.

I grinned. "Me too. She forced me to be her friend."

Mindy waved her hand back and forth like a scale weighing judgment. "Eh. Forced or persuaded. It's a fine line. Now, let me work on that frustrating man. He still thinks you're just being nice."

I groaned. "What else am I supposed to do? I already showed him my boobs. And he was such a gentleman he didn't even look below my eyes."

That had them howling with laughter.

I downed my wine in one go. I wasn't sure how Mindy could help, but I would give it another try. I never backed down when there was something I wanted. Why stop now? Even if my heart was screaming at me to protect it.

CHAPTER NINE

LACHLAN

I didn't have time to take off from my business, but if I didn't unpack my apartment today, it would've never gotten done. I'd have lived in boxes forever, a constant reminder of the upheaval I put myself through. So today, we needed to tackle it head-on.

Thank God for Mindy. I honestly didn't know what I'd do without her.

Mindy fluffed a decorative pillow and placed it on my bed. I didn't care about decor, so I let her design my bedroom. Usually, it was merely a place to crash in between all my work. Especially during the summer months when wedding season was in full swing.

"Ta-da!" she cheered.

"We still need to finish my kitchen."

She waved me off. "That's unloading dishes. It'll be a piece of cake."

While it had been a long day, had she not been a drill

sergeant about going room by room, box by box, we'd never have gotten it done.

She floated into the kitchen, and I followed behind her.

"So..." she started.

Oh, here we go. I was waiting for the other shoe to drop when she brought up why I passed off Willow's photos to her.

"Spit it out, Min."

"Why do you want me to handle processing Willow's photos? You love perfecting your art. Especially with our boudoir photos."

"You need the practice," I lied.

Okay, not quite a lie, but not the whole truth either. I handled a lot of editing, but she was more than capable of doing it. I usually was a control freak about it.

She shot me an annoyed look. "We both know that's a lie."

I groaned and muttered under my breath.

"What?"

"I used my bedroom voice on her."

Mindy's eyebrows rose to the ceiling. "Really? How?"

"I growled at her to drink her water."

Mindy stared at me for what felt like years but was truthfully only seconds, and then she burst out into laughter. "What's with you Doms and telling people to drink their water?"

"I'm not a Dom."

She rolled her eyes. "Stern Brunch Daddy, then."

What the fuck was that?

I didn't consider myself a Dom. I respected the BDSM community and even had some boudoir clients who incorporated the lifestyle into their photos. But I wasn't in the community. I liked to be dominant and obeyed in the bedroom, but only then.

"Why is that a problem?" Mindy asked.

"It was inappropriate," I explained. I strode over to her and took the glass out of her hand, putting it in the right cabinet. I might reorganize that later since she put some of those where I didn't want them.

"Control freak," she mumbled under her breath, but loud enough that she wanted me to hear it. "She's been asking you out, and you're too oblivious to notice. She probably liked it."

I shook my head. Definitely not. Those photos weren't for me. "Can you please handle the editing?"

Her eyes narrowed to slits. "Fine. But this isn't the end of this conversation."

It was if I had any say in it, but she kept her mouth shut as we dug into my kitchen boxes for the next hour.

Afterward, I slumped onto my couch in defeat.

Mindy grabbed her purse off the armchair and slung it over her shoulder. "I'm outta here."

"Hot date?" I joked.

"You know it."

She was out of my apartment before I could give her the third degree about it. I grabbed my laptop off the coffee table and sunk into work. I was still working through the photos from Kai and Aspen's wedding, in addition to other editing projects that had piled up by taking two days off.

I worked for the next few hours until my phone kept buzzing.

FINN: Summer concert tonight, remember!

Good thing I lived twenty feet away from the town square. I already heard his band from here.

I finished editing my current photo, backed up my work, and closed my laptop. I grabbed my camera and put it around my neck, then left my apartment.

Now that my place was put together, my chest felt lighter. Like I had been holding all my anxiety about the move there. As I walked down the street, the universe whispered to me the answer to the question that had been on my mind since I moved.

This is where you belong.

I spied tables and booths dotted along the walkway of the square as I made my way through the crowd. The parking lot in front of the square had been blocked off and replaced with a stage. Front and center, my brother Finn tore it up on his fiddle, his red hair waving with his movement and his kilt blowing in the summer night air. Truthfully, I loved photographing him in motion while he played. It made for great action shots.

I worked my way through the aisles of people crowded in front of the stage. Once they saw the camera around my neck, they let me through, assuming correctly that I was with the band.

I shot different angles while the band played on, even getting one of Finn and Eilish as they faced each other to play their respective instruments. I felt like I'd have to shove that one in his face, so he'd see the love they had for each other. Give him a taste of his own medicine.

Satisfied with my work, I waved at Finn, who nodded in thanks, and Eilish smiled at me through her singing. Damn, she was belting out that Cranberries song hard tonight. The band was on all night during the farmer's market, so I'd get more shots later. It gave me the opportunity to check out all that was available at the various stalls.

One thing I loved about Drakesville was all the community events, and local produce was cool. I loved supporting my community rather than a multibillion-dollar corporation.

When I first opened the studio, I didn't hang around town, so it was nice to see different community members out and about tonight. I liked that the farmer's market here was a fun nighttime event.

I strolled through the tables, picking up a block of goat cheese and a loaf of artisan bread, before I stopped short at the booth for the coffee shop.

Willow gave out coffee with a smile on her face. She was dressed casually in a Drakesville Drip t-shirt and jeans that hugged her curves, and her dark hair was pulled up in a loose ponytail. Why did I immediately think about pulling on that while doing something completely inappropriate?

But those thoughts zoomed out of my brain when I saw Bob Douglas marching over to her, his face red with anger. I inched closer to her booth, my hackles raised at how the larger man encroached into her space and boxed her in. I didn't like that at all.

I stepped closer, hoping to see what all the fuss was about.

"We have a contract," Willow told him, her tone firm but polite. "I'm happy to renegotiate upon its expiration."

Bob stuck a finger in her face. "Listen here, little girl."

Oh, hell no.

I might not use my fists like Killian or have muscles like Ronan to back up my words, but that didn't mean I'd stand by and watch someone be talked to like that.

I cleared my throat. "Everything alright here?"

Willow's head jerked over in my direction, but Bob's glare cut like a knife. "Stay out of it, boy."

Willow rolled her eyes. "This is not the time nor place to discuss this. If you want to break our contract, please refer to the terms and the fee associated with that."

Whoa, total boss lady coming out tonight. That was hot. I liked a lady who knew how to handle herself.

I swore Bob had steam coming out of his ears. "I'm not fucking paying that shit!"

I spied my brother Ronan coming up behind Bob. "Do we have a problem here?"

Bob jumped at Ronan's presence. Ro was a commanding force, and with his big arms crossed over his chest, he was a formidable opponent.

"Do we?" I asked, leveling Bob with a hard stare.

He shook his head. "Uh...no. No problem."

"You're lucky I still even sell to you, Bob," Willow said, her voice harsh but unwavering. "I'm truly sorry about your dad, but he would've never spoken to me that way."

"Tell her you're sorry," I growled out. I clenched one of my hands into a fist and shot daggers at this insufferable asshole who thought shouting at a woman was how he got his way.

A proud smile built across my brother's face at the sound of my voice. Bob muttered a lousy apology and stomped off.

What a dick.

"You good, Will?" Ronan asked.

She gave a slight tilt of her head. "Mmmhmm. He's a bully."

I reached a hand out toward her and put it on her arm in comfort. "Are you sure?"

Her gaze shifted upward toward me. We stood staring

like that for only a few seconds, but my heart skipped a beat at the look in her intense amber eyes. "I'm good. Thanks for coming to my rescue. Let me get you a coffee on the house."

I shrank away from her, my hand immediately going cold at the loss of her touch. "Oh, that's okay. Anyone would've done the same."

"I'll take that coffee," Ronan piped up.

She grabbed a to-go cup and poured a hot cup of coffee for Ronan. He fixed it with milk and took a sip. "What about you?" she asked me.

"Black coffee."

A ghost of a smile edged around her mouth. "I knew that, but what roast do you want? I have my new dark roast Drakesville Night or my standard Drakesville Morning."

"I like the Drakesville Morning."

She poured me a cup and handed it off. "Enjoy." She eyed the items in my hands, and her eyes lit up. "Oh! That's the best goat cheese I've ever had."

I lifted the package in my hand. "Oh? Yeah, I like a good cheese board."

"I have a great wine that goes perfectly with that."

"Oh. Cool."

She pushed a strand of hair behind her ear. "Maybe you could come over sometime, and we can trade."

"Um..."

"If you want..."

"Uh...sure," I mumbled. She was for sure being neighborly again. I held up my camera and pointed toward the stage. "Well, I gotta get going. Finn needs me to take more photos."

Disappointment flashed across her face, but only for a second. I wouldn't have noticed it had I not been so focused on staring intently at the raven-haired beauty. I didn't wait for her to respond and walked away before I did something rash.

She was so cute, but I wasn't one that messed with someone in a relationship.

Ronan shook with laughter as we walked together toward the stage.

I nudged his shoulder. "What?"

"She was asking you out, you numbskull."

I shook my head. "She was being polite. Besides, she's dating someone."

Ronan gave a slow shake of his head. "She's not."

He didn't know that. He wasn't the one behind the camera taking those photos of her. Maybe her relationship was new, and people didn't know yet. Aspen mentioned Willow and her girlfriend broke up last winter. She probably didn't want all of town talking about her new relationship yet.

"Bro, you're too in your own head about this," Ronan said. "She was giving you the eyes."

I scoffed. "What eyes?"

"The please 'fuck me' eyes."

We made our way to the front of the stage, and I brought my camera to my face again, snapping a few additional shots of the band. "No. She wasn't."

"You're hopeless."

"You're one to talk," I whispered under my breath.

Ronan didn't respond. I lifted my camera from my face and turned to him. Only to find his eyes following a pretty blonde walking with the chief of the volunteer fire company and holding onto a leash with a big Dalmatian on the end.

"You sure are on my ass for someone who salivates anytime you notice Freya Reynolds. Why don't you ask her out?"

He glared at me. "Stay out of my love life."

"Good. Stay the fuck out of mine, then."

God, I loved my brothers, but I also wanted to strangle them. There was no in-between.

I took that as my sign to get out of there.

I walked the short distance back to my apartment. I ate a donut at the market, so I heated something quick for dinner and got back to work.

I loaded the photos I took and started the culling process. I knew what Finn was looking for, so that was easy. I worked hunched over my laptop on my couch for a couple of hours until I noticed how late it was.

Checking the time on my phone, I saw a text from one of my other needy brothers.

> KILLIAN: Can you take photos of Siobhan's baby shower?

> ME: Mom already asked. I'll be there.

> KILLIAN: Thanks, bro. You better now?

I ignored that last part.

I ran through my calendar for tomorrow. No shoots again, so I could sleep in after a late night working. I had a wedding Friday and another one Saturday, then the baby shower was Sunday. It was going to be a busy weekend.

I grabbed one of my Moleskine notebooks off the coffee table and wrote out my to-do list. There was something so satisfying about physically crossing things off a list.

To-do:
Send Finn band photos

Send proofs & set up video conference for the Rachels Wedding

Finish culling photos for Kai & Aspen's wedding

Begin retouching Kai & Aspen's photos

Send proofs & set up video conference for Kai & Aspen

Begin culling Willow's boudoir photos

I paused my pen on that last one. Mindy saved my ass by backing up those photos. I hadn't been able to look at them since I shot them.

Against my better judgment, I opened the folder on my computer. The first image was of Willow wrapped in the bi flag. Mindy put that first to see if I'd ask to put it in my upcoming art show. The angle I took had just the right light and shadow that it hid her nudity. It was subtle, but it spoke to me on a deeper level as a queer person in tune with themself. It was perfect for the exhibit showcasing Queer Joy, but I'd never ask her to display it. These were her personal photos, not to stroke my ego.

I scrolled through more of the photos, deleting ones out of focus, and trying to think of Willow as merely a subject. I dragged out a breath when the photos of her in that blue lingerie set popped up on my screen. She lay on the bed, her hand on her lips suggestively and her curls around her head like a halo. I couldn't help the way my body reacted, even though it was unethical.

I saved my work and shut my laptop, placing it back on the coffee table. I needed a cold shower to forget how inappropriate this was.

I got up and walked into my bathroom. I stripped down and turned the water on, then stepped inside, letting the cool water wash down my aching muscles. But as soon as I closed my eyes, the image of Willow was there behind them. Like the sexy coffee shop owner was branded into my brain.

"Fuck it."

I turned the water to hot; this wasn't working anyway.

I ran my hand down my abs and wrapped it around my dick. I might go to hell for this but fuck it. I stroked slowly as the images of Willow flowed through my imagination. They shifted from the actual photos to a fantasy of her in my bed waiting for me, wearing that set and looking up at me with those hopeful eyes.

As my fantasy took over, I stroked hard. Images of me ripping that lingerie to shreds and fucking her until she screamed came to me in a flash. I groaned and came over my hand as I imagined wrapping it around her throat.

Yup. I was fucked. God, why did she have to be so damn pretty and yet unattainable?

CHAPTER TEN

WILLOW

I held up a cute white maxi dress with blue flowers in one hand and a navy sundress with little white dogs all over it in the other.

"Which one?" I asked Mindy.

She leaned back on the edge of my bed, her face telling me she was weighing the options. "Maxi dress."

I put the blue dress back in my closet and held out the white dress. I pulled the material to the side to show her the long slit in the leg. "It's not too much for a baby shower?"

"Let me see it on."

I obliged her and stripped down to slide the dress on. At my height, maxi dresses were always a toss-up. They were either perfect, or they dragged on the ground. This one was perfect, and I loved it.

Mindy spun her finger in a circle, and I gave her a little twirl.

"It's cute, but with a subtle sexiness."

I ran my hands down the material of my dress. My

hands were freshly painted in an intricate flower design from earlier when Mindy called me up and said, 'Let's go get our nails done.' I had told her no at first since I was at the coffee shop, but she showed up, and my employees told me to enjoy myself.

I walked over to my bed, and Mindy grabbed my hand. Her own manicure was in her signature pink, but she had an accent nail on each hand with a pink flower design blocked out in white. It looked great against her tanned skin.

"She did a good job," Mindy said. "My girl in the city's amazing, but I'm impressed with yours."

My nail tech was a genuine artist, and I hadn't been to her in ages. As an artist myself, I loved the interesting designs she came up with. Kacey always made fun of me for spending so much money on something stupid. Why did she have to hate something that gave me such joy?

Huh. Aspen was right. She was mean. How had I never noticed that before? I thought our break-up was amicable, and her reasons for doing it made sense. I buried myself in my work, but perhaps there was more to it. I might have dodged a bullet there.

"Small town's not so bad, huh?" I teased Mindy.

Her smile was sly. "Maybe..."

"Doesn't the commute bother you?"

She waved me off. "It's not so bad. So anyway...what are we gonna do today?"

"Flirt with Lachlan. Shamelessly. Ask him out again," I recited.

When we were getting our nails done, I relayed how Lachlan came to my rescue at the farmer's market. Then she started to strategize. I wouldn't admit it to her, but I thought it was time to cut my losses. The man mumbled or ran away whenever I asked him out. A no would be better, at least, than I'd know where I stood.

I sat at my vanity and did my makeup while Mindy chatted with me about her latest hot date. She was so funny. She told guys exactly what she wanted, and they either ran for the hills or thought she was a challenge. She was a woman who knew what she wanted, and I admired that.

I did my makeup subtly, in a natural style I liked to do. I slid out of my chair and wandered over to my closet. I pulled out a pair of white wedge heels and held them up for Mindy. She shook her head, and I dug in my closet for my white strappy stilettos.

"He likes those," she said.

I raised an eyebrow. "Do you know that from experience?"

"Mmmhmm. But it made me taller than him, and he got self-conscious about it."

"Oh. That's because his brothers have called him 'shrimp' his whole life," I explained.

The Murphy Brothers were giants, except for Lachlan. Being so tiny, I didn't need a six-foot-three partner. That made things more difficult.

I strapped on the shoes. "Why did you break up?"

She pursed her pink-tinted lips. "We were more friends than lovers. Don't get me wrong, the sex was great, but we realized our kinks didn't match up. We were still figuring those things out."

I felt my cheeks get hot. Should I ask what those kinks were?

She let out a light laugh. "Don't worry. I can read you like a book, and you're well-matched. We're great friends and work well together, so it's all good in the end."

"I get that. My first boyfriend was my first employee, and now he handles my roasting facility."

"Interesting."

It wasn't, but she'd understand that more if she knew what it was like growing up here.

I crossed the room and picked up my present for Siobhan. I got her this cute fox security blanket that was on her registry, but I also made her some paintings of woodland creatures that would match the wallpaper she had in the nursery. Their fox theme was so cute that I had a lot of fun painting it. I hoped it fit in their nursery and they liked it.

I did a little spin again for her. "How do I look?"

She got off my bed and angled her head, studying me. "It's cute. Go get him."

I didn't question why she wasn't coming with me. She was Lachlan's bestie, but I got the feeling she didn't know Siobhan all that well. We walked out of my apartment together, and I locked the door behind us before walking down the stairs to the street.

I yelped as we bumped into Lachlan.

"Fancy meeting you here," I teased.

"Um...hi."

"Are you heading to Killian's?" I asked, gesturing to the gift in his hand.

"Walk together," Mindy insisted. "And hold the lady's gift; it's too heavy for her."

I frowned at her. "I'm fine."

"Well...I'm off," she said and tore off in the opposite direction.

Lachlan and I stood there on the sidewalk, watching her go. I shifted the gift bag into my other hand, and I was surprised when Lachlan took it from me. "Oh, you don't have to do that."

"It's fine," he said.

His eyes traveled up and down my body, inspecting my appearance. I swore heat flashed in his eyes, but I must have been seeing what I wanted to see.

"I was gonna drive," I explained.

Siobhan and Killian's house was within walking distance, but with how heavy my paintings were, driving was the logical solution.

"Nonsense. Drakesville's so walkable. I can carry it for you. What's in here anyway? Do babies need bricks?"

I laughed at his joke and started walking down the street. He quickly got in step with me. "Paintings for the nursery."

"To match the mural?" he asked.

I nodded. "I would have loved to paint that for her instead of them using wallpaper. I hope they like it."

"Siobhan loves handmade things. She'll love it."

That was true. Siobhan was a knitter, and she was constantly handing out scarves and gloves. I cherished the royal blue pair she made for me last year. They were made with such care and love.

The conversation died as we walked further on. I bit my tongue instead of saying what I needed to say.

It didn't take long to get to Killian's house. Lachlan opened the door for me, and I stepped inside. There were more people than I expected inside, but we found Siobhan sitting on the couch talking to one of Brian Murphy's daughters. She was the spitting image of Brian, with her blue eyes and red hair. Although her mother had even brighter red hair, so maybe she got it from Kelsey.

"Uncle Lachs!" she squealed and then jumped up, attacking Lachlan.

I grabbed my gift from him just in time.

"Hey, pipsqueak," Lachlan teased.

She hugged him tight and began chatting away at him.

Siobhan gave me a smile. "That's a cute dress. Lachlan, doesn't Willow look pretty?"

I glared at her, knowing what she was doing.

His niece hugged his leg. "I like your dress."

"Thank you," I told her with a smile.

"She looks pretty, Uncle Lachlan. Right?"

Lachlan nodded, his gaze piercing me. "Yes. The blue flowers look good on her."

"Thanks, it's my favorite color," I explained.

Siobhan smiled at me. "I'm glad you started wearing it again."

I dipped my head down. I hadn't realized how much Kacey dimmed my light. I shifted my gaze to Lachlan, but he was busy taking photos of his niece. She was posing and being the center of attention, but it was cute how he appeased her.

Siobhan laughed as she watched. "She's a little ham."

I held up my present. "Where do you want gifts?"

"Ooh. Gimme. My mom's driving me up a wall, and it's my shower, so I'm opening it now."

I handed the bag off to her, and her brow knitted at the weight. "What's in here?"

"Something for the nursery."

She dug into the bag, pushing the tissue paper aside. She unwrapped the first framed artwork of a cute raccoon on a tree stump. The second one was of a fox in the same wooded background, and then the last one was of a little deer. When she pulled out the security blanket, she blinked back tears.

"Oh, Siobhan," I sighed.

"It's the hormones," she explained, brushing away the tears. "Did you make these?"

"Only the paintings."

"These are beautiful. How long did it take you?"

"Not long," I lied.

As soon as she shared she was pregnant, I asked for her registry. Once she finally gave it to me and I saw her theme, the ideas circulated. Painting the set together had been fun, and then I saw what Killian had done with the nursery, and it felt like the universe had pulled everything together.

She hefted herself off the couch but ignored my offered hand. "Let's go take these upstairs."

I followed her up the steps and into the nursery. She held up a frame against the blank wall. They fit perfectly. I noticed there was another wall where maternity photos hung. The love she had for Killian showed in them.

"Oh. Wow, these photos are great," I said.

She beamed. "Lachlan took those. Apparently, he shoved them in Killian's face and told him to admit he loved me."

That was rather sweet.

"The nursery looks great. I was worried the paintings wouldn't go."

She gave me a big hug. "They're perfect. Thank you so much. And for coming. I know kids aren't your thing."

I shook my head. "Don't want them myself. But I'm glad you get to have the life you want."

Siobhan leaned the painting against the wall and placed a hand on her stomach. "So, can I ask the real question I want to ask now?"

"What's that?"

"Did you and Lachlan come together?"

I shook my head. "No. We bumped into each other and walked over together. I don't think he's interested."

"Yeah...you didn't notice how he looked at you when I told him to say you looked pretty. That man's hungry," she told me with a smile.

"Then why does he keep rejecting me?"

She frowned. "I think that's a question for him. I'm not sure why. It's obvious he's interested."

I don't know why everyone in Lachlan's life seemed to think that because the man had proved repeatedly he wasn't.

I couldn't argue my point because Killian walked into the room with a relieved look on his face. "Oh, there you are."

"Willow made us something for the nursery," she explained.

She showed the paintings to him, and he nodded. "Thanks, Will. My brother finally ask you out yet?"

I sighed.

Killian ran a frustrated hand through his hair. "Christ, he's a dumbass."

"I need a drink. You have alcohol for the childless people?" I joked.

Killian laughed. "Sure, Will. Let's get you some of that good punch Mom makes."

"Sounds good to me."

"I can't wait to have this baby and get to drink again," Siobhan said.

The corner of Killian's mouth tipped up. "That's not the only reason. You can't wait for us to meet Bean."

She reached up and met him in a gentle kiss.

I took that as my leave to go find said punch.

In the kitchen, I found Mary Pat Murphy. "Willow, it's

great to see you. I love what you're doing with the coffee shop."

"Oh, thank you, Mrs. Murphy."

She waved me off. "None of that. It's Mary Pat. What can I get you?"

"I heard there's some good punch."

She grinned. "Of course."

She grabbed me a cup, and I chatted with her politely. Mary Pat came into the shop a couple of times a month, and she was always the nicest, asking how my parents were and how business was going. Talking to her was like a warm hug.

She got distracted by another guest, and I slipped away into the backyard. Finn and Ronan waved at me, and I returned it, but I was more interested in their youngest brother.

I eyed him in the backyard, taking photos of his two little nieces. I sipped on my punch, which was way stronger than I realized. By the time I left here today, I was going to find out why Lachlan kept rejecting me. One way or another.

As the party wound down, I found Lachlan putting away his camera. "Hi."

"Uh...hey," he greeted, that stutter back in his voice.

"Do you want to walk back together?" I asked.

"Sure. I have to say bye to everyone, or Mom will get upset I was rude."

I nodded.

I made a quick bathroom trip and then met him outside. We walked together in silence while the question I wanted to ask was on the very tip of my tongue. He hadn't tried to avoid me the entire party, but his mom put him to work as her personal photographer. I got the feeling he did that often, but he was too polite to say no.

"So...did you enjoy the party?" he asked, clearly making small talk.

"Sure. But babies aren't my thing. Happy for Siobhan, though."

I dried Siobhan's tears over her previous pregnancy losses and then again when her late husband died. We had become fast friends after that, and it broke my heart that she didn't get what she wanted out of life. Watching her and Killian slowly fall madly in love made all her struggles worth it. It made my heart happy to see my friend get the things she deserved.

He nodded. "Yeah. I hope that's not catching."

I laughed. "So, you're a part of the no kids club too?"

"Hell yes. That's hard when you're in a big family, and your mom demands grandbabies. Even with Bri and Kels having baby number four on the way, she doesn't get it."

"Oh, try being an only child. My parents have come to terms with it but still make snide comments. I love kids, but that life isn't for me. I'm much too busy with the shop."

He nodded. "Yup. I love my brother's kids, but Christ Bri's can be little terrors. I love being the fun uncle."

Why did that make him hotter? Kids were a deal breaker for me. In college, I dated this girl I really liked, but she wanted a family, and I didn't. Same thing with the guy I dated after her. Kacey didn't want kids. Like me, it had been a hard no.

Huh. Maybe that's why I put up with her bitchiness disguised as teasing for so long.

We lapsed back into silence as we walked back to our

respective homes. I was working up the courage to ask him what I really wanted to know.

He spun on his heel as we approached his front door. "Well this is me. I'll see you around."

"Why don't you like me?" I blurted out, the words coming out too fast based on the confusion marking his face.

His brows knitted together. "What?"

"Why don't you like me?" I asked again, firmer and more determined.

"What makes you think that?"

I wrung my hands together. "If you're not interested, say no and reject me already."

"What are you talking about?"

"I keep on throwing myself at you, and I get nothing. I ask you out, and you either mumble or literally run away! And then I freaking tried to seduce you with those photos and NOTHING. If you were so—"

"You fucking what?" His voice was strained, and he clenched his teeth while his eyes begged for an explanation.

I dipped my head. I didn't mean to blurt all of that out.

He lifted my chin to look up at him, his eyes searing into my soul. "Say that again."

"I tried to seduce you," I whispered.

"Wait...you said those boudoir photos were for someone."

"Lachlan," I said in a low, sexy whisper. "They were for *you*."

He swallowed hard. "They weren't a sexy gift for your partner?"

I slid my hand up his chest, a jolt of energy coursing through me at touching this man. "I don't have a partner. I was trying to be subtle. But then you kept brushing me off every time I asked you out."

Relief washed over his face. "I thought you were being your typical nice self, and I wanted to respect your partner."

"You really couldn't tell I was interested?"

He gave me a sheepish look. "You know, you come back to town, and you run into old friends, and they say, 'hey, let's grab a drink sometime,' but then you never do. I thought you were just aggressively friendly."

I gave him my best sultry smile, trying to channel the vixen from that day in his studio. "Well, now that we've cleared that up, let me ask again: how about I buy you that beer now?"

A small smile barely ghosted across his lips. "Okay. Let's get that drink."

A spark of giddiness shot through my chest. Perhaps my relentless pursuit of the quiet artist hadn't been for nothing after all.

CHAPTER ELEVEN

LACHLAN

I breathed out a shaky breath. Holy shit, she didn't have a partner. I had a feeling I knew whose idea it was to 'seduce me' with a boudoir shoot. I'd be having some words with Mindy later, but tonight, I was getting to know the pretty coffee shop owner.

"Let me drop off my camera," I said to her.

"Okay..."

I left her in the street and climbed the stairs to my apartment. I dropped my camera on my coffee table and went into my bathroom.

I ran a comb through my hair and misted on cologne. Rubbing a hand through my facial hair, I debated shaving, but it would have taken too long.

I inspected my outfit. If we were going to the brewery, my loose-fitting t-shirt and jeans were fine. I was half tempted to ask Mindy if I should change, but I was a little miffed at her for encouraging Willow to do that shoot and make me think it was for someone else.

Fuck it, it was fine.

I left my apartment and found Willow waiting for me on the street. She was a sight for sore eyes in that pretty dress and winning smile.

"Ready?" she asked.

"Ladies first. Let's go to the brewery."

No way in hell I was rolling up to Sullivan's Irish Pub where two of my nosy brothers worked. Both of which had left the baby shower early for closing shifts. It would be a front-row seat to a first date, and I wasn't giving them that satisfaction. Going to the brewery meant I had a little more time before they found out I went on a date with Willow. I was already prepared for the 'I told you so' teasing they'd give me.

She filled the walk with small talk, and I tried to tell the horny bastard inside me to stop walking two paces behind her so I could watch her ass. The material of her dress swayed against her hips, allowing my imagination to run wild.

I held the door open for her, and the hostess led us to a table. The brewery was busier than I expected for a Sunday night. A sign of how successful the MacGregor Brothers had made it over the years. Back in the city, anytime a friend tried to turn me on to a cool new brewery out in the 'burbs, it filled me with hometown pride to find it was this one.

Willow situated herself across from me and scanned the draft list. "What do you like here?"

I shrugged. "Whatever's good."

"Wanna get a flight? I love the hefeweizen."

"Whatever you want."

We ordered a flight of Mac Daddy (the hefeweizen), Radle My Cage (The lemon radler), Montco Porter, and

Tattooed Mamas Drink Beer (the IPA collab with the tattoo shop next door).

"It's cool that they do so many collabs," I commented as we waited for our server to bring our flight.

"I'm doing one with them."

"Really?"

Her chest puffed out with pride. "The brewmaster reached out to me personally. He wants to use my beans for a coffee porter."

"That's cool. So, tell me how you got into the coffee biz."

Her eyes lit up as she told me the long-winded story. Describing going to business school because it was what she was supposed to do, even though she didn't love it. Her dad wanted her to work for his company, but she wanted something more fulfilling. Throughout college, she worked as a barista at one of the big-name coffee chains, but she always preferred those smaller local shops that felt like a part of the community.

She was still giving me the rundown by the time our flight was dropped off.

"After I graduated, I had to give my dad a business plan so he'd let me use my trust fund for capital. He wanted me to use it for my wedding or a house. But I started small with a coffee truck, and then the stars aligned."

"How so?"

"The old shop closed, and it was waiting for me to revitalize it. My dad wanted an updated business plan to make sure I wasn't blowing my money," she explained. "I'm really privileged that money wasn't an issue, but I've worked so hard to make the business successful."

"I never said you didn't."

She frowned. "Sorry. I'm used to having to defend

myself. The shop's been open for five years, but people still see my baby face and youthfulness and want me to fail."

"You don't need to do that with me." I turned my attention to the beer flight in front of us and picked up Mac Daddy, taking a sip. It gave off a great hint of the banana and clove flavor. "Oh, this is good. My brothers usually have the lager on hand."

"The lager's good, but I prefer this one," she explained. She reached out for the IPA and took a sip. She wrinkled her nose and put the glass back. "Yeah, IPA's still a no for me."

I laughed. "They're good."

Her eyes crinkled with a smile. "If you like trees."

Oh, the girl's got jokes. For once, I didn't feel awkward around her. Maybe it was because she looked at me like she was ready to pounce on me. Or the alcohol had calmed my nerves.

I tried the radler next and thought it was too sweet. I drank down the IPA instead. It was good if you liked a hoppy IPA, which I did. We both agreed that the porter was good if you were in the mood for it. A good beer for the winter but not in the dead heat of a humid Pennsylvanian summer. We talked about all the holiday beers that would come out in the fall and how she was excited about Christmas. Her giddy little smile at the prospect was so adorable.

She sipped on her beer, but her eyes sparkled under the dim lights of the brewery. She was so pretty it hurt.

Her gaze shifted to the small menu at the end of the table. "Are you hungry?"

"I could eat. What's good here?"

"Cheesesteak. I'm partial to the grilled cheese, though."

"Basic," I teased.

"Classic," she shot back.

Our server came back around, and Willow gave him a thousand-watt smile when she asked for a menu. He returned seconds later, and we flipped through the pages silently.

My brain was spinning out that I was here with the girl who invaded all my teenage fantasies. I still couldn't wrap my head around the fact that she had been flirting with me this whole time.

"Do you like Bavarian pretzels?" she asked.

I shrugged. "Who doesn't?"

A sly smile edged around her lips. "Let's get that."

We decided on appetizers since my mom had enough food for an army at the baby shower. My family didn't do small, and baby showers were no exception.

Willow gave our server her winning smile again while ordering the pretzel and an order of crab fries. A woman after my own carb-loving heart.

She downed the last of the Mac Daddy and pulled up the draft list again. "Do you wanna do another flight?"

"Sure."

Her eyes grew wide and pointed at the menu. "Ooh, this is new!"

"What?" I asked, my curiosity piqued at the light in her eyes.

"New summer beer," she read off. "Drakesville Summer is a wheat ale with citrus and a blend of lemon and orange peel. A perfect light and refreshing beer for summer."

I scanned the beer list. "Okay, how about that, Old Man Sullivan and... What else?"

She gazed at the beer list in thought. "How about the lager and 611 Ale?"

I nodded in agreement. She probably didn't like the last

one that much since it was an ale that erred more on the hoppy side. It was nice she chose one I'd like.

When the server discarded our flight, I ordered a new one.

Willow dug into her purse and pulled her phone out. She began furiously typing away at something.

"Everything okay?" I asked.

She held up a flower-painted nail. "I just got an idea... hold on." She went back to typing and then quickly put her phone away. "Sorry. The idea of coffee flights for the shop came to me. I don't know, though. I have to run the numbers first."

The way she spoke so passionately about her business reminded me of myself. Another thing we had in common.

She shook her chestnut locks. "Anyway, enough about me. I want to know what made you move back."

A knot formed in my stomach. I told everyone it was because I opened the studio, but the real question was why I rented one out in the suburbs if I lived in the city. Something told me Willow would detect my lie.

"The commute was killing me," I told her. Not entirely a lie. I hated driving back and forth from Drakesville to Philly all the time.

"Hmm. Then why rent here?"

"Cheaper rent," I half lied again.

She peered at me like she caught the lie, but she didn't call me on it. "Is it weird being back?"

"Nah. I come home every weekend for family dinner."

The server came back around again to drop off our food and our second flight of beer. I ripped off a piece of the pretzel while Willow picked up one of the flight glasses and held it to her lips. She took a sip, and then her eyes lit up.

She handed me the glass. "Try this."

I took it from her and raised it to my own lips, letting the golden-colored liquid slide down my throat. Citrus and what I could only describe as 'sunshine' burst onto my taste-buds. It was a good mix between the radler and the hefeweizen. The perfect summer beer.

"Wow, that's good," I agreed.

She beamed. She reached for the 611 Ale and took a dainty sip, only to scrunch up her face and set the glass back down. "Yeah, that's still a no for me."

I laughed. "Then why did you try it?"

She gave an apathetic shrug and swiped a fry out of the basket. "Had to know for sure. What if I changed my mind?"

I took a few fries of my own, watching her in amusement as she chowed down on half the pretzel. We chatted while testing the new beers and munching on our appetizers. The conversation between us never faltered, like we had known each other for years. Which I guess we had, but not like this.

This was probably the best first date I'd ever been on, and I would've moved it to my place later had I not noticed the glassy glaze in her eyes. All of that could wait until we were both sober.

"You wanna get outta here?" she asked after we finished our beers and demolished the food.

"Sure."

I tried to beat her to the check, but she snatched it out of my hands. "I asked you out. It's my treat."

I let her pay, and we walked outside into the warm summer night together. She clung to my arm, laughing while she stumbled down the sidewalk. Another sign of why I should wait to get to know her better before getting physical. I wanted her to remember it. Plus, consent was always important to me with any of my partners.

The walk back to our respective apartments was short, and as much as I didn't want the night to end, we'd have to pick this up later.

"I had a great time," she told me.

"Me too."

She gestured to her door. "Do you want to come up?"

I gave a slow shake of my head, and that crestfallen look on her face punched me in the gut. "Not tonight."

"Oh," she squeaked out in a voice so low I barely heard it. "Do you not—"

I didn't let her finish. I pressed her against the door of her apartment and showed her a preview of my plans for when we were both of sound mind. When our lips met, sparks trailed down my spine. Kissing her was as good as I imagined. So worth the wait.

She let me lead, and I took her mouth roughly, showing her what I wanted. Like a good girl, she obeyed.

I pulled back, and her eyes were wild.

"Lachlan," she panted out. "Come upstairs."

I tilted her chin up to look at me. "Later, sweetness. We're going slow. I want to take my time with you." I gave her one last scorching kiss. "Off to bed. You have an early day tomorrow."

And in a daze, she obeyed, entering her apartment without another word.

At the sound of the door slamming behind her, I huffed out a shaky breath. That was ballsy as hell, but it was clear we were on the same page. Now I needed to plan our next date.

CHAPTER TWELVE

WILLOW

I should be walking on cloud nine after a great first date with Lachlan. But as soon as I flipped the sign on the shop's door to open, I was engulfed in chaos. Siobhan couldn't open today because she had a doctor's appointment, so I was on my own. Usually, that was fine, but then the milk order never showed up, and I had a line of customers out the door. A few hours later, Jack called and said one of the roasters broke down. And to top it all off, my new hire, Tameka's, car broke down, so she couldn't come in.

I wanted to cry. I even went so far as to check my lunar calendar to make sure it wasn't a full moon. That would have made sense. But alas, just a series of bad luck.

Like any good businesswoman, I didn't cry and instead plastered on my best customer service smile and apologized for the inconvenience. Did I still get cussed out? Well, only once. Sometimes, small-town living, where everyone has known you since you were a toddler, had its perks.

I didn't have a spare minute to think about last night until Siobhan showed up for the afternoon shift.

"Oh honey," she sighed. "Bad day?"

"The worst."

She wrapped me in a warm hug, and we laughed together at her big belly pressing into me. She only had a couple more weeks until her baby was here. I couldn't believe she was still on her feet. Killian would have my ass for that.

She let me go and tied her apron around her waist. Thankfully, the rush was finally over, and she could manage the front while I sifted through resumes in the office. I could also go over to the roastery.

I rubbed my temples. I was too hungover to go there today. Jack could handle it. He only called to keep me in the loop. A good businessperson knew when to delegate.

Siobhan began cleaning up the espresso machine. I had been a coffee-making tornado, and without a second set of hands, I got lax cleaning up.

"I heard a rumor about you..." Siobhan said while she worked on cleaning our machines, and I wiped down the counter.

Wow. The gossip mill in Drakesville was quick. Although I heard about every time she and Killian were spotted together when she first got pregnant, so I shouldn't have been surprised.

"And what's that?" I asked.

She gave me a teasing smile. "That you were seen with Lachlan Murphy at the brewery last night."

I felt a tug at my lips but tried to tamp down my excitement. "I was."

"Finally! Was it good?"

"Mmmhmm."

Siobhan gave me the side eye. "That's all I get?"

I shrugged. "It's a start. He wants to take it slow."

That was interesting to me. I saw the heat in Lachlan's eyes last night, so I knew he was interested. But the splitting headache I woke up with explained why he put the brakes on something more than a kiss. Although the one he gave me had me wanting for more.

I understood what Mindy said about us being well-matched. He practically used his Dom voice on me to tell me to go to bed. Like when he told me to drink my water during the photoshoot. I didn't hate that. Not one bit. I loved the reward of being a good girl.

Siobhan finished cleaning off the espresso machine and put her rag away. "I think he's more cautious than Killian. Not everyone needs to get pregnant first before falling in love."

I rolled my eyes. "That's a hard no for me."

She laughed. "I'm aware. But I'm glad you finally went out! It took that man forever to get with it."

"Apparently, he thought I was dating someone. He was trying to be respectful."

"Ah. Makes sense. So, when's the next date?"

I frowned. "Unclear. I need to chase him down again."

She fiddled with the quartz hanging from her neck, deep in thought. I gave that to her when she was struggling with morning sickness, and it made me smile that she kept it.

The bell on our door sounded, forcing us to lift our heads and greet our next customer. In walked the object of our conversation. My face hurt at the bright smile I plastered across it.

Siobhan nudged me. "Well, there's your green light."

Lachlan stepped up to the counter, that shy look on his face again. "Hi."

"Hi. Black coffee?" I asked.

He held up the white coffee cup with the bi flag in the shape of a heart that I had mistakenly put in the reusable cup bin. I had been looking for that but hadn't noticed who picked it up. "Yes, but it occurred to me I don't have your number."

I took the cup from him and turned around to pour Drakesville Morning from the drip machine into it. I spun around to face him and handed back the cup. "You always know where to find me."

He pursed his lips together. "True, but I wanted to figure out our schedules."

"Schedules?"

"So, I can take you on another date."

He rubbed the back of his neck and gave me a hopeful look. Wasn't sure why he was so nervous. Last night, I was ready to take him upstairs and rip off his clothes. Of course, I wanted to go on another date with him. And then maybe drag him to my bed and find out if what he said last night showed what he was like in bed.

"You don't need my number for that," I explained. I pulled my phone out of my apron pocket, unlocked it, and slid it over to him. "But I can't wait to go out again. I had a good time last night."

He took my phone, pressed a few buttons, and then handed it back. "Me too."

"So where are you taking her?" Siobhan cut in.

I jumped at her intrusion. I had forgotten she was still in the room with us.

"Somewhere fun," Lachlan said coyly.

"Well, I'm free mostly nights. Even on the weekends," I explained.

He cringed. "Summer's super busy for me — wedding season. But how about tomorrow night?"

"I can do weeknights!"

God, I hope I didn't sound desperate. I was shocked he came over so soon, asking to see me again. That had to be a good sign.

"Good. Wear old clothes."

Err. What?

He gave me a sly grin and then walked off with his coffee in hand. I was glad only Siobhan was in the shop because I definitely stared at his ass in those tight jeans as he walked out.

That smile hinted at the man I wanted to see, not the man shy enough to question if I was still interested. I couldn't wait to peel back the layers on Lachlan until he showed me his true self.

"What did he say again?" Aspen asked from her perch on my bed.

"To wear old clothes," I called back to her while digging through my closet.

What did that even mean? He texted me earlier asking if tonight was still good but wouldn't budge on giving me a hint on where we were going. I tried to prod Mindy, but she said he was mad at her and wouldn't tell her.

"So, what are you gonna wear?" my cousin asked.

I put my hands on my hips and surveyed my closet. That was indeed a good question and why I asked her over.

But she was scrolling through her phone while lying on my bed, being completely useless.

Loved her, but she was not helping right now. If this was what it would be like to have a sister, I was glad I was an only child.

My phone buzzed in my back pocket.

I groaned, wondering what else was wrong at work. With one of our roasters down, I was worried about output, but Jack was working on it. Yesterday, I sifted through all the resumes I put in the 'maybe' folder, and there were obvious reasons why I never called them. I was running on empty, and in the back of my mind, trying to pursue Lachlan impeded my work.

I pulled out my phone, and that thought melted away at a text from the man in question.

> LACHLAN: Pick you up in a half hour.

> ME: Do I get any hint of where we're going?

> LACHLAN: Nope. It's a surprise.

Frustrating man.

Well, if he wouldn't tell me, I was still going to wear something cute. And summery. I pulled out a black crop top, ripped shorts, and my jean jacket. I changed into it and put on my black wedge sandals.

I strode across my small bedroom and spun around for my cousin to inspect. "Cute," she agreed.

I toyed with the frays of my shorts. "I hope it's okay. I don't care what he said; I still want to look cute."

"You do."

I settled on the bed with my cousin, catching her up on the gossip at the shop, and she bemoaned how Mom-Mom was already asking her when she was having a baby. Unlike me, Aspen wanted kids, but she and Kai literally just got married.

"I'm sorry, hun," I told her. "You know how our family is."

She gave me a weak smile. "I know. It must be worse for you."

I grimaced. She had no idea. At least she and Rowan could tag team with their parents. Me? I was dodging my parents' calls and telling them I was too busy with the shop in chaos. Which wasn't exactly a lie.

I checked my phone, and Aspen jumped up from my bed. "You look amazing. He might not want to take you anywhere."

I grinned. "Here's hoping. I don't get why he wants to take it slow."

"Maybe it's a good thing."

"Why?" I whined.

"You always jump two feet into relationships. It might be good to take your time with this one, really get to know him."

Okay, she didn't have to call me out like that, but perhaps she was right.

"Plus, it's always nice after a little edging to get it in."

We laughed together. Totally didn't want to know that about her, but I got what she meant. There might be some truth to that.

She made her leave, and a few minutes later, my phone dinged that Lachlan was downstairs. My heart leaped up into my throat with anticipation. I checked my makeup in my bathroom one last time and then ran downstairs to meet him.

He wore his leather jacket over a plain black t-shirt and

a pair of faded jeans. It looked good on him, but nothing that really said these were 'old clothes.' Where was he taking me?

"Hi," I greeted.

He scanned me from head to toe, not being able to stop the way his gaze bore into my exposed skin. That was what I was talking about. I'd handle taking things slow with him, but it was nice to know how much he was holding back. Made me think it wouldn't take long until I found out if it was true what they said about the quiet ones.

He lifted his eyes to my face and literally had to shake himself out of his daze. "You look great."

"Thank you. So, where is this mysterious date?"

He held up his hand, showing me a six-pack of Drakesville Summer. "Have you ever done those paint and sip classes?"

"Oh! Those are so fun."

That explained the old clothes. I was a skilled enough painter to not get it everywhere. Plus, those classes were easy, and I did my own thing.

"So not a completely uncool idea?" There was a shaky quality to his tone of voice that surprised me again. This man didn't get how into him I was.

"It should be fun," I reassured him. "Lead the way."

He led me to his car, and we drove the short distance to the neighboring town of Green Willow. We walked into the shop together, and the instructor led us to where we could set up and put our beer down. A lot of these places were BYOB, which was fun. I loved that Lachlan brought the beer from the other night. He sure did pay attention.

He cracked open a beer for me and handed it over. I took a sip, reveling in the delicious taste of this new beer. I couldn't wait to taste the coffee beer the brewery was going to make.

Lachlan opened one for himself. "How was your day?"

I blanched. "Let's not talk about work."

That piqued his interest. "Oh?"

I sighed. "It was chaotic today, and I'm super busy."

"Oh. If I'm keeping you from—"

"No," I interrupted and placed a hand on his arm. "I want to spend time with you."

"If you're sure..."

"I chased after you long enough. I want to see where this goes."

The corner of his mouth twitched into a half-smile. "Alright. Then let's get to painting."

He rolled up the sleeves of his jacket and holy forearms. I felt my mouth get dry at the sight. I watched his hands at work, mixing paint onto his palette.

He turned back to me with a bemused look. "You okay?"

My brain was fried by hot forearms. "Mmmhmm."

I had to drink my beer to calm myself down.

There was no way in hell I wanted to take it slow with him. I wanted to see what else those hands could do.

CHAPTER THIRTEEN

LACHLAN

*S*he was so cute when she stuck out her tongue while she painted a particularly challenging part. I was mesmerized by the way she moved her brush across the canvas, not paying attention to the instructor but bringing the painting to life in her own way. I didn't have to be an art school graduate to recognize raw talent.

The class tonight was specifically designed for couples, and our paintings were a set. It depicted two sides of a tree with heart-shaped leaves and a pretty sunset background.

Okay... yeah, it was super-duper cheesy, but Willow's sweet smile made me lean into it and have fun with it. And that was exactly what I wanted for tonight.

I held my paintbrush in the air as I watched her work. I couldn't help myself, drinking in the sight of her tanned skin exposed by her tiny crop top. Or how those short shorts made her legs miles long.

Why was I being so insistent on taking things slowly? The way my body reacted told me I wanted her as badly as she wanted me. The other night was the correct choice. She drank too much, and I wanted us to be sober. But...tonight? I wasn't so sure I could hold myself back.

I set my paintbrush down and took a sip of my beer. I checked my phone and rolled my eyes at all the notifications. My brothers had been razzing me non-stop since they found out I finally took Willow out. I should have known going out in our small town was a bad idea. Hence, the painting class in the next town over.

I swiped the notifications away and then saw a message request on one of my social media accounts.

> Henry: We both know you'll come crawling back. So, stop playing around.

And...that was exactly why I pumped the brakes with Willow. As much as I wanted to bury myself in her and see what we could be now that we both were single, a part of me was afraid I was replacing him with her. And that wasn't fair to her. I needed to ease back into dating. To make sure this person was the one I truly wanted to be with before she broke my heart, too.

"What's wrong?" Willow asked, her voice a low whisper of concern.

I slid my phone back into my jacket pocket. "Nothing."

She peered at me like she saw through me. "Are you sure? Is it Siobhan? Is the baby okay? You look really upset."

This woman was too sweet for words. Henry would have never asked if something was wrong with my family. He never particularly liked them, and that was even before Killian rocked his shit.

"No, Will. Siobhan's fine. Work stuff."

I don't know what made me lie to her. Probably because I felt like I could open up to her, and once I told her what was going on, I'd be spilling my guts out to her. And nobody wanted that on a second date.

It was a good idea to change the subject. I pointed to her painting. She had already filled in the tree and was working on the sunset. "I have a question for you... How come you never went to art school?"

Her mouth turned down into a frown. "Because my parents expected me to follow in their footsteps. I tried to take a painting class in college, but apparently, it was a senior class, so I had to drop it," she explained.

She set her paintbrush down and took a sip of her beer. She grimaced at her painting. "I suck at blending."

I gestured to her canvas. "Can I help?"

"Sure."

Instead of simply showing her, I positioned her body in front of the canvas and put the paintbrush in her hand. I was aware of how my body reacted to being pressed up against hers, but I tried to ignore those carnal urges.

"You've almost got it," I whispered in her ear. "Just need to even it out."

I guided her hand with mine, moving the brush together across the canvas.

"Good?" she asked. Her voice was shaky but in a good way, like she was nervous to please me.

I pushed her hair off her shoulder and pressed a small kiss below her ear. "Very good."

She shivered, but not because of the cold. Damn, that might be too fast for a second date. I pulled away and walked over to my painting to take a sip of beer to cool myself off.

"It looks like I have professionals in this class," the instructor said from behind us.

"Just him," Willow explained. "He's the art school graduate."

The instructor shook her head. "Nonsense. I know talent when I see it."

She flitted off to the next couple, and I nudged Willow. "See? Anyone would recognize you're an artist."

She wrinkled her nose. "I love painting. But I've never felt like I was a 'real' artist."

I frowned at that. I hated the notion that to be an artist or any type of creative, you had to spend a lot of money studying. Some people had a natural talent for the arts or were self-taught. Sometimes, they were even better than all those pretentious art school people.

"You're an artist, or I wouldn't want that painting in the coffee shop so bad."

The corner of her lip crooked up into a smile. "You can't have it!"

I picked up my paintbrush and dipped it into the paint. I stroked across the canvas, materializing the sunset into the blank space.

"What made you decide on this for a date?" she asked. Her attention was on her painting, but her body language was still engaged.

I didn't look up from my canvas as I answered her. "I thought it was a good way to get to know each other."

"Get to know each other? Lachlan, we went to high school together in a tiny town."

"Yeah, but we didn't really know each other back then," I argued.

"Okay, fair. So...what's your favorite color?"

I turned toward her. "That's what you want to know?"

Her grin lit up her face. "Sure!"

I dipped my brush into the dark blue paint on my

palette and mixed it until I got the shade I wanted. I spread the pigment across my canvas before answering her. "Blue like the night sky."

"Mine too!" Her sunny disposition was infectious.

"I know. You said that at the baby shower. You look good in it, too."

Her cheeks tinted pink, and I wondered if she was thinking about the photo shoot like I was.

"That's why I wore it during the shoot," she said in a low whisper.

Okayyy... Message received.

"So... Do you still like Celtic music?" I asked, lobbing another question so my dick would be quiet.

She broke out into laughter. "Lachlan, I said I liked Finn's band to impress you."

I side-eyed her. Had I been so clueless in high school? "Really?"

"Yes. But Eilish's always trying to get me to come out to shows."

"I forgot you were friends."

She shrugged. "Technically, my ex. She also introduced me to my last girlfriend. Probably should have heeded her warning."

I set my brush down and took another sip of beer. Small-town dating was worse than dating in the art world. It was like six degrees of who fucked who. Especially if you were queer. Queer in a small town? We all dated each other.

"Who's your ex?" I asked. Eilish had the worst taste, and maybe the nosy part of me was resurfacing. This town did that to you.

She dipped her head down. "Kacey Reed. Why?"

It was good she couldn't see my face, or the hardened look on it might have scared her.

Kacey was Eilish's ex that Killian banned from the pub. She was the worst. She hid her asshole tendencies behind a teasing tone. She made digs at Finn's weight all the time, which he laughed off, but it made Eilish protective of him. Kacey never said that shit in front of Eilish, and the one time she did, Eilish went full-on hellcat, according to Finn. He might be more clueless than I was with the object of his affection.

"What's wrong?" Willow asked, snapping me out of my memory.

"Kacey's..."

"An asshole," Willow finished my sentence.

"You deserved better than her."

She gave me a sad smile. "I know."

I lifted her chin. "You do."

She pressed her hand against my chest. "I know. That's why I've been chasing you."

My lips curved up. "I kinda like this chase. Making you work for it."

That got me a raised eyebrow. "Oh, yeah?"

"Mmmhmm. Finish your painting, sweetness."

Willow was not a girl who disobeyed. I loved that and the way her cheeks got pink at her dirty thoughts. Besides, making her wait a little could be fun. I was evil like that.

We spent the rest of the date playing twenty questions, and I found I didn't know her at all. In high school, we sat beside each other and talked about music. I had been too shy to ask her all the rapid-fire questions she was asking me now.

"How do you not have a favorite movie?" she asked, her amber eyes wide in shock.

I laughed. "Hard to when you're forced to watch whatever your big brothers want to."

"But not a single movie you'd say is your favorite?"

I shrugged. "Ehh."

Lie. My favorite movie made me a bisexual stereotype, and I knew it. She'd laugh if I told her the truth.

I watched her run her paintbrush across her canvas, finishing out the skyline. I had finished a few minutes ago, but watching her craft her art was a turn-on. The beauty and personality that shone onto her canvas were the things I always tried to bring out in my photos.

She put the last stroke on with a flourish and then stepped back to survey her work. She peered over at mine. "Yours is better."

"Nah, we have different styles. They complement each other."

"If you insist," she conceded.

"I do."

The instructor announced class was ending, and we began packing up our things. I tossed our empty beer bottles in the recycling bin, and Willow helped clean off our station. We carried our paintings to my car, where I carefully laid them down in my backseat.

I climbed into the driver's seat and started my car while she buckled herself into the passenger seat. The night was still young, but she had to be up early to open the shop, and I wanted to respect that we were on different schedules.

"I had fun tonight," she said a few minutes after we were on the road.

"Me too."

"So…"

I grinned. "So what?"

"Where to now?"

We passed the welcome sign for Drakesville, and I turned down onto Main Street, passing Sullivan's Irish Pub until I found our street.

"I figured you had to be up early to open the shop."

"I do," she admitted, but in a voice that told me she didn't want the date to end here either.

I did a few circles around the block until I found a parking spot on one of the side streets behind our shops.

"We could finish the rest of the beers upstairs," she offered.

I cut the engine and put it in park. "Maybe."

"Lachlan, are you even interested in me?"

I spun in my seat and grabbed her jaw, then took her mouth like she wanted. She melted into me, kissing me back with all the fervor I could want. But this was merely another preview.

She was breathless when I pulled away. I gave her another sly grin. "I don't put out until at least the third date."

Although if she tried to convince me, I might have caved on that and given in to our shared desires.

"I better make it a good one, huh?"

I lifted her mouth back to mine again, kissing her nice and slow one more time.

She gripped my shirt and deepened the kiss, and it took all my willpower to pull away.

"So, you do want me?" she asked.

I trailed a finger down her cheek. "More than you can know, but let's ease into this, okay?"

She let out a shaky breath. "Okay. But the next date is on me."

"Can't wait. Now be a good girl and get up to bed."

God, she was so stinking cute when her cheeks burned

red. Our tastes definitely matched up, and it would be exciting when we finally explored those. But with patience. I wanted to make sure this Willow was real to me and not the one I had made up in my head.

I got out of the car and helped her with her painting until she unlocked her front door. I made sure she was inside and then got my painting and the rest of the beer out of the car. I trudged up the steps of my apartment next door. After unlocking my front door, I set my painting down against the wall in my living room and slumped on my couch.

Giddiness spread through my chest at seeing a text message from the woman in question already.

> WILLOW: I had a great time tonight. Can't wait to do it again :)

> ME: Your move, sweetness. Name the time and place.

> WILLOW: On it!

CHAPTER FOURTEEN

WILLOW

*L*achlan proved to be a hard man to find time with. Not that I was much better with the number of interviews I had this week. But with wedding season and my need to get another barista in the shop, our schedules had yet to match up for another date.

Based on our text conversations, he was still interested. The upside was that it gave me more time to figure out a fun third date. So far, everything felt too boring. Aspen recommended doing something in the city, but I wanted to show him the magic of our town. If we went into Philly, he might remember why he left Drakesville.

My new hires were working out so far, but I still wanted a replacement for Siobhan. I wasn't convinced she'd be returning to the shop after her maternity leave. Juggling two jobs and a baby, even with Killian also working, would be a lot. I loved that for her, but I needed another permanent employee. So back to the resumes I went.

I didn't mind waiting to find time with Lachlan again.

To be honest, dating someone who understood the demands on your time was a pleasant change. He didn't complain that I had to spend more time at my shop, and I didn't whine when he was running from photoshoot to photoshoot.

My phone vibrated in my apron pocket, and I pulled it out, checking it quickly.

> MINDY: Can I put in a food order?

> ME: Kitchen's closed, my friend.

> MINDY: It's for Mr. Grumpypants. Please?

She sent me a series of pleading face images that made me laugh.

> ME: Fine! You're annoying.

Kelly had a handle on the front, and we had a lull, so I walked into our kitchen. Should I make exceptions for my friends? No, but I was going to do it, anyway. Plus, it was an excuse to see Lachlan again.

A text came through with Mindy's order, and I punched it into our POS system and comped it. I turned on the grill and got to work.

Before I hired a cook this year, I was the person slinging eggs and rolling burritos. It had taken Matteo and Kelly begging me to hire someone before I took the work off my plate. I made quick work of preparing the food and then packaged it up to take next door. Kelly had coffees ready when I walked out to the front and even made me one of my newest combinations—a coconut caramel cold brew. I called it a Coconut Delight.

"I'll be next door if you need me," I told her.

"Take lunch. You've earned it."

I didn't know about that. There was still so much to do around here. I felt guilty taking this lunch break.

I took the coffee carrier and my bag of goodies and walked next door. When I entered the studio, Mindy was on the phone and had a grimace on her face.

She inclined her head at me in a silent greeting while carrying on the conversation. "Yes, I understand, sir, but we have a contract. That your wife, not you, signed. So, we will not be returning your wife's money unless she calls us."

I quirked up an eyebrow, and she gave me a roll of her eyes.

"Well, take it up with your wife. That's not my problem." She slammed the phone down dramatically. "I'm sorry. Dealing with some bullshit today."

I handed off the coffee and burrito. "You okay?"

"Oh. Yeah, I can handle him. What an asshat."

She pointed toward the hallway. "Lachs is in his office. Can you pull him out of his mood? He doesn't do well with confrontation."

Hopefully, seeing me would lift his mood. I took his boring black coffee and burrito with me down the hall. His office door was open, but he sat at his desk with his head in his hands. My eyes widened at the number of photos spread out across the desk.

The first one that caught my eye was the same one he had at the entrance of his studio — of him at Pride wrapped in the bi flag. As I took in the others, there was a pattern to the images. A wedding of two brides, a family portrait with two dads, a drag performance, and more from Pride. Whatever was bothering him had nothing to do with the customer who yelled at Mindy.

I cleared my throat. "Is this a bad time? I come bearing coffee and food."

He jerked his head up suddenly. "You scared me."

"Sorry. Coffee break?"

He nodded and pushed out of his chair. "Let's go for a walk. I need to shut off my brain."

I handed him his cup of coffee, and we left his office together. He remained silent as we walked down the hallway until we were back at the reception desk.

"Did you handle that a-hole?" he asked Mindy.

"Got it, boss. Go have lunch with your girl and calm down."

Warm fuzzies fluttered in my chest at her words. Although, I'd feel better if Lachlan had said it.

He led me outside, and we walked toward the square. Eating lunch in the gazebo would be perfect, and there was a nice shade from the hot summer day. I liked how he thought.

"Everything okay?" I asked.

He took a sip of his coffee. "No. I did a bridal boudoir shoot, and the husband got mad."

"Why?"

"Some guys get defensive since I'm a male photographer. Mindy was there, and I checked in with the bride the whole time. She was so excited about the photos."

"So, he's a misogynistic dick?"

"Yup."

We came up on the gazebo, and despite the nice weather, it was open for us to sit in. Ever the gentleman, Lachlan gestured for me to go in first. I stepped inside and took a seat on the bench. Lachlan was close behind and dropped into the seat next to me.

I handed him his burrito and unwrapped my own.

"Does that happen often?" I asked.

"Yeah. Guys get all aggro that only they can see their wives like that. I feel bad for those brides."

We ate in silence for a couple of moments. Lachlan had been so respectful when he did my shoot, even though I had ulterior motives.

"Is he gonna write a bad review?" I asked.

"Probably. Whatever." He took another bite of his burrito. "This tastes different from the last one I ordered."

"I had to 86 cheese when I made them."

"You made them?"

"Yeah. Technically, my kitchen's closed, but Mindy begged."

His lips dipped down into a frown. "You didn't have to do that."

"I wanted to. That jerk wasn't the only thing bothering you, huh?"

His frown deepened. "I have an art show and need to decide on what I'm featuring."

"Oh! That's exciting. Is there a theme?"

His expression changed, his eyes sparkling. "It's about queer joy. My clientele has always been from our community, so I want to showcase that. My friend Hayden's an amazing painter, and they convinced me to join."

"That's awesome. Tell me when it is—I'd love to come."

He dipped his head down, his ears turning red again. This man was such a conundrum. He kissed me with confidence but got shy about his work.

"Your work's outstanding. You deserve the recognition."

He muttered a thanks and finished his burrito. I chewed on my own and basked in the afternoon sun.

"How's the shop?" he asked.

I swallowed a bite. "Good. But I'm still looking to replace Siobhan after she has the baby."

"Kill's freaking out."

I pictured Siobhan rolling her eyes when she complained about his overprotectiveness. Sometimes, she was too annoyed to see the beauty in how he loved her.

"They'll be fine," I reassured Lachlan.

I finished my food and crumpled up the wrapper. Lachlan gathered up our trash and threw it away. When he returned, he slipped his hand into mine.

"Sorry we haven't connected again," he said.

I gave him a warm smile. The butterflies in my chest were now a roaring stampede. "I have an idea of something fun for our next date."

"Okay, what's that?"

"A taste of Drakesville."

His lips twitched. "Okay you wanna explain what that means?"

"We go on a food tour of town," I explained.

Aspen thought it was a dumb idea, but it was the perfect way to show him Drakesville was cool, too. Then he'd see why he should stick around. Perhaps then I'd get more than some chaste handholding and kisses that didn't lead to the bedroom.

"That sounds cool. But not the pub. My nosy brothers work there."

That was a given.

He rubbed his thumb against the back of my palm. "I'd like to spend more time with you."

God, he was sweet.

"Then... What are you doing tonight?"

"Doing a food tour of my hometown with the cute local coffee shop owner."

I grinned. "Oh, anyone I know?"

He brought my hand up to his mouth and kissed it. "You, sweetness."

"Then it's a date."

"Can't wait."

I slipped my hand from his and reluctantly stood. We walked out of the gazebo, but he grabbed my hand again once we were on the sidewalk. I tried not to skip for joy.

We walked back to our respective shops, but before he let me go, he pulled me toward him and planted a quick kiss on my lips.

"See ya later, sweetness."

"Can't wait."

My phone buzzed as I was putting on the final touches of my lipstick. I grinned at Lachlan's message.

LACHLAN: Ready when you are.

Tonight was going to be fun. I stepped back and judged my outfit. A simple tank and jeans were perfect for a night out in town. It made it appear like I hadn't thought too hard about my outfit. Despite the tornado of clothes strewn across my bed.

I put on my wedge heels and grabbed my purse before walking downstairs. Lachlan stood on the street, waiting for me. His lips twitched as he took me in. It was nice to see that reaction again. He was dressed casually in a plain black t-shirt, jeans, and, of course, his signature leather jacket.

"Are you gonna be cold?" he asked, his gaze lingering on my exposed skin.

"Nope!"

"Okay. Where's the first stop?"

"Old York Grille."

He slipped his hand in mine. "Lead the way."

I squeezed his hand and led him on the short walk up the street. The proximity to our businesses was why I had picked it. It wasn't your typical diner open twenty-four-seven with burnt coffee. It was bougie as hell—another reason I picked it because I wanted to show Lachlan that our town wasn't boring.

As we approached the door, he removed his hand from mine and held the door open for me. When we walked inside, it wasn't that busy, so we were seated quickly.

Lachlan furrowed his brow as he perused the menu. "What are you thinking tonight?"

"The Fruity Pebbles French toast."

"You sure live up to your nickname, sweetness."

"Um. You started calling me that well before you knew of my sweet tooth."

"It's because you've always been sweet, Willow. Even to people who don't deserve it. Plus, you were always a sucker for the skittles I'd pass you in class."

I had forgotten about that completely. "You remembered that?"

He flipped through the pages of the menu. "How could I not?"

"You said your mom put them in your lunch, and you didn't have the heart to tell her you hated them."

He rubbed the back of his neck, and I laughed at how oblivious we both were back then. Just like how I pretended to love his brother's band, he gave me his candy to make me smile.

He flipped the menu closed. "Are we having breakfast for dinner?"

"Yes!" I squealed. "I didn't even think of that. But yes! Breakfast for dinner here, then a beer at Drakesville Tavern."

He wrinkled his nose. "Nobody goes there. It sucks."

"That's why I want to check it out."

"If you say so."

He ordered the chicken and waffles, and I got my too-sweet French toast. I tried their coffee and blanched. This was burnt.

Lachlan snickered. "Are you a coffee snob?"

My face grew hot with guilt. "Sometimes I can't turn it off."

"I get that. When Mom asks me to take a family photo, my brothers audibly groan because they know I'm gonna reposition them and wait for the perfect light. And take too many shots. I get one snap in before they all bolt."

I laughed at picturing his brothers darting away from him. "So, we both take pride in our work."

"Nothing wrong with that."

When our food came, we dug in, and I couldn't help but moan at how good it was. I pretended not to notice how he shifted uncomfortably in his chair or how his eyes burned into me. My plans for seduction appeared to be working.

"Did you figure out what photos you want to use for the art show?" I asked.

His mouth turned into a thin line. "Not yet."

"Well, I'm sure you'll figure it out."

He nodded, but his expression didn't conceal his uncertainty.

I made small talk, changing the subject until we were

finished at the diner. Then I fought him for the check. His smile told me he let me win.

We walked hand in hand over to the tavern. Sullivan's was closer, but I respected him not wanting to be harassed by his big brothers.

Turned out the Drakesville Tavern did suck. We waited for ten minutes to get a table and then another fifteen for anyone to acknowledge our existence. When warm beers were slammed down on our table by a grumpy bartender, Lachlan had enough.

If the place had been busy, I'd understand it a little more, but there were only two other customers in the whole place. Lachlan slapped cash on the table for our untouched beers, and we tore out of there.

And our date had been going so well.

"I'm sorry," I said.

He squeezed my hand. "Told ya it sucked."

"Wanna go to the brewery instead? Or if you're still hungry, we could grab a slice of pizza."

"Nah. Fuck it. Let's go to the pub."

Now that surprised me, but I knew better than to ask twice. We walked the couple of blocks to Sullivan's Irish Pub, laughing at the bizarre treatment at the tavern, and theorized how they stayed in business. I was convinced it was a front for something sinister, but Lachlan said Killian used to work there, and the owner never paid his employees on time. So just someone who was shitty at business. That made me itch with hives. Not being able to pay my employees was my biggest fear.

As we approached Sullivan's, Lachlan held the door open for me, and we stepped inside. Of course, Brian Murphy spotted us immediately, much to my chagrin.

"Well, look who it is!"

Lachlan shot his oldest brother an annoyed look. "Don't even start."

"Has he been grumpy on your date, Willow?" Brian asked me.

"No. We tried to go to the tavern, and it was less than desired," I explained.

Killian walked over to the host stand. "That's because that place sucks."

Then Siobhan waddled over. "Put them in my section."

Now I understood why he didn't want to come here. I wasn't sure I loved all the attention from his family.

Brian leveled an eyebrow at Lachlan, who nodded, and we were directed to an open booth. We slid into seats across from each other, and a few minutes later, Siobhan made her slow way over to us.

"Are we just doing drinks?" she asked.

I gave the menu a cursory glance. "Maybe a plate of fries, too."

"Can I get a beer?" Lachlan asked.

"Which one?"

"Drakesville Lager."

"What about you, Will?" Siobhan asked me.

"Oh. Espresso Martini if Kill will make it."

Siobhan glanced back at her boyfriend. "He will. Be right back."

"She looks ready to pop," Lachlan said.

I grinned. "Any day now."

A few minutes later, Siobhan wandered back over to us with our drinks. At the bar, her baby daddy wore a frown.

Lachlan took a sip of his beer. "How annoying is he being?"

Siobhan laughed. "You know your brother. He doesn't like that I'm still on my feet. But what else am I gonna do?"

"Rest?" I offered, taking a sip of my martini. Perfection.

Killian was an artist behind the bar. Even if he was a huge grumpypants.

"It's because he loves you," Lachlan told her.

Her eyes got shiny, and she put her hand on her belly. "I know. I love that stubborn man so much."

On instinct, I handed Siobhan a napkin to wipe her tears. She laughed while she dabbed at her eyes, and Lachlan gave her a kind smile.

"Anyway!" she exclaimed, trying to lift the mood. "Enjoy your date. Finally!"

Lachlan turned to me when she had walked away. "Did everyone know you were interested in me?"

I gave him a hapless shrug.

We sipped on our drinks and chatted more about our prospective weeks. When Siobhan waddled back over, we ordered some appetizers, and surprisingly, his brothers only bothered him a few times. The disaster at the tavern was now long forgotten.

I ordered another martini and laughed at Killian's frown while he made it.

Lachlan shook his head. "Don't mind him. He's a dick."

"No. He's got a gooey center. You didn't watch him fall in love with Siobhan."

"Oh, I sure did."

He then launched into retelling me the story of how Killian roped all the Murphy Brothers into helping move Siobhan into his house. Then, on Christmas Eve, he sent an SOS text to the family group chat, asking them to go to the Christmas Tree Farm with him. I couldn't believe their luck at finding a tree that Ronan's friend who owned the place had stowed away. But Lachlan admitted he added some fake branches to fill it out and make it look nice because it was a little bare.

We ordered a third drink when I spied Eilish and Finn setting up equipment in the corner. Eilish's eyes lit up when she spotted me, and she barreled over to us.

"Oh, your brother owes me money," she told Lachlan. "I'm so glad you finally went out. Girl here was getting desperate."

Oh my God. Eilish had such a big mouth. I wanted to melt into the seat, but the corner of Lachlan's mouth twitched into an almost smile.

"Hey, Lish," he greeted her.

"Hi! Are you still coming to the fair tomorrow?"

"Yes. I'll get more shots."

"Yay!" she exclaimed. "Invoice me. You know your brother."

As quickly as she charged over, she sprinted back to help Finn and the rest of the band set up.

"You're working at Summer Fest?" I asked.

Summer Fest was a big summer carnival put on every year in a nearby town. It was organized by the same people who ran the Harvest Fest in the fall. I always had a booth at both events.

"Yes, but it's not for Celtic Kiss," he explained. "I was hired by the organizers to shoot the whole thing. It's a good way to be involved in our community."

My heart warmed at his words. The sense of community was what I loved about this town.

"I love that. Stop by for some coffee."

He grinned. "Maybe I will."

We listened to Celtic Kiss play a set and then called it a night. Lachlan won the fight for the check, and then we walked home together, hand in hand.

He leaned me against my door and kissed me until I had to come up for air.

"Tonight was fun," he said.

"It can be more fun if you come upstairs…"

"Soon, sweetness. Be patient."

I pouted. "I don't want to be patient."

"I promise to make it worth your while."

Oof. That didn't make me want to be any more patient. It made me want to jump him.

He gave me one last kiss goodnight. "Now head up to bed."

"Lachlan…" I whined.

"Bed," he growled out. "Behave."

I usually behaved, but he was holding out on me, and I didn't understand why. That commanding tone was so firm and stern that it made me listen, even though I didn't want to. The quiet ones always made it worth my while, but I was tired of waiting.

Okay, we were back to Operation Seduce Lachlan Murphy. I'd get him to break soon.

CHAPTER FIFTEEN

LACHLAN

*L*ast night with Willow had been fun. She was so cute, and I knew what she was doing with her idea of exploring our town. She was scared I'd move back to Philly. But the longer I put down roots here, the more I realized this was where I wanted to be.

"You're smiley today," Mindy commented as she breezed into my office.

I glanced up from my computer, where I had been editing photos from Willow's boudoir shoot. These photos might be the sexiest I'd ever done, and even though I knew it was all a part of a ruse, I still wanted her to have them. I had been working hard on them because I wanted to bind them up and deliver them to her soon.

"Ready to go?" I asked Mindy.

She peeked at my screen. "Oh, these are great. You need to ask her about the flag one for the art show."

I shut my laptop lid and got up from my desk. "No. These are for her."

Mindy peered at me. "You're still wound so tight. But you went out last night... Oh my God, have you still not slept together?"

I grabbed my equipment bag. "Not your business, Min."

"Sure, it is. I'm your best friend."

"More like a pain in my ass," I muttered under my breath and walked out of my office.

She was like a chihuahua nipping at my heels. "Well... have you?"

"No."

"Why not?"

"Because I wanted to get to know her better. I wanted to make sure..."

"You don't rush back to Henry," she answered.

I frowned. "Yeah. You ready or what?"

She dropped the interrogation, and we walked outside together. "Wanna get coffee for the road?"

"Nah. There's a cute barista already there who has a coffee with my name on it."

Mindy laughed. "Oh, no way you're running back to that douche-bag. You're in love."

I scoffed. "No, I'm not. We've gone on like three dates."

"You forget how much I know you."

She skipped off into the coffee shop while I loaded up the car.

I wasn't in love with Willow. At least not yet. I had strong feelings for her, and I had fun on our dates. It was hell going home and only having my hand to take the edge off. But for whatever reason, I kept edging the both of us. I couldn't explain why. It wasn't like she hadn't shown her interest.

I slammed the trunk of my car shut, and Mindy sauntered out of the coffee shop with her ridiculously sugary drink. "Let's go, boss."

Sometimes, I wondered who the boss was.

I got in the car, and we drove off to the fairgrounds. It was an old farm that had been converted into a festival space. I spent so many years here as a kid for the Harvest Fest and various summer carnivals. It was a joy to be hired to showcase that.

When we arrived, Mindy helped me unload our equipment, and we came up with a game plan. This was a day-long shoot, and I wanted to hit all the good shots. Entrance, kids, rides, various vendors, and, of course, a lot of the stage. Celtic Kiss I had to shoot, but Mindy and I strategized to get shots of all the bands playing today.

"Good. Find your girl first. You need caffeine," she told me and wandered off with her camera ready to shoot everything in sight.

I wandered around the field, taking it all in and thinking about the best shots I wanted to get in today. It was still early in the day, so it wasn't too crowded yet.

I stopped when I came upon the Drakesville Drip's booth. Willow stood at attention, kindly directing her employees on where she wanted everything. Her pretty hair was up in a high ponytail, and the ends were curled. It reminded me of all those times in high school when she wore that bow in it and had on her little cheerleading outfit.

Damn. I wondered if she still had that thing.

She spoke to a man I didn't recognize who had a curly-haired toddler on his hip. I approached the table, and Willow spotted me immediately. "Hey! I have a coffee with your name on it."

"That's my girl."

Her cheeks pinkened, and the man beside her coughed

to cover up his laugh. She quickly busied herself with fixing my coffee and turned her back to me.

I took the man in, trying to place this dark-haired stranger. The beard made Jack unrecognizable.

"Jack, hi, uhh... Good to see you," I stumbled with my words.

"Lachlan. I heard you were back in town. Good to see you. And good that someone made this one stop thinking about work for once."

"Yeah...um... Oh, that's me."

He laughed, shifting his kid onto his other hip. "I heard the studio's doing well. Knew both you and our girl would take over this town."

Willow turned around and handed me my coffee. I pretended not to notice the glare she shot Jack. "Thanks, sweetness."

Her expression morphed into happiness at my honeyed tone. Her eyes lit up again, and a smile tugged at her lips. "Last night was fun."

"It was."

"I heard about it," Jack chimed in.

"You did not," she scoffed. She turned back to me. "Ask me why I hired my ex to run my roastery?"

I took a sip of my black coffee and glanced between them. There was no love between them. Her wrinkled nose was the expression I'd make at Killian.

"Because I'm the best, Will," Jack teased.

"Full of it."

I raised my cup. "If he helped make this, I'm on board."

Jack grinned. "Knew I liked you."

"Are you shooting all day?" Willow asked me, ignoring Jack.

I nodded. "Yup. Min's wandering around already. I better get to it."

"Come by later. I'll probably still be here."

"I will. Promise."

I left her to bicker with Jack and drank my coffee while making a mental map of the day. I'd have to ask her about why her ex-boyfriend was one of her employees. But who was I to judge? Outside of Henry, I was still friends with most of my exes.

I drank my coffee bitterly at the thought of my ex. He hadn't quit trying to contact me. Hayden called me the other day to discuss the art show and let it slip that Henry kept asking about me. That meant he was desperate.

As I finished my coffee, the crowd started pouring in, and the rides got turned on. It was gonna be a busy day. I threw my coffee in the trash and began shooting.

I shot the scrambler and the Ferris wheel and various food vendors. The brewery had a booth that I did a few shots at, and then I went over to the stage. My brother's band wasn't on yet, but I took shots of the opening act. They were...not good, but that was to be expected at these types of things.

On my lunch break, I swung back around to the coffee shop's booth, but Willow was nowhere to be seen.

Her manager—the girl with the curly blonde hair—noticed me. "Oh, she went to get lunch at the burger stand."

I nodded my thanks and headed that way. I found her at the back of the line. She felt me come up behind her and turned around to give me a big smile. "Hey, stranger."

"Wanna have lunch together?" I asked.

She beamed. "Yes! Good shoot so far?"

"Busy. But an easier gig than a wedding. Maybe."

We moved up in the line, and she ordered a bacon cheeseburger; I did the same. We opted to split an order of fries. She fought me to pay, which was adorable, and I let her. We headed over to the tent where tables had been set up to eat.

I couldn't help myself by snapping a photo of her before she took a bite of her burger. The sunlight shone off the highlights in her hair, and she looked so pretty.

"Stop!" she laughed.

"Sorry. You're too cute, I had to. Those are the rules."

She flipped her hair back, giving a little pose as I took another shot. "I didn't know I was dating the paparazzi."

A smile tugged at my lips at her joke. This woman was funny. I didn't remember that when I was the shy teenager sitting next to her in class. I put my camera into my equipment bag and gave her my undivided attention.

We devoured our burgers in silence and scarfed down the fries, making both of us laugh.

"We both had a busy morning, huh?" she asked.

"Yup."

She checked her phone. "Celtic Kiss doesn't go on until later."

"Yeah, but I'll get more of the other acts as well. Plus, Mindy's around here somewhere, too."

"I told Eilish I'd come watch them perform, so maybe we can meet up again later."

"Sure."

A heavy weight fell in the air, and I needed to ask what had been on my mind all morning. "How come your ex works for you?"

"I was wondering when you'd ask that," she said with a sigh. "Trust me, that wasn't easy."

"How did that happen?"

"After college, I moved back and was working on my

business plan before my dad let me use my trust fund. I spent a lot of time at the bagel shop studying their business. Jack worked there, and when I rented the old coffee shop and put the help wanted sign on the door, he was the first person to walk through it."

"Is it weird working with your ex?"

She frowned. "You work with your ex."

Okay, she caught me there.

Her eyes twinkled. "Why Lachlan Murphy! Are you jealous?"

I rubbed the back of my neck and shifted my gaze to the table.

Damn, she was right. I was still jealous of Jack. That was some high school bullshit.

A laugh erupted out of her. "Aw. Don't worry about that. I wouldn't have been chasing you so much if I still had a thing for my ex. Jack and I didn't work out, and we made peace with it. We were young and not suited for each other. Besides, he and Kelly have the cutest little girl. And I love that they found love in my shop."

Hang on. Now I remembered the little girl in Jack's arms this morning, who bore an uncanny resemblance to her curly-haired manager. Oh.

"Is it bad I was jealous?" I asked.

She reached out for my hand and stroked a finger down my palm. "Nope. But maybe you can show me later why I'll never be interested in someone else. Give into that jealousy."

"Maybe..." I said coyly. Even though I was thinking of how quickly we could get out of here. Why the fuck had I been waiting so long to have her in my bed? That was a stupid idea.

Her phone vibrated, and her face fell. "Sorry. I'm short-staffed at the booth and need to get back. I'll see you later."

She darted away, but I'd be a liar if I said I didn't watch her cute little butt on the way out. I was toast. We weren't going to wait this out much longer, and that was totally okay.

My brother's band went on at dusk, right as the sky turned into that mix of pink, orange, and purple. These shots would be amazing.

My camera clicked away while Eilish belted out a sad ballad. In Irish. I had no fucking clue what she was singing, but it was pretty, and the crowd was enraptured by her. As was my lughead of a brother. He looked focused on playing his fiddle, but his attention was on the tiny redhead in front of him.

Was I this oblivious with Willow? My brothers were right to call me a dumbass because Finn was hopeless. So was Eilish, for that matter.

After they played a few more songs, I found Willow in the crowd. She gave me a quick pose as I shot her picture. Most of my relationships got annoyed with that, but she took it in stride.

She let me work until the band's set was complete, and then she sauntered over to me. "Hi."

"Hey, sweetness."

"Are you off the clock yet?"

"Almost."

Mindy was already begging me to let her go home. It had been a long day, and I was tired. We got a ton of shots, but I was waiting for the lights to turn on the rides, and then I'd get a few more for good measure.

"Wanna join me while I finish up?" I asked Willow.

"Sure. My employees told me to go away because I was being a micromanager, and they had it handled."

Well, that sure sounded familiar.

She regaled me with tales of annoying customers she had to manage today while I got a few more shots in.

As nighttime set in and the lights flipped on, she gasped. "Oh, it's so pretty."

I couldn't help but snap another picture of the wonder on her face. The lights on the Ferris Wheel were a perfect backdrop, making her look ethereal.

I grabbed her waist and pulled her toward me, planting a kiss on her lips. Underneath the lights of the festival, kissing her felt like a dream. She melted into the kiss, letting me take the lead.

I had to pull away before I dragged her to my car and got her in my backseat. "I haven't kissed you properly yet today."

She grinned. "I was waiting for that."

I caressed her cheek. "You look so pretty under these lights."

She beamed. "I'm glad we got to spend some time together today."

"Me too. I like spending time with you. I'm sorry my schedule is all over the place."

She waved me off. "I, for one, understand that completely."

I hung my camera from around my neck and slid my hand into hers. A satisfied smirk spread across her face and made me squeeze her hand. She was so damn cute.

"I'm glad you get that," I told her. "Sometimes it's hard

when the person you're dating doesn't understand all the hours you have to put in."

She nodded.

She got it, and I loved that about her. It made us fit. Was it frustrating that we had to work around our schedules? Yes, but she didn't complain, and that made everything so easy. Maybe that was why I held off getting intimate with her. I was waiting for the other shoe to drop.

"Do you want to get dessert?" she asked.

I chuckled at her sweet tooth again.

"Come on, Lachs. Let's get some ice cream."

"You can, and I'll use you as my model."

She grinned and dragged me over to the ice cream cart. She got a cone, and when her tongue flicked out, I had to remind myself to get a picture for the festival. Then she kept doing it. Slower. Licking longer. Little seductress did that on purpose.

"Sweetness," I gritted out, my voice thick with desire.

"What? Aren't I a good model?"

I pulled my camera away from my face and narrowed my eyes at her. She gave me a playful little smirk.

I led her away from the ice cream cart, casually snapping photos as we walked over to the stage. A new band was on the stage, and I got in a couple more shots while she stood quietly beside me.

I felt my phone vibrate in my jeans. I rolled my eyes at Mindy's text.

> MINDY: I'm done! I'm hitching a ride home.
> See ya later.

It surprised me it took her that long to ditch me. It was time to pack it in. We got a buttload of photos to sort through tomorrow. I put my camera away in my equipment bag and then wrapped my arms around Willow's waist from behind.

"You are so bad," I whispered in her ear.

She giggled. "Well since someone said I have to wait, I need to have fun somehow."

"I told you to be good. Don't you want to be good?"

"Maybe..."

I held her to my chest while we watched the band on stage in front of us. She leaned back against me, and I breathed in her hair. She smelt of coffee beans and vanilla, a sweet combination for my sweet girl.

After the next band's set finished, she spun around to face me. "When can we go out again? This doesn't count. This is in between work."

I sighed, thinking of my jam-packed schedule this week. Oh. There was one opening. "Maybe next Friday? I had a wedding cancellation, and I'm free."

"I heard there's a brewery in Green Willow, and I wanna check it out."

I noticed they had a booth here at the fest while I was shooting today. I loved breweries, and getting a little ways out of town would be good. Away from the prying eyes of my family.

"Let's check it out."

Her face lit up. "Great. Friday it is. I have to get back and make sure we're all packed up."

I grabbed her around the waist and stole one last kiss. "See ya later, sweetness. Can't wait until Friday."

She reluctantly pulled away, and as I watched her leave again, I realized I was done with waiting. Willow would be mine. But first, I had to do something for her before our next date.

I took some more night shots, and then I headed home.

At the studio, Mindy left a note about backing up her files already. I did that too, and instead of going upstairs and slumping into my bed, I opened Willow's boudoir photos again.

I had a week to complete this and hand off the booklet to her, showing her how beautiful she was. Then I'd finally take her to bed like she wanted. It was time. No more slow. No more edging. I was ready to uncage my inner beast with the sweet barista next door. My good girl had been so patient, and I was ready to give her what she wanted.

CHAPTER SIXTEEN

WILLOW

*I*n anticipation of our date tonight, I got my nails redone on my lunch break. I told my artist I wanted blue and summery, and she delivered with a dark blue marbled-styled design that looked like the ocean waves.

Then I went back to the shop and took care of business until Matteo told me to get out of there. I loved my employees, but sometimes they were so bossy.

I had another interview this week, and I offered them the position, so my stress level was easing up. Siobhan was due on Sunday, and today was her last day at the shop. She would have worked until the minute she gave birth, but Killian had been extra annoying as they got closer to her date. She looked ready, though. Sad as I was to see her go, I was happy for her and couldn't wait to spoil her baby. I might be an only child, but I could be the fun aunt to my friends' kids.

"Are you sure you're good?" I asked Matteo while I checked the register again.

He physically pushed at my back to get me out from behind the cash register. "Boss lady, go get ready for your hot date."

I put my hands on my hips. "How did you know I have a date?"

"Fresh set," Tameka said, eying me up and down. "The fact you've been bouncing up and down all day."

"You're all annoying busybodies."

They laughed.

"Go," Matteo urged. "Get on out of here and go get hot for your man."

Sometimes, living in this town drove me up a wall.

Listening to my employees, I left the shop and trudged up the steps to my apartment next door. I tore off for my shower, stripped off my clothes, and began getting ready. I scrubbed my body until I was squeaky clean.

After drying off and doing my hair, I strode into my bedroom and surveyed my closet. Going to another brewery spelled casual attire, but I wanted to impress Lachlan so much that he finally took me to his bed tonight.

I flicked through my hangers until I landed on a blue sun dress to match my nails and pondered what shoes to wear. Wedge heels would be more casual, but I remembered the heat in Lachlan's eyes when he saw my stilettos at my cousin's wedding. Stilettos it was. It was still a cute summer date outfit.

Against the wall next to my vanity, I had a triangle-shaped display shelf meant for my crystals. The bottom of it depicted the phases of the moon and had hooks where I hung my various crystal necklaces. My friend Gemma made them, and while she was a firm believer in the power and meaning behind the stones, I merely thought they were a cute accessory.

I plucked off the rose quartz crystal, thinking of Gemma mentioning that this one was great for opening your heart to love. That made me think about the gemstone bracelets around my wrist. I usually wore a combination of bracelets made up of blue stones like sodalite or lapis lazuli and the unique piece Gemma created for me to mimic the colors of the bi pride flag. I always wore that one. But when Lachlan still wasn't taking a hint, Gemma came into the shop and handed me a set of three new bracelets she said were a part of her 'love and connection' set. I had shoved them onto the shelf, but now the rose quartz, blue lace agate, and rhodochrosite bracelets stared back at me.

I liked my crystals and my Celtic decorations, but I wasn't as 'woo-woo' as Gemma. My cynical side ignored that and grabbed the new jewelry. I slid my current bracelets off my wrist and replaced them with the new ones. I could use all the help I could get to seduce Lachlan Murphy.

I sat at my vanity and did my makeup, opting for a more subtle, demure look tonight. Leaning into that cute girl next door aesthetic had always been successful for me, even if I rather put on a bold lip.

My phone vibrated against my vanity, and butterflies danced in my stomach.

> LACHLAN: Ready when you are,
> sweetness.

I should hate that cheesy nickname, but I loved it. Especially when he gave me that wicked smirk.

Ugh! Why wouldn't he let me see his inner beast yet? I was so ready to be his.

I grabbed my purse, locked my apartment, and sprinted downstairs. Lachlan leaned up against his car, waiting. He wore a pair of jeans and a nice button-down with the top button undone, making him look so sexy. He looked so effortlessly hot. His gaze ran down my body, and heat grew in his eyes as he noticed my heels. That had been the right choice.

"Ready to go?" I asked.

"Uh-huh."

"Lachlan."

"Huh?"

"Eyes up here."

He shook his head and opened the passenger side door for me. I stepped inside, and he shut the door behind me before running around to the driver's side.

He put a hand on my thigh. "You look nice tonight."

I beamed, knowing I got a lustful reaction out of him.

He drove off to Green Willow, and we tried to find the brewery. It was in a weird location behind a warehouse near the train station. Not the best location, but understandable if they were brand new.

The place wasn't big, with only a few tables scattered about. We found an open one and checked their menu. There were a lot of IPAs on their draft lists and not much else.

"You want food?" Lachlan asked.

"Do they have any food?"

"Yeah... not much, though."

I turned over the back of the menu and saw they had some food, but it was done by a different company. That was common for breweries, but it was one reason I loved the MacGregors. They were a full-functioning brewpub. This brewery didn't have servers, as we had to order everything on our phones. It might have been because I was also in the service industry, but that didn't sit well with me.

"I think we need to order beers from the bar," Lachlan said.

"Oh. What do you want?"

I wasn't sure I'd like any of their beers. There was a fruity beer I'd probably like, but it put me off because it was called 'Chick Beer.'

"Why don't we get a flight?" Lachlan suggested.

We decided on their core IPA, a porter, a pale ale, and the 'Chick Beer.' So maybe not the best place, but I'd make the most of it since I was here with Lachlan.

I waited at our table while he grabbed the beers. He came back over a few minutes later with our flight of beers. His smile reminded me it didn't matter if this place wasn't that good. What was important was the person I was here with. Spending time with Lachlan was the real purpose of this outing.

He took a sip of the IPA and wrinkled his nose. "You won't like it."

I took it anyway and tried it. It was not good, and not because I didn't like IPAs. It felt like they dumped way too many hops in the batch.

Lachlan snickered. "Told ya."

I tried the porter next, which I liked, but it felt too thick in my throat for how hot out it was. Lachlan thought that was good as well, but he liked the pale ale the best. Chick Beer was my favorite, but the name made me roll my eyes.

I handed it to Lachlan, and he tried it. "Needs a better name."

"Mmmhmm."

Our food was taking a long time, but I wasn't sure I even wanted another beer. Having the brewery in town spoiled me, but it was good to branch out sometimes.

"How was your week?" he asked me.

It warmed my heart that when he asked, he genuinely cared about the answer. It wasn't like we didn't see each other this week since he stopped in for his morning coffee almost every day. And yesterday, I dragged him away from his desk to eat lunch with me. That had been at Mindy's behest to get him out of his own head.

"It was good," I answered truthfully. "It was Siobhan's last day, but I hired a new full-timer, so I feel better about everything."

"You feel you can relax."

"Exactly. I could always use more help, but I feel better now. Some days, I can do the business stuff instead of being behind the counter."

He nodded. "I hate that part, though. That's what Mindy's for."

I laughed. "She's good at that, though. You're the artist. You work well together."

A food runner dropped off our baskets of food. I was so hungry, I scarfed down half the chicken sandwich I ordered. It was...okay. The grimace on Lachlan's face told me he felt the same way.

"Sweetness, what's wrong?"

I sighed. "I feel like I picked the wrong place again."

His eyes softened. "No, that's not your fault. We can go somewhere else."

"Can we?"

"Of course. Fuck it, let's go to the pub."

"Are you sure?"

He nodded. "We tried it. It was an adventure. Let's go home."

We had already paid for our food and drinks, so we left in a hurry. Lachlan guided me toward his car, and we drove back to town.

I hopped out of his car once he parked in front of his studio. He was two steps behind me, but he eyed my heels. "Can you walk in those?"

I shot him an annoyed look. "Yes, I can walk in these. Now let's go. I want food that doesn't taste like they put it in a microwave."

He laced his hand through mine, and we strolled up through town together. Drakesville could be so picturesque, and I loved that everything was in walking distance. It only took us a few minutes to get to the pub, and since it was Friday night, it was busy. I spotted two seats at the bar and made a beeline for them.

Killian nodded at us, began pouring a beer, and handed that over to his brother. He winked at me while he made a complicated drink and then slid an Espresso Martini over to me.

"Oh, yay! You remembered," I cheered and took a sip of the drink.

He leaned over on the bar top. "Surprised to see you two here again. You said me and Bri were nosy."

"You *are* nosy," Lachlan scoffed.

I slid my hand onto his thigh and squeezed gently, telling him to be nice. He laid his hand on top of mine, and I laced our hands together.

"Did Siobhan have the baby yet?" I asked Killian.

He gave me a dirty look. "You think I'd be here? Nah. She made me pick up this shift tonight, so I didn't burn a hole in the floor pacing it."

A loud laugh erupted on the other side of us, and I noticed Ronan sitting at the bar. "Oh, hey, Ronan."

A sly smile spread across his lips. "Hey, Willow. Glad my dumbass brother finally took the hint."

Lachlan took a bigger sip of his beer. "You're one to talk."

Ronan waved him off, but his gaze was on something on the other side of the pub. I turned my head and saw Freya Reynolds looking bored and scrolling through her phone while a man with bright blonde hair and a polo shirt ranted at her.

I've witnessed Freya on a lot of these boring dates. She ate those men for breakfast. It was impressive. Actually... Now that I thought about it, she and Mindy were so similar. Formidable women who took what they wanted and told everyone to shove it if they had a problem with it. They looked similar, too. Hmm.

I'd have to ask Lachlan what was the deal with Ronan and Freya later. They'd be cute together, but Freya didn't do commitment. Everyone in town knew that.

Lachlan pulled a menu off the bar. "What do you want?"

"Wanna split a flatbread and some fries?"

He nodded and rattled off our order to Killian, who punched it into the computer at the bar.

I drank my martini while Lachlan rubbed a hand on the back of my neck. I don't think he realized he was doing it.

"How was the week for you?" I asked him.

He blew out a breath. "Busy. Lots of editing, and then I have weddings tomorrow and Sunday. Rinse and repeat."

I slid my foot up his leg. "Well... tonight we can relax a bit."

"I might need something to take the edge off..." he said in a low whisper. "Something sweet and obedient."

I gulped.

It was always the quiet ones.

He slid his hand down my back and played with my hair. "You know something like that?"

"Uh-huh," I panted out.

Killian set down our food, causing our sexual tension to fizzle out. "Christ, get a room."

I let out a giggle but then took a slice of the flatbread. That brewery in Green Willow had sucked, and I loved the pub. If we had to endure Lachlan's brothers teasing him, it was a fair trade for good food.

Lachlan ignored his brother and ate a fry. We devoured our food, a sign the other place had been such a disaster, and we had been trying to make the best of it. We ordered another round of drinks.

Lachlan played with the crystals on my wrist. "These are new."

"Not new. Just haven't worn them yet."

He ran his finger along the inside of my wrist, and a shiver went down my spine. "They're pretty."

"My friend Gemma makes them."

"I'm also friends with Gemma."

Oh right. After he and Kai broke up, Lachlan dated Gemma for a little before we all went away to college. How did I always forget how interconnected this town was? Especially the queer people. We all seemed to date each other. Sometimes, we were all too much of a stereotype.

He kept rubbing my wrist, setting me off like a live wire. "Lachlan."

"What's wrong, sweetness?" he asked with a wicked grin on his face.

"Why are you being such a tease?"

He bent his head to my ear. "Let's get out of here."

I never jumped up faster. Fucking finally.

CHAPTER SEVENTEEN

LACHLAN

*W*as it mean to make her squirm tonight? Yes. Did I enjoy the way she wanted to combust if I didn't get her into my bed? Also, yes. I was evil like that.

I ignored my brothers' smug 'I told you so' looks and cashed us out. Then we sped out of the pub toward our apartments. She was bouncing on those killer heels, excitement dancing through her.

"Your place or mine?" she asked, frowning at the crosswalk still blinking red.

"Mine. I want to show you something."

She gave me a seductive grin, and then we walked across the street toward our apartments. "Oh. I've wanted to see that for a while."

Heat climbed up my face at this brazen woman. But that's not what I meant at all. I gestured to the door of my apartment. "Not that. I have to show you something else first."

I opened the main door and led her up the steps. She stepped inside, and I closed the door behind her. She surveyed my place, taking in my decor, her eyes fixating on the signed and framed hockey jersey on the wall.

"Why do you have a signed Blaise Holmstrom jersey?" she asked.

"You like hockey?"

She shook her head. "Not really, but Blaise is the only out bisexual player in the league, so I love him."

"He's a client. He found out I was a fan of the team and gave me that. It makes my brothers jealous."

She laughed. "I like your place. It's orderly."

I gestured to the couch. "Sit. There's something I've been meaning to give you."

She gingerly sat on my couch, and I squeezed in beside her. I took the photo album off my coffee table and handed it to her. Her artfully manicured hands ran over the leather-bound book, trailing over the letters 'For your eyes only' embossed on the cover.

"Is this what I think it is?" she asked.

"Yup."

"You didn't have to do that. That was a ploy to seduce you."

"These are for you. Everyone should see themselves the way my camera does."

She flipped open the book to the first photograph of her in the blue sweater, kneeling on the bed with a demure look. She scanned to the next page of the different poses I had her in on the bed and then the close-ups of her knee-high socks. Those were the sexiest ones.

Her mouth dropped open, and she put a hand to her lip when she turned the page to the silhouette of her standing against the window. That was one of my favorites. She looked like a goddess at how the light shone in from the window.

"I love that one," I told her.

She flipped to the next page, the images of her in that sexy lingerie set coming up next. "More than these?"

"You'd be sexy in a garbage bag."

She let out a short laugh. "You're full of it. These are fantastic."

That stroked my ego more than anything else she could have said.

Her eyes sparkled as she went through the entire book, only to end at the image of her wrapped in the bi pride flag. Then she frowned. "What's this?"

"Huh?"

She tore off a sticky note and handed it to me. I scowled at Mindy's handwriting with the words, 'Ask her about the art show.' Why was my best friend so meddlesome?

I crumpled up the note and tossed it on the table. "Don't worry about that. Do you like the photos?"

She shut the booklet and held it against her chest. "Lachlan... is that how you really see me?"

"That's how I always saw you."

Her eyes were as big as saucers. "Really?"

I set the booklet on the table and cupped her face. "Yes, sweetness. You've always been a goddess. You haunted my fantasies."

"Was it hard to take those photos?"

I groaned. "So hard. I was hard."

She laughed. "That was the point. It was supposed to get it through your head that I was pursuing you. When I dropped that flag, I wanted you to drop the nice guy persona and take me. Right then and there."

"I was trying to be a professional. I—" I shook my head. She didn't need to know I jacked it to fantasies about her.

Her hand danced up my thigh and rubbed my crotch over my jeans. "You what, baby? Did you touch yourself and think of me?"

I grabbed her wrist. "Behave."

"Haven't I been good enough?"

"So good, sweetness. But let me kiss you before I get you on your knees."

Her cheeks reddened, but I didn't give her time to think before I crashed my lips on hers.

The kiss was needy and rough, our desperation for connection seeping out into it. She let me lead her as I angled her head to get better leverage. I licked across the seam of her lips, and she opened to me obediently, letting my tongue graze over hers.

We kissed until there was no air left in the room. I only broke it to pull her into my lap and run my hands up her bare thighs. She ran her hands over my scruff. "Lachlan, I've been giving you the green light for weeks."

"I know, sweetness. I needed time. Thank you for being patient. You've been so good."

"I like being good, but you're testing me too much."

I gripped her thighs and took her mouth again, slow this time, savoring her with each brush of my lips. She snaked her hands around my neck, threading her fingers through my hair and deepening the kiss. With every brush of lips and tongues, my hands inched higher until I pressed my hand against her center.

She buried her head in my neck. "Please."

Holy hell, her pleading voice set me off. "Please, what?"

She rocked against my hand, desperate for the friction. "Please give me what I want. I've been such a good girl."

"Yes, you have."

"Take me to bed. Please."

Okay, that was enough toying with her.

I wrapped my hands around her waist and stood. She clung to me as I carried her into my bedroom. Once inside, I set her down and plucked at the hem of her dress. "Can I take this off?"

"Please."

I searched for the zipper but discovered it was one of those wrapped sundresses. With a quick flick of my wrist, I undid the knot, and the straps fell away. I tugged at the material, and my dick hardened as I was met with white lace underneath. She helped me pull the dress off, dropping the material to the floor.

She was an angelic image in a matching set of a lacy white bra and underwear and those heels. She bent to unstrap one.

"Leave them," I ordered, my voice stern.

Her eyes widened. "Oh...okay."

"You wanted those photos to be for me, right?"

She nodded.

"Let's take some more."

She cocked her head at me, but I held up a finger and bound over to my bedside table. I pulled out my personal camera, the one that was never used for work. The one wiped after every relationship was over.

"You won't share these?" she asked.

"Never ever. These are for us. And if things go south—"

"Don't say that!"

I grabbed her jaw, forcing her to look into my eyes. "If that ever happens, I won't keep them. You have my word. These get deleted right away. They'll always stay between us."

"I trust you."

"Good. Now on the bed, sweetness."

She obeyed, laying back on the bed and spreading her legs for me. I snapped photos of her, directing her where I wanted and at what angle. She was so good at that. Obeying my every word and giving me exactly what I wanted out of these shots.

Her hand kept sneaking up my leg when I was bent over her, getting close-ups of her face. I wrapped my hand around her wrist and held it against the bed. "Behave."

"Take a photo of you holding me down."

I took a shot of my hand on her wrist, the veins in my hands bulging, a perfect seduction shot. But then I moved and wrapped my hand around her throat. "Who's the photographer here?"

"You are."

"You okay with this?"

I snapped a close-up of my hand around her neck, getting more turned on by each snap. That was probably a shitty shot, but these weren't professional. These were for me. For her. For us.

"I love it. I take direction well," she purred beneath me.

I slid my hand down her chest. "Yes. You do."

"You never answered my question."

"What's that?"

"Did you touch yourself to my pictures?"

I took her hand and put it against the bulge in my jeans. "So much."

"Did you imagine me in your bed?"

I gulped. Oh God, how did she know that?

"Yes," I admitted.

She rubbed her hand against my jeans. "Did you come all over your hands?"

"You know I did." I moved her hands off me and stepped off the bed. I gestured to her undergarments. "Get those off. I want to see all of you."

She reached behind her and undid her bra. She threw it to the side, revealing her breasts. They were small but fit her frame. I snapped another photo. "Good girl, now take those panties off. I want to see that pretty pussy."

The blush spread from her face to her beautiful chest.

I snapped photos of her shimming those tiny panties off her legs. I nearly died when she spread her legs, bearing herself to me.

"Gorgeous," I purred.

"Can I see?"

"Later."

I placed my camera on my bedside table and walked around to the front of the bed. She stared up at me, waiting for my next command.

I stripped my shirt off. "Do you love being my muse?"

"Yes."

I undid my jeans and slid my boxer briefs down my legs. Without direction, she flipped around so she faced the bed, her heels up in the air. She wrapped her fingers around my cock and stroked.

I groaned.

"Good?" she asked.

"You want to know what I thought when I saw those pretty blue nails?"

"That you wanted to see them wrapped around your cock?"

"Mmmhmm."

She stroked slower, teasing me. "How's it look?"

"Fucking beautiful."

She gave me a mischievous look. "I have a better idea."

She bent her head and took me into her mouth. I nearly crumbled at the sensation of her wet mouth combined with her slow strokes.

I reached down and grabbed her hair, pressing her down onto me. She took the direction so well, letting me press her deeper onto it. I wished I had taken a photo of this. But that might have been a little too pornographic, even for my private collection.

She pulled off and looked up at me. "You want a photo of this so bad, huh?"

I nodded.

She licked the head of my cock, teasing me. "How bad?"

"Sweetness, it doesn't matter. Be good and keep sucking."

She did as she was told, taking me back inside and stroking me with her hand at the same time. I let her continue working me over until I couldn't take it anymore.

She frowned. "Why'd you stop?"

I flipped her around onto her back and dragged her legs closer to the bed. "My turn."

I spread her legs and took that first lick. She cried out, and I kept doing it, kissing, nipping, and sucking in equal measure.

"There you go," I purred. "Come for me."

"Lachlan," she cried.

"So goood," I moaned and drowned myself in her again.

Until she cried out my name on one long note, coming all over my face.

This was like all my high school fantasies had come true.

I moved her legs off my shoulders. "Look at you, sweetness. All sexy and sated."

She looked down at me. "That's so fucking hot."

"You enjoy watching me make you come?"

"Mmmhmm."

I pressed my thumb against her clit. "You want to be a good girl and come again?"

Her face was a crimson shade, but she slowly shook her head. "I want you inside me."

I grinned and climbed up the bed toward my bedside table. I grabbed a condom and slid it on. I kneed her legs apart again and positioned myself between her thighs.

I lifted one of her heels over my shoulders. "I love feeling these."

She placed her other heel on my chest, pressing in lightly. "You like a little pleasure with your pain, huh?"

I lifted the other leg over my shoulder. "You know it."

Before she could respond, I found her entrance and slid home. She gasped but then moved with me as our bodies became one. She met me with every thrust, keeping pace with me as I rocked inside her.

"Lachlan," she moaned. "Please."

"Easy. You're doing so good, sweetness. Let me get you there."

She grabbed one of my hands and wrapped it around her throat.

Oh. Fuuuck yessss.

I gave into what she wanted, choking her gently with every urgent stroke. I released her just in time for us to both cry out and come apart together.

Willow clung to me, curled up in my lap while I stroked her hair. Her heels were still on, and we had been pressed together in silence for a while.

"Talk to me," I urged.

She buried her head in my neck, muttering something I couldn't hear.

I tilted her head to look into her eyes, studying her. Did that feel as intense for her as it did for me?

"Sweetness, what's wrong?" I asked.

"I feel overwhelmed. Overstimulated. It was…intense."

"I'm sorry."

She shook her head. "No! In a good way. I'm just feeling…"

"You need aftercare. What do you need?"

She frowned. "Um…"

Her uncertainty had my hackles raised. Had none of her partners been kind enough to give that to her? Shit, should we have talked more about what I wanted in the bedroom?

I slid her off my lap and sank to the floor. I undid the straps of her heels and rubbed her feet, loving how she moaned at the sensation. "What do you need, sweetness? I'm sorry, we should have talked about limits and safe words."

"Well… maybe, but I was on board with all of it. I like being choked and told what to do. I spend so much time making the rules, having to make all the big decisions at the shop, that coming home, I need to lie back and let someone else be in charge."

"You need it to relax you," I said, understanding her need to be dominated by me.

"Do you ever want that?" she asked.

"Sometimes I like it. When it's something my partner needs. But I prefer to be in charge."

"I like you being in charge."

"I know, sweetness."

She looked down at me, kneeling at her feet. "Can you get back up here and cuddle me?"

Whew. I felt like I had been an asshole. I slid back into the bed and pulled the comforter around us. She laid her head on my chest, and we stayed like that for a couple of minutes.

"Did the photos worry you? I can delete them. I will never ever share those."

"No. I love being your muse. Intense is good. I like intense, but I need to come back down from it."

I caressed her cheek. "Anything you need, tell me."

"Was it overwhelming to you, too?"

"Yes. But good. Better than my fantasies."

She purred like a cat, satisfied with my answer. "Good... because I wanna do it again."

"Oh, yeah?"

She kissed down my chest, and I felt myself grow hard at where her hands ran down. "You've been holding out on me."

"Made it worth it though, huh?"

"Mmmhmm," she murmured against my skin.

And nope, she didn't get to be in charge. I flipped her over and held her wrists down on the bed. "Not so fast."

She arched up, begging for a kiss, but I went to her neck first.

"Mean!" she play-cried.

"You fucking love it," I growled.

She rocked against my hands. "Lachlan, please. Show me how good I am."

"So good..." I purred and then took her mouth again.

We kissed until we couldn't breathe, until we were desperate for more.

I yanked open my bedside table again, grabbing a

condom and sliding it on. I kneed her legs apart and sank into her again, both of us sighing in relief.

She wrapped her legs around my waist and rocked against me, wanting me to move inside her, but I held still. I laced our fingers together, holding her wrists down against the bed so she couldn't dig her nails into me.

"Patience," I growled.

"Please?" she begged.

And there it was, the desperation I needed.

"You're so pretty when you beg for it, sweetness."

"Lachlan..." she panted out. "Please."

I slid out of her and then back in, slow and torturous. If I went too fast, we were gonna go too soon. I wanted to give my good girl what she deserved. She moved with me, letting me go as slow as I wanted but matching my energy as she clenched her legs tighter around me.

"Willow," I warned. "I won't last long if you keep on doing that."

"I don't care. I want it. Please."

How could I say no to that?

I quickened my pace, keeping her wrists held down while I got better leverage, sliding in and out faster than before. When she cried out her orgasm, I let go and kissed her through my own release.

We were a mess of sweaty limbs and panting breaths. I released her hands and kissed the back of her palms. "So worth the wait."

I slid out of her and got rid of the condom. She cleaned herself up in the bathroom while I lay back against my bed.

She strolled into my bedroom, looking for her dress. "I gotta open the shop in the morning."

I patted the space beside me. "I have to be up early for a wedding in the Poconos. Stay. Please?"

She chewed on her lip, her brain turning, but then she crawled into bed beside me and onto my chest. I could get used to this. Of her in my bed every night.

"What the fuck had I been waiting for?"

"Huh?" she asked.

I twirled a piece of her hair around my finger. "Did I say that out loud?"

"Yes. What had you been waiting for? I was ready weeks ago."

My phone vibrated on my bedside table, but I ignored it. "I wanted to get to know the adult Willow. I didn't want my high school crush to make you out to be someone you weren't."

"Oh. Well... Aspen said I always jump into relationships, so I think it was good for both of us. I've had fun getting to know you over the past couple of weeks."

My phone vibrated again. And then a third time.

"Do you need to get that?" she asked. "Oh my God! It could be about Siobhan and the baby!"

I checked my phone and groaned. Nope. That interruption I would have welcomed. Just my annoying ex who kept harassing me under different numbers now. Why couldn't he get the hint that I was done? Philly was in my rearview mirror, and settling down in Drakesville was my future. Maybe with the cute woman beside me.

> UNKNOWN: You'll be back.
>
> UNKNOWN: You always are.
>
> UNKNOWN: Quit playing around Lachs. You know you want me back.

I left him on read and dropped my phone back on the table.

"Not Siobhan," I reassured Willow. "Just spam."

There was a furrow in her brow that told me she didn't believe me, but when I kissed her again, she settled down.

I kissed her hair. "Let's get some sleep."

She curled into me and obeyed like the good girl she was. I loved that.

CHAPTER EIGHTEEN

WILLOW

$\mathcal{I}$ was walking on cloud nine after my date with Lachlan, only for the rest of the weekend to be busy as hell. My new hire to replace Siobhan started on Saturday, and I spent the day training her. She picked it up quickly, and after another day of training, I was confident in my decision to hire her.

I hated losing Siobhan, but it gave me the kick in the pants to fill out my staffing. Now that I had, I could focus on all the admin work I had been letting slide.

After we closed the shop for the night, I stayed behind working on the schedule for the next week. For once, delegating to my baristas didn't give me hives.

My phone beeped, and I saw a text from Siobhan.

SIOBHAN: She's coming!

I grinned at Siobhan's daughter being as punctual as she was.

ME: AHH! Congrats. Let me know if you
need anything.

SIOBHAN: Gotta get this baby outta me
first. I'll have Lachlan send photos later.

Lachlan said he was on baby watch today, so we hadn't made any plans. I wished I could go to the hospital and be there for Siobhan, but my mom came into the shop today and cornered me about dinner with her and my dad. That was fair since I had been skirting my parents' dinner invitations for weeks.

No doubt the gossip mill in town was why Mom came hunting me down. Several people had asked me today if Lachlan and I were dating. I was in such a good mood from the other night that instead of playing it coy, I said yes. Might as well tell everyone the truth.

I worked for another hour, making the schedule, doing inventory, and checking in with the roasters' output. Everything was in order, and for the first time in years, I felt like I could breathe a sigh of relief.

I shut my computer down before I got sucked into more work and headed upstairs to my apartment. I took a quick shower, so Mom didn't comment on me smelling like coffee, and changed into a dress she loved.

I loved my parents, but Mom was a little high maintenance about appearances. It was easier to appease her than argue. Arguing with a lawyer was a nightmare. Hence, I never got away with anything when I was a kid. Mom always had a rebuttal.

I headed down to my car and drove over to the other side of town. My parents lived on the more affluent side of town in a five-bedroom, Tudor-style home. Growing up, I knew my parents worked hard for their success, but they always reminded me of my privilege. I wouldn't have been able to open the shop as quickly as I had without their backing. I appreciated them for that, even if people always assumed I was a spoiled brat.

I drove up the long drive and parked. I checked my makeup in my car's overhead mirror before heading inside.

I found my mom in the kitchen pouring a glass of wine. "Hey, honey."

"Hi, mom."

"Busy day at the shop?" she asked while pouring another glass for me.

I took the offered glass. "As always."

"You need to get more help."

I forced myself to not roll my eyes. "I've hired four more people this summer. I'm solid."

She took the mac and cheese out of the oven, and I helped with bringing out the other side dishes onto the patio. Dad waved his grill spatula at me while he flipped burgers and chicken on the grill. It was the perfect summer afternoon for a barbecue. Although my dad had been known for firing up the grill in the dead of winter, too.

"Perfect timing, pumpkin. Food's almost ready," Dad said.

Mom settled into a seat at the patio table. I sat next to her and sipped my wine, enjoying the breeze of summer before my parents started in on me.

A few minutes later, Dad brought a plate of burgers and grilled chicken over to the table, and we served ourselves.

"You've been busy, pumpkin?" Dad asked through mouthfuls of food.

"Yup. Siobhan went into labor, so I hired someone new in the nick of time."

"Aw," Mom cooed. "Did she have the baby yet?"

I checked my phone, but there was no news yet. She'd likely take a while until she finally came out. "Not yet."

I took another sip of my wine, waiting for my parents to mention how much they wished they were grandparents. They surprised me when they didn't have a comment. Perhaps they learned that my choices for my life were my own and not theirs.

"So, what else is new?" Mom asked.

I swallowed my bite of burger. "Mom, ask about Lachlan already."

Dad frowned. "Who's that?"

"Lachlan Murphy," Mom reminded him. "You know. Mary Pat and Colin's youngest. He opened his own photography studio. I've been meaning to talk to him about getting new headshots done."

Dad's frown deepened. He was great with faces but terrible at names.

"His studio is next door to the shop," I reminded him.

Recognition crossed my dad's face. "Oh! That boy you had a crush on in high school."

I tipped back my glass of wine, drowning myself in embarrassment. Seriously, had everyone known about that?

Mom let out a light laugh. "So, what's going on with you?"

"We're dating. It's still new," I explained.

He wasn't even my boyfriend, but dating was accurate. I wasn't sure if the boyfriend/girlfriend conversation was on the table yet. The man had been wanting to take things so painfully slow; I didn't want to drive him away.

"Well, you should have him over for dinner one night," Mom said. "Now I know why you've been avoiding us."

Lachlan wasn't the reason I had been avoiding them. I truly had been busy running my business. Sometimes, it was like they didn't understand all the responsibilities I had.

Dad came to my rescue. "Nonsense, hon. Our Willow's a busy woman with a successful business. Have you thought more about expanding?"

Geez, what was with them tonight? Wasn't having the shop and the roastery good enough?

"I'm happy with where we are right now. I'm excited about the brewery releasing the coffee beer using my beans in the fall," I said.

"That's amazing," Mom said, her praise genuine. "We're so proud of you. We only harp on you because we know you can be bigger and better."

"I'm happy with my life and the shop's progress."

My parents meant well, but their quest for constant success wasn't one I shared. I didn't need the big house or the fancy cars. I was happy with my little shop in town and my cozy apartment. Sometimes, they didn't understand that.

I distracted them from the conversation about my life by asking Mom about her latest court case and then Dad about how the business was going.

After dinner, I told my parents to stay seated while I did the dishes, and they relaxed in the backyard. I spied them from the window in the kitchen. My dad reached out and grabbed my mom's hand. One thing they always instilled in me was how much I wanted a love like theirs. One day.

I finished cleaning up and joined them on the patio again. "Thanks for dinner."

Mom smiled at me. "Anytime, sweetie."

Dad swirled his wine glass. "So, this Lachlan boy…"

I tried not to roll my eyes. Lachlan was in his late twenties like me, but to my dad, he was still a boy. "What about him?"

"Is he good to you? Not like that Kacey girl, right?"

I frowned. "Oh. No. He's nothing like Kacey. He's not a man of many words, but yes, we're enjoying our time together."

Dad nodded. "As long as he makes you happy, we're happy, pumpkin."

"He does."

Was it weird to say that this early in our relationship? Perhaps, but once Lachlan realized I was interested and we started going out together, everything with him felt light. He didn't make me feel bad about myself and told me not to wear certain colors. He listened when I talked. And he was kind. I was falling hard for him, but it was way too soon for those feelings, so I pushed them down.

"We're happy for you," Mom reassured me. "Now bring him to dinner one night to meet us."

That time, I did visibly roll my eyes. "Is there dessert?"

Mom jumped up at the prospect of dessert, and I went home shortly after.

I climbed the stairs of my apartment and lay back on my bed. I had two other employees opening and training the new hire tomorrow, so I didn't need to be in the shop. But there was still lots to do on the backend. It felt nice that I had space to do that with my staff in place.

I checked my phone, but still no news of the baby.

> ME: Did she have her yet?

> LACHLAN: Not yet.

> ME: Do you want me to come?

LACHLAN: Nah. I'll keep you in the loop.

I frowned, but I looked at how long a typical labor was, so they might be there for a while.

ME: Please let me know.

LACHLAN: Sure thing, sweetness.

I melted into my bed, thinking about the other night, and couldn't wait to do it all over again.

The next morning, my body roused me early, as if I was opening the shop again. I'd always been a morning person, so my body naturally acclimated to these early morning hours.

The first thing I saw on my phone was a text from Lachlan. It was a photo of Siobhan and the baby. Siobhan was sweaty, and her hair was in a messy bun, but her aura was joyous, and I couldn't help but be happy my friend was getting the life she'd always dreamed of.

Since I didn't have to be in the shop today, I had a better idea. I texted the new father.

ME: I'm doing a Murphy family coffee run. Who's all there?

KILLIAN: You're an angel. Please. I'll have Mom text you. You'll learn quickly this family is all up in each other's business.

ME: No need. I know everyone's orders!

I had already learned that, but I didn't mind it. I might

not have a million siblings like Lachlan, but my family was equally annoying. In their own endearing way.

I made a mental note of everyone's coffee orders. Unsure if Siobhan would drink caffeine yet, I went with the decaf and put an order into the shop. Matteo would see that in a few minutes when he turned on the lights.

I threw on comfy clothes and slipped into my flats before walking downstairs. My staff already had the sign flipped on and the coffee brewing. Pride billowed in my chest that I had them trained to be self-sufficient. It made my job as the owner that much easier. In truth, Kelly and Matteo could do a lot of the admin work I insisted on doing. I could sit back and let them run the shop, but I was a hands-on owner.

"This is a big order," Matteo said.

"Siobhan had the baby," I explained. "Let me comp that. I'm taking coffee for the family. Look how cute she is."

I pulled out my phone and showed them all.

"So cute," Matteo agreed and got to work on the orders.

I came around behind the counter to help, but he hip-checked me to get out of there.

"We're staffed enough behind here. Let me handle it."

"I still have so much to do."

"You'll learn she's a control freak, Mel," Matteo joked to the newcomer. "But she's the best boss I've ever had, so you learn to live with it."

"Hey!" I protested.

All three of them grinned at me. I let them fulfill my order while I checked around the shop, making sure tables were wiped down, and the condiment station was stocked. I checked in with our cook, who was prepping for the day.

Before I could go into the office to do invoicing, Matteo had my order up. Okay, invoicing could wait until later. I grabbed two of the cardboard drink containers, and Matteo brought out the third one to my car. Okay, this was a lot, but I'd call Lachlan to help me when I got to the hospital.

Before driving off, I double-checked I had accounted for everyone. Black coffee for Lachlan and his dad; coffee, cream, and sugar for his mom; decaf and an extra coffee for Siobhan if she wanted caffeine today; cold brew for Finn; Americanos for Brian and Kelsey; Latte for Killian; a cappuccino for Ronan. Oh, wait, I forgot me!

Matteo knocked on my window, and I rolled it down. "You forgot yourself, boss lady."

He handed me an iced vanilla latte, my summer go-to. "Thank you. I'm sure I'll be back later."

"You've been working non-stop for months. We have the staff. Delegate. Boss lady gets to sit back."

I didn't like that philosophy. Instead, I thanked him and drove to the hospital in one of the neighboring towns. Drakesville was too small to have our own.

When I arrived, I called Lachlan.

"Coffee delivery!" I cheered.

"Oh, Kill said you were bringing some. You didn't have to do that."

"Nonsense, I wanted to, but I need an extra hand."

"On it."

I got out of my car, placing one container on my roof while I grabbed the others. Lachlan didn't meet me outside, but Ronan did and grabbed the container on the roof and one from my hand.

"Lachlan's still snapping away photos," he explained.

"Oh. Well, thanks for coming to help. I figured everyone was tired."

"We are."

We walked together into the hospital and found the rest

of his family in the waiting area. I doled out the coffees to the family members there. As I finished, Lachlan came out, and his parents jumped up and sprinted in the direction he had come.

Before I could hand him his coffee, he greeted me with a kiss. "Hi."

"Hi," I said back, ignoring the hoots and hollers from his brothers.

My heart hammered in my chest at how that small kiss wrapped joy around me. Was it bad that I had missed him when it had only been a couple of days?

He brushed my hair out of my face. "I missed you."

My chest warmed. "I missed you, too. How's Siobhan?"

"Good. Baby's good. She's a cutie."

I held up the to-go container. "I brought you a coffee."

He took his black coffee from me and sipped it slowly. "You're the sweetest. You didn't need to do that."

I beamed. It was a gracious gesture I wanted to do for everyone, but he made it seem like it was the best idea ever.

"I like free coffee if you keep on dating her," Ronan called out, breaking our connection.

"You should charge those jerkoffs," Lachlan joked.

I laughed and took a seat next to Ronan. Lachlan sat next to me and slipped his hand into mine, playing with the bracelets on my wrist.

"How was dinner with your parents?" he asked.

I blew out an annoyed breath. "Fine, but they're nosy. They want to meet you."

"My mom also wants you to come to the next family dinner."

"Of course I'll come. Your mom's so nice."

He held up his cup of coffee. "You won her over with coffee."

I shook my head with a shy smile. I highly doubted that. Mary Pat Murphy was a nice lady, and I loved chatting with her when she came into the shop.

A few minutes later, Lachlan's parents came out of the maternity ward. Mary Pat smiled at me. "Siobhan wants to see you."

I grabbed the last container of coffee, and Lachlan walked with me into the room Siobhan was in. Inside, she lay in the hospital bed with the baby in her arms, and I'd never seen her happier.

"Hi," I whispered. "I come bearing coffee."

"An angel—thank you," Killian said and grabbed his coffee.

"Shev, are you doing caffeine yet?" I asked.

Siobhan chewed on her lip. "I'll take the decaf."

I handed it to her. "How are you doing?"

She beamed. "I'm amazing, Will. She's so beautiful."

I swore Killian puffed out his chest. "She's the best thing that ever happened to me. They both are."

Aw.

Killian eyed his brother. "You sure you never want one?"

Lachlan shivered. "It's a no for me. I get to be the fun uncle."

God, I was so glad we were on the same page with that.

"Well, you two are well-matched," Siobhan laughed. "I'm glad Lachs finally figured it out."

The tips of his ears went red, but I smiled at his shyness, given how he was not shy in the bedroom. He was such a contradiction.

We spent a few more minutes chatting with the happy couple, but as soon as the baby woke up and started crying, we were out of there. We said goodbye to his family and headed to the exit.

Lachlan laced his hand through mine while we walked to my car. "I'm glad you came. It meant a lot."

"Of course. Siobhan's my friend, too. Can I admit something terrible?"

"What?"

"Her late husband was an asshole. She never saw how he belittled her, but how people treat service workers is how I know they're a good person. He was not."

"Wow."

"Too harsh?" I asked.

He shook his head. "Nope—truth hurts. I'm glad she could get my brother's head out of his ass. I love that they're happy together."

"Me too."

We stopped when we reached my car, and Lachlan bent to give me a quick kiss goodbye. "I gotta book it to an engagement shoot. See you later?"

"Mmmhmm."

He kissed me again, slowly this time. It was a promise of more to come later, and I, for one, couldn't wait.

CHAPTER NINETEEN

LACHLAN

"Ask her," Mindy urged, shoving the photo of Willow wrapped in the bisexual pride flag into my face again.

I sighed. The art show in Philly was a couple of weeks away, and my bestie had been all up in my business about it. That was her job, but she was grinding my gears when I had a million other things to do today.

"I'm not asking her that," I growled out. "Those photos were for her. And I don't appreciate you sliding in that note in her booklet."

Mindy raised a blonde eyebrow at me. "Did she have any objections?"

Well, no, but I also told Willow to ignore that note, and neither of us brought it up again.

"Why are you on my ass about this?"

Mindy crossed her arms over her chest. "Someone's gotta be. Have you even made any decisions?"

Hayden's art show was all about showcasing queer joy,

and I had a handful of selections that made the cut already. I had a lesbian wedding and a family portrait where the adults were two dads, my self-portrait at a pride parade, and some photos of various queer identities at that same pride event.

I pulled the photos out of my folder and spread them across my desk. "Here's what I've got so far."

"These are good, but I love this photo of Willow. You captured her essence, and I know bi representation is important to you. It's who you are."

She was annoying when she was right.

"Those photos were for Willow, not an audience."

"No, those were for you, but you were too far up your own ass to notice."

I shot her an annoyed glare. "Yeah... when are we gonna talk about you butting into my love life?"

"Shut up, you love me."

"Pain in my ass."

"Just ask her! She'll say yes."

"End of discussion."

Mindy threw up her hands and walked away. That wasn't the first time this week we had this argument, and it wouldn't be the last.

I shuffled the photos into my folder and went back to editing. Taking photos and shooting was fun, but it was the tedious fine-tuning that was the actual work. That was where I had to put in more hours than was in a day. But I wanted my business to be a success, so I'd sacrifice my sleep for it.

Weekdays were usually in the office days behind my computer, especially during wedding season when I was hauling ass to various locations all weekend long. I'd like to say I took time off, but I didn't.

I sent over proofs to the bridal client, and my calendar chimed with an appointment.

I rubbed a hand over my face. Shit, did I forget about a shoot? When I opened my calendar, a grin spread across my face at the appointment titled 'Lunch with your girlfriend. Take a break, you jerkoff.'

Someone needed to reprimand my assistant, but I was too tired to do it. Also, Willow and I hadn't discussed the boyfriend/girlfriend thing yet. But calling her my girlfriend made that old high school crush sing.

I shut the lid of my laptop and ambled out of my office.

Willow stood at the reception desk chatting with Mindy with a takeout bag in her hand. She shouldn't be that cute in her Drakesville Drip t-shirt and ripped jeans, but she was.

She handed off an iced drink to Mindy. "I think you'll like this one. It's not that different from your regular order. I call it Sweet Summer. It's an iced latte with honey and caramel. Oat milk for you."

"You're the best," Mindy told her and took a sip from her straw. "Ooh. I do like that."

"I can't wait until fall when I have all my apple and pumpkin drinks. They're amazing." Willow stirred her own concoction in a glass Drakesville Drip reusable tumbler. "This one is a Summertime Sun, but I'm not sure I love the orange flavor with coffee."

"Ooh. I'll have to try that out too."

"Can't you people drink regular coffee?" I interjected.

Willow's eyes twinkled when she saw me. "Only boring yet so sexy photographers do."

Mindy pretended to gag while I crossed over to Willow and planted a quick kiss on her lips. "You think I'm sexy, huh?"

A wicked grin tugged at the corner of her mouth. "You

know it. Do you have time for lunch? I grabbed sandwiches from the diner."

"Someone put it in my calendar. I'm all yours."

I led her to our tiny break room, and we unpacked the food together. She handed me a coffee cup that I thought was single-use but was actually a reusable cup with her shop's logo on it.

"Hey, these are new," I said.

"Yup. New way I'm trying to be sustainable. Some people still want the paper ones, but I'm trying." She opened her purse and pulled out a new bag of beans. "I also brought you more coffee. I noticed you were running low when I was here yesterday."

The benefits of working next door to Willow meant she strolled over with coffee or lunch when I was in the office all day. It was a perk I had been loving.

"Thank you. But you better invoice me for that."

"Mindy already took care of it."

She took the new bag of beans over to the counter and placed it next to the coffee pot. I grabbed her around the waist before she could sit down again and pulled her into my lap. I devoured her mouth, holding her jaw firm as I kissed her as if I hadn't seen her in weeks instead of mere hours.

"Hi," she whispered after cutting the kiss off before we got carried away.

"You're so sweet to bring me lunch."

"Our schedules are challenging. It's fun to have these little lunch dates."

She slipped off my lap and sat beside me. We ate together and talked about our respective days, reminding me of how normal this relationship was. Things with Henry had always been a mind game, always guessing about what he'd do to test or betray me next. The drama had been exhilarating for a time, but not now. Now, I wanted the ease and comfort that came with the girl next door.

My brain wanted to tell me I settled, but that wasn't it. When I stared into Willow's eyes, I saw a future. One where I didn't have to second guess every sentence. A future with someone who loved me for me.

Whoa. Love? I was getting way ahead of myself there. The woman wasn't even officially my girlfriend. It was like I made us wait so long to be intimate that now my heart was speeding down the highway.

"So, when's that art show?" she asked.

I swallowed slowly; my hackles raised that Mindy sent her to convince me about the photo. "In a couple of weeks."

"Oh, great. I'd love to come."

"Okay."

She chewed on her lip. "Mindy said you were undecided about one of the photos, and I should tell you yes. What does that mean?"

I took another bite of my sandwich and chewed even slower. "Do you remember that note in the photo album I gave you?"

She gave me an understanding nod.

"Mindy thinks I should include that photo of you. But..."

"What's the problem? Do you need my permission?"

I nodded. "Yes. Your permission if I'd add it, but also, that photo wasn't meant for the public. It's private."

She stared back at me. "What's the theme again?"

"Queer joy."

She sipped on her coffee, swirling the ice around in her tumbler, her thoughts going a mile a minute. "Do you want to include it?"

"Yes," I admitted.

It was a damn good photo, and it showcased everything I wanted to do with the theme of the show. At the same time, I wanted to respect Willow's privacy. When I thought those were for a loving partner, I gave it my all, making them as sensual as possible.

"Then use it," she said. Her voice dropped to a low, sexy tone. "We can always take more private photos. Maybe tonight."

"Oh, yeah?"

"Mmmhmm."

Her foot rubbed up against my leg. "Use that photo for the show, and I'll let you take better ones tonight. Ones just for you."

I checked my watch. How bad would it be if I threw her over my shoulder and took her upstairs to have my way with her? Bad. I had too many photos to cull this afternoon.

Did that stop her from rubbing her foot against my leg or giving me a seductive smile? Nope. Where was my good girl?

"Willow..." I growled out in my bedroom voice, firm and commanding.

She squirmed in her seat. "Y-yes?"

"Enough. Later."

"Come over for dinner?" she asked, her big amber eyes hopeful.

"Maybe..." I said to be a tease.

"Lachlan," she whined.

I grinned. "I'm just teasing you. I'm available tonight."

She clapped her hands. "Yay! I have an idea for a fun dinner and a movie date."

Her joy was so infectious that it didn't matter if she fixed peanut butter and jelly sandwiches and made me watch Real Housewives. Actually...that could have been fun, too, as long as I was with her.

"Great. It's a date," she said.

We wrapped up lunch and cleaned up the break room together. I realized she asked me to come over tonight because the rest of my week was an absolute shitshow with wedding and engagement shoots. I loved that she was thoughtful enough to consider that and work around it.

Before she left, I snagged her in another kiss that was a promise of later. "Thank you."

"For what?"

"Working around my busy schedule. Sometimes it's too much for people."

She gave a happy shake of her head. "Not for me. I like a challenge, and you, Lachlan, have been my biggest one yet."

I kissed her one more time, but she pushed me away before I dragged her upstairs. I had no idea what she had in store for me tonight, but I didn't care.

After I had enough of staring at my computer all day, I ran to the florist before they closed. As I surveyed the various bouquets around the shop, it dawned on me that I didn't know if Willow had a favorite flower.

Mindy and Willow had grown close in the last couple of weeks, so maybe my best friend would know. I shot off a text to her, but she proved to be useless. I went to Aspen next.

ME: Does your cousin have a favorite flower?

ASPEN: Not a clue.

So helpful.

The pretty blonde at the counter eyed me, looking lost. "Do you need help?"

"My girlfriend likes blue. Do you have any recommendations?"

"Oh, yes."

She showed me an arrangement of blue hydrangeas and delphiniums with white roses and button poms. It reminded me of the dress Willow wore to the baby shower. And her nails.

Now I thought of how those nails would look later. Hmm. Maybe keeping my inner beast locked away inside for so long had been a mistake. He was insatiable now.

I thanked the shopkeeper, bought the arrangement, and drove home. In my apartment, I set the flowers down on my coffee table and took a shower. I didn't know what Willow had in store for me tonight, but it sounded like a casual night in. I, for one, was in favor of that. Going out with her was fun, but I traveled a lot for work, and having a chill night in front of the TV sounded heavenly.

After toweling off and putting on the woodsy cologne she liked, I threw on a t-shirt and a clean pair of jeans. I never thought too much about my outfits before, and I adhered to a casual look, but a part of me wondered if I should try to impress her more.

Nope. That was overthinking. I hadn't heard from her yet, so I flopped down on my couch, but then I made the mistake of checking my email.

Great. Another wedding cancellation.

That was common in our business. Sometimes, people didn't realize until they were at the altar that they weren't right for each other. I'd photographed many weddings where I knew without a doubt the couple wouldn't last past the honeymoon. That didn't mean it forced my worries away. Thank God I always had a non-refundable deposit.

My response to the bride was polite and understanding of her situation. She told me all the business about her asshole groom, which I had clocked at our first consultation.

A text popped up from Mindy.

> MINDY: Stop checking email & relax with your girlfriend.

> ME: Micromanager.

> MINDY: Somebody's gotta be.

> MINDY: Go get laid.

Such a pain in my ass lately. What was with her?

I got what she was getting at. There was no use crying over a cancelled wedding. There would be more than I cared for this season anyway.

I flipped over to Willow's contact in my phone.

> ME: Hey, sweetness. Let me know when to head over.

> WILLOW: Whenever! See ya soon.

Her excitement radiated even from her text messages. She was so adorable.

I slid my phone into my pocket and stood. My feet froze in place as I thought about tonight, and then I double-backed to grab the camera on my bedside table. I shoved that into a bag, grabbed the flowers off the coffee table, and headed downstairs. I frowned at finding the outer door to

Willow's apartment opened, but I trudged up the steps to her main door. After a quick knock, she opened it and let me inside.

She tilted her head at the flowers in my hands. "What's this?"

"For you. They reminded me of what you wore to Siobhan's baby shower."

She took them from me and gave the petals a big sniff. "I love getting flowers. So pretty."

Noted.

"What's the grand plan tonight?" I asked.

"I hope you like fondue. I thought it would be fun. Aspen said she got two fondue pots after the wedding, so she pawned one off on me."

"Do you want help?"

She waved me off. "Nope. Sit your cute butt down on my couch, and I'll bring it over."

My lips twitched. "I got a cute butt, huh?"

"Mmmhmm. Now sit."

I did as she asked, strolling over to her couch while she put the flowers into water. Her apartment was about the same size as mine next door, but her decorating was cozy and eclectic. I went for the more minimal style, while everything in her apartment was colorful and alive. From her blue velvet couch to the walls lined with paintings of fairies and moon phases. There was another bi pride piece like the one in her coffee shop. She had some bookshelves against the wall decorated with various candles and crystal paperweights. I had a feeling those came from our mutual friend Gemma.

I took off my shoes and stretched out my legs while she brought over a plate of roasted broccoli and cauliflower. Next was a plate of potatoes, bread, and grilled chicken.

Then she brought over the pot with skewers and plugged it into an extension cord.

"Can I admit I've never had fondue for dinner?" I asked.

She grinned. "It's fun. After dinner, I can clean out the pot and make chocolate for dessert. I have fruit ready."

She sprinted back into the kitchen for one last plate of pot stickers and empty plates we could pile our meals onto.

"So, what's on deck for a movie?" I asked.

"Glad you asked. I want to figure out your favorite movie."

"Why?"

"Because it's fun."

She stabbed her skewer into a piece of broccoli and dipped it into the fondue pot. She put it to her lips and moaned. "Oh my God. This was such a good idea."

She speared a piece of chicken next and moaned again, making my dick rise at the sounds coming from her mouth. So innocent, yet so dirty. Trying a piece of bread and then some veggies in the cheese had me moaning, too. This was a fun date.

"Good, huh?" she asked.

"Yes. How are the potatoes?"

"Like round cheese fries. Yum." She swallowed another bite and then stood up to survey her entertainment center. "Okay... Cheesy action movie? Or something classic like *The Godfather?*"

I turned the question on her. "What's your favorite movie?"

"You won't believe me."

"Try me."

"*Indiana Jones*. But not the new ones. The first one is the best."

That was not what I expected her to say, but... everyone joked *The Mummy* was their bi awakening, so not that far off. That was why I refused to tell her it was mine. It was too big of a joke in the bi community. She wouldn't have believed me. I had her pegged for someone who went for a rom-com or even a superhero film. Not an action-adventure movie from the eighties.

"Put it on," I told her.

She did as I asked and came back to the couch. We ate in silence for the first couple minutes of the film, both of us too engrossed in the delicious food.

"So..." she began. "Your mom came into the shop today and invited me to dinner on Sunday."

Yup, knew that was happening soon.

"What did you tell her?"

"That I wanted to discuss it with you first."

"You're invited."

She set her plate on the coffee table. "Do you want me there?"

I grabbed her hand. "Yes. But my family's gonna give you the third degree. And prepare for my mom asking for more grandbabies."

"Well, don't worry because you're not off the hook. My mom cornered me about you coming over for a barbecue next week. She even called the studio and had Mindy check your schedule."

Damn, Mrs. Rivers didn't fuck around. I'd heard she was intimidating and not a person you wanted to tangle with, but I hadn't expected that.

"My mother is a force to be reckoned with," Willow explained with a grimace.

"Well, I can't wait to meet your parents, too."

She frowned. "I don't think you'll be saying that after my mom talks to you like you're on trial."

I laughed. Oh, she'd be saying that same thing after dinner with my mom. Mary Pat Murphy wasn't a badass lawyer like her mom, but she was equally intimidating.

She played with the hem of her shirt. "Lachlan, I need to ask you something."

"Anything."

"Are you my boyfriend?"

"Do you want me to be?"

She frowned. "That's not what I asked."

"Yes. I'm your boyfriend. I'm not seeing anyone else. Mindy entered our lunch date on my calendar as 'Lunch with your girlfriend.' You're not seeing anyone else, right?"

"Of course not. I wanted to make sure we were on the same page."

I set my plate of food down and pulled her into my lap. "You were worried about that? After everything?"

She tucked her chin into my chest. "Yes."

"Don't. It took me far too long to realize you were into me. I'm not letting you escape that easily."

"I don't want to escape."

"Good. Now give me a kiss."

Before she could say anything else, I silenced her with a tender kiss.

CHAPTER TWENTY

WILLOW

*A*fter dinner, Lachlan helped me clean up and make dessert. He prepped the fruit while I cleaned out the fondue pot and made the chocolate sauce. We ate at my tiny kitchen table, and I didn't miss how he stared at my lips while I licked chocolate off my fingers.

I might have moaned exaggeratedly to tease him. "So good..."

"Willow..." his voice came out shaky.

I licked my lips. "What's wrong?"

"You know what you're doing."

I gave him a sultry smile. "What? I'm enjoying dessert."

"I'd like to enjoy something else," he muttered under his breath, like I didn't want to hear it.

Bingo. There was the inner beast I was waiting for.

"Well, I have a surprise for you."

"Yeah?"

I unplugged the fondue pot and took his hand, guiding

him toward my bedroom. On my bed lay three sets of lingerie. One was the same royal blue one I had worn for the boudoir shoot, but next to it lay a baby blue version and then a black one that was mostly see-through. They were all sexy as hell, and I wanted to model them for him.

"Pick one, and let me be your muse," I told him.

He stared at the skimpy clothing on my bed. "The baby blue one. We already have photos of you in dark blue."

I grabbed his choice off the bed, although I wanted him to say all three. Maybe later.

I sauntered off toward my bathroom and tore off my clothes. I had dressed in a comfy t-shirt and shorts tonight to make it easier to slip into one of these sets. This one didn't have the matching choker, but only a skimpy bra and G-string that barely covered anything. I connected the garter belts to my thong and slipped on matching heels. Because I had planned ahead and left options in my bathroom.

The prospect of being Lachlan's sexy muse set a thrill through me. It was like as soon as he finally let us be intimate, a valve had been turned on inside me that couldn't be set off. I was turned on all the time with thoughts of being with him again. Of being his good girl who did whatever he asked.

I strutted into my bedroom and found Lachlan sitting at the foot of my bed. His eyes scanned across my body, and a tingle went down my spine at the attention. And he hadn't even touched me yet.

"Oh... sweetness."

I did a little spin. "You like?"

"Yes."

His voice was hoarse, like he was trying to contain himself. Mmm. I didn't want that. I wanted him to unleash his inner beast on me.

I stalked over to him. "Did you bring your camera?"

"Yes." He slid his hands up my thighs. "Will you model this for me?"

I nodded.

The world spun as he tossed me onto the bed. "Stay."

I did as I was told, lying back on my bed while he rustled around in the living room for the bag he brought over. He returned with his digital camera and began clicking away. How hot was it that my sexy photographer boyfriend got off on taking spicy pictures of me? So hot.

He directed me into different poses for a couple of minutes. On my knees and being patient, with my arms and legs spread wide, and close-ups of my face. I especially loved when he wrapped his hand around my throat and snapped a photo of that.

"Willow," he whispered.

I pressed a hand against his chest, and he loosened his grip on my throat. "Let go, baby. You can unleash it with me."

"Unleash what?"

"That beast inside you."

"Not yet." He pressed me down on the bed and slid my bra strap down. "I'm not done cataloging your beauty."

He pulled the cups of my bra down, revealing my breasts, and he snapped photos of that. He traveled down my body, taking pictures as he went. I nearly cried out as he palmed the thin scrap of material that was my underwear.

"I wanna rip this off you," he growled.

"Do it."

He plucked at the G-string. "Quiet. I'm the boss in here."

Arousal danced low in my belly. I fucking loved that.

"Then boss me around."

Much to my annoyance, he didn't rip it off and take me right then and there like I wanted him to. Instead, he pushed the material to the side and plunged two thick fingers inside me. I bucked against him, wanting to get the friction he provided.

"There's my girl," he purred.

"Mmm."

"So good."

I nodded my enthusiasm and closed my eyes, giving in to the pleasure he provided. My patience had been a virtue, and now, he gave me my reward. The click-click-click of his camera mixed with the sounds of my cries, turning me on even more. I loved this photo kink of his.

His fingers pressed deep inside me, pumping fast. My world collapsed, and I cried out in ecstasy.

"Goooood…" he whispered. "There you go. Come back to me, sweetness."

I cracked my eyes open, finding him leaning over me and cupping my face. "Am I a good muse?"

He set his camera down. "You're such a gorgeous sight. I love photographing you."

I crooked my finger at him. "Come get it."

The purr of my voice must have set him off, or he decided he couldn't handle it anymore. He tore his t-shirt off, flinging it to the opposite end of the room. His jeans and boxer briefs were next, but he paused first to grab a condom, then he was on top of me and kissing me.

I deepened the kiss and ran my hands through his hair. The scruff on his jaw scraped against my face but in the most delicious way possible. He plunged his tongue inside my mouth, greedy and demanding. I submitted to him, letting the pleasure take over.

He pulled back and plucked at my bra strap. "This is pretty, but I want to see you all."

I reached behind me, ripping the bra off and unhooking my garter belts to shimmy out of the thong. He guided my shoes off my feet and helped me out of the rest. He sat back on his heels and stared down at my naked body.

"Can I?" he asked.

I nodded, understanding his question.

He grabbed his camera and took a photo of me like that, ready and waiting for him. I gave him a couple more poses, getting more turned on at how much he loved photographing my naked body.

Then he set it on my bedside table and kneed my legs apart. "You've been so patient, huh?"

"Yes, baby. I'm ready."

"Yes, you are."

He held my wrists down again, and I watched immobile as he grabbed the condom wrapper and made quick work of getting it on his cock. He gave it a few good pumps, and then he slid inside me. I sighed when he finally gave me what I wanted.

"Yesssss..." I drawled out and rocked against his hands.

He withdrew from me and then slid back in, torturing me with his slow pace. I wanted him to take me. To rut on top of me hard and fast until he exploded. To hear that guttural moan when he finally came.

I wrapped my legs around his waist and thrust up at him, meeting his movements. His hips rolled against mine as we moved in sync. In bed, we were so well matched in our tastes. In how we slid together like two puzzle pieces finally fitting together.

He slid one of his hands from my wrist and wrapped it

around my throat. Those ocean-blue orbs asked for consent, and I gave him a quick nod. Delicious pleasure coursed through me when he squeezed. He took my body like I belonged to him, unleashing the inner wild man he kept hidden.

But not from me. No, this man matched my energy in the best way possible.

"That's my girl, taking it so good," he whispered, his voice husky and on the edge of pleasure.

With his hand around my throat, I couldn't speak, and that was the thrill. His soft voice and the kindness in his eyes told me I could trust him. That this man would never lay a hand on me or hurt me intentionally. Unless I asked.

"You've been so patient with me," he said. I could only nod while he took me harder and rougher than before. He released his hold on my neck. "Who's been a good girl?"

"Me," I squeaked out. "I'm such a good girl."

"Yes, you are. Now be a good girl and come for me."

He squeezed my neck again, and then we both came undone.

It was always the fucking quiet ones. And I loved it.

It was then that I realized the truth. I was deeply in love with this man, and there was no going back. But I bit my tongue instead of voicing that. It was far too early for those feelings. But that wasn't unusual for me. I always said I love you first. But with Lachlan, I knew to hold my tongue. For now.

"What about this?" I asked Lachlan, holding up a modest maxi dress with flowers.

Lachlan lay back on my bed in defeat. "Sweetness... stop fretting. It's only dinner."

"But I want your parents to like me!"

"They do like you."

To say I was nervous about dinner with his parents was an understatement. Mary Pat came into the shop occasionally, and she'd always been nice to me, but Lachlan was her baby, and I wanted her to approve of us dating.

The dress was pretty and not revealing. It was a perfect Sunday dinner outfit. Casual enough that it didn't look like I was trying too hard. But I was. I was trying so hard to win over his parents.

I changed into the dress and a pair of sandals and then found the perfect jewelry to match it. My manicure needed a refresh, but there wasn't time for that.

Lachlan lay on my bed with a frown on his face as he stared at his phone. Whatever was on there had him upset, and it hadn't been the first time I noticed it, but I didn't want to pry. I hoped that guy who complained about his wife's boudoir shoot wasn't causing him problems. That was only a small portion of the photography he did, and I had heard the talk around town. People loved his work and how he was invested in our community.

Lachlan climbed off my bed and came up behind me, pressing a kiss behind my ear. "Beautiful. You ready?"

"Mmmhmm."

I followed him out of my apartment, stopping to lock up behind us, and then climbed into the passenger's seat of his car. His parents lived on the other side of town, so we had to drive. We could walk, but it would have been quite the hike versus a three-minute drive.

I wiped my sweaty hands down my dress while he drove us, my nerves all over the place. We agreed to go to my parents for a barbecue next weekend, and then Lachlan would be in the hot seat. Hopefully, he wouldn't be as stressed out as I was.

Lachlan pulled into his parents' driveway and cut his engine, then he grabbed my hand and gave it a reassuring squeeze. "Relax. It's only dinner."

I squeezed his hand back. "I'm nervous."

"Don't be."

He let me go, and we got out of the car together. He walked up toward the door and headed right in, calling out that we were here. His mom's booming voice replied that we were just in time.

Eep. That was my fault we were late.

Lachlan led me into the dining room, where his family was gathered around a large table. His parents were at the two heads of it, while Brian, Kelsey, and Finn were on one side of the table, and Ronan was on the other. We slid into the empty chairs beside Ronan. Not surprisingly, Siobhan and Killian were absent. With having a newborn, that was to be expected.

"You made it," Mary Pat Murphy said.

"My apologies," I told her.

She waved me off. "We just sat down."

She began handing off dishes so we could each take our fill. She made grilled chicken with green beans and roasted potatoes. It smelled delicious. I took a thigh of chicken and a healthy helping of potatoes and green beans and passed it on.

"It's good to have you," Lachlan's dad, Colin, told me with a nod.

"Thank you so much. Everything looks amazing."

I cut off a piece of chicken and took my first bite. Oh wow, this was good. I'd have to get the recipe from Mary Pat. I wanted to laugh at how Lachlan shoveled it in, but I held back so as not to make a fool of myself in front of his family.

"I'm bummed Shev couldn't bring the baby," Kelsey said. "But they look like such blobs at that age."

We all laughed at that.

Mary Pat pointed at her. "You're next."

Brian put a hand on his wife's pregnant belly. "Soon. And the last one."

"You said that last time," Ronan joked.

I braced myself for the kid conversation being thrust on me. Lachlan visibly shuttered next to me, and Mary Pat locked onto that.

"Do you want kids, Willow?" she asked.

"Oh no. It's not for me. But I'm excited for Siobhan and Killian. They deserve it."

"What is with this generation?" his mom huffed out.

"Hon," Colin warned.

"Not everyone wants kids," Ronan said, coming to our rescue. "And that's okay. Bri and Kels had enough for the family as it is."

"Hey!" Kelsey burst out with faux indignation.

"What? Is he wrong?" Finn asked.

Brian laughed. "Nope. Wasn't expecting it after I got the ole snip."

"I don't get it. Doesn't everyone want kids? That's what you're supposed to do!" Mary Pat exclaimed.

"Mom, some people can't have kids, and some people don't want them," Ronan countered. "It doesn't make you incomplete because you can't or won't. People can make their own choices. We don't have to do something just because we're supposed to."

There was a hint of hurt in Ronan's voice, but it was rude to ask what he meant. I agreed with him that just because you thought you were 'supposed to' didn't mean you had to. Many people shouldn't be parents, me included. I was not fit for motherhood, and I knew it.

"Mom, will you stop?" Lachlan asked through gritted teeth.

Uh-oh. Better defuse the situation quickly.

Brian picked up on it, too, as we locked eyes. "So, Willow...how is the coffee shop? It always looks so busy."

"Oh, it's great! We're working with the brewery on a coffee beer that I'm excited about. And I'm thinking of offering coffee flights, too."

"What are coffee flights?" Finn asked.

I was chewing on a big bite of green beans, so Lachlan answered for me. "Like beer flights, but coffee.

"That sounds exciting," Mary Pat said.

I laughed. "I have some ideas that I think will be profitable. I need to research and run more numbers."

Colin pointed a fork full of chicken at me. "And that, boys, is why this young lady is successful. She's methodical and thinks things through. Youse all could learn a thing or two from her."

I beamed at the high praise from a man who barely knew me.

"I can't wait to not be pregnant again," Kelsey lamented. "Your coffee is so good. But you don't have a decaf."

Oh. That was right—we didn't brew a decaf. Huh. I put that to the back of my mind to consider down the line. Had to research the market for decaf coffee drinkers to consider if that was viable. After the coffee flights. I had done some experimenting already, but I wasn't sold on launching it yet. I had to discuss it with my staff further.

Lachlan smirked. "You already got her wheels turning, considering that."

"I'll take it!" Kelsey cheered.

"I gotta do market research, but it's a great suggestion. I'm always looking for how we can improve."

Colin gave me another smile. "You got a good one. Not like that last one."

Lachlan's brothers and Kelsey all groaned in unison.

I raised my eyebrow at Lachlan.

"Oh, right. That Henry guy wasn't right for you," Mary Pat agreed.

Henry? Who was Henry?

I peered at Lachlan, who shook his head. "Can we not discuss my ex in front of my new partner?"

His brothers exchanged glances, and a part of me wanted to ask more questions, but this wasn't the time or place.

Kelsey jumped in her seat. "Oh, the baby kicked."

"AW!" Mary Pat cooed.

Kelsey winked at me, telling me that the baby had not, in fact, kicked, but I gave her a smile in thanks.

I ate my dinner while the conversation turned to what names they were thinking for the new baby.

Why had Lachlan never once mentioned his ex? It must have been bad if he didn't want to talk about him. Not like I talked about all my exes with him, but my intuition screamed at me to prod him. Lachlan's face had turned to stone from the moment his parents mentioned Henry.

The rest of dinner went off without a hitch, with Mary Pat telling embarrassing stories about Lachlan that made his face turn red. Much to the delight of his brothers.

After dinner, Mary Pat brought out a tray of homemade ice cream sandwiches, store-bought vanilla ice cream smashed between two of her famous chocolate chip cookies. It was a perfect summer treat.

I offered to help with the dishes once dessert was over. Mary Pat told Kelsey to rest, so I was stuck in the kitchen with my boyfriend's mom. I rinsed off the plates and handed them to her to put into the dishwasher.

"Thanks for dinner. It was great," I told her.

"My pleasure. I'm so glad Lachlan found someone like you. I didn't like his ex-boyfriend."

"Uh-huh."

"He hurt him so bad it forced him to move home. Bringing my baby home was the only good thing that man ever did."

She shouldn't be telling me this. This was a conversation Lachlan and I should have had.

"He was hurting when he moved back, but I'm glad he found love again with you. You sure you won't change your mind about kids?"

"Lachlan doesn't want them, either. But no. I'm solid in that decision. I can always be the fun aunt."

She frowned at that. I'd never get someone of her generation to understand my stance on not having kids. It was a useless argument.

"I want my boys to be happy. Even if I don't understand their choices."

"Of course. That's what good moms want."

I handed her the last dish, and she put it in the dishwasher. We found everyone crowded around the TV in the living room.

Lachlan and I stayed for another hour after dinner, and then he made an excuse that I had to be up early to open the shop. Technically, that was a lie since my staff allowed me to not do that anymore.

We said our goodbyes and drove back over to our apartments. The car ride was tense, filled with an uncomfortable silence. My question was on the tip of my tongue, but if Henry hurt Lachlan as much as his mom said, he wouldn't want to talk about him.

"I'm sorry my parents talked about my ex and the kids' thing," he offered after he parked his car in front of my shop and turned the engine off.

"Oh."

"I don't want to talk about him. He wasn't a good person," he said, his voice a firm 'no.'

That made me have so many more questions. I wanted him to confide in me. To tell me all the hurt he'd been through before so I could make it better. That's what partners were supposed to do. But his tone of voice was like he erected a wall in front of him, locking me out. It hurt more than I cared to admit.

"Did my mom lay on the kid guilt when you helped her clean up?" he asked, changing the subject.

"Nothing I can't handle."

"Okay. I'm sorry."

"Baby..."

His eyes lit up at the pet name. "Yeah?"

"It's okay. I was prepared for that. Wanna come upstairs?"

"Fuck yes. I need you beneath me, screaming my name."

I grinned. "I think I can handle that."

I still wanted to ask about his ex and why it made him move home, but I would respect his boundaries. I couldn't help thinking about the wall between us now and how it made my unease blossom into worry. What if the reason he didn't want to talk about his ex was because Lachlan wasn't quite over him? What if asking about Henry made Lachlan realize his life was in the city? The thought of losing him forced my mouth to remain shut.

Instead, I climbed the stairs to my apartment and let my boyfriend have his way with my body. I'd never complain about losing myself in the man I loved. Even if I wasn't ready to admit that to him yet. Now that really would have had him running screaming back to the city. Maybe into the arms of the man he was trying to get away from.

CHAPTER TWENTY-ONE

LACHLAN

*I*n between weddings and engagement shoots, I had been running back and forth between the city and Drakesville all week to prepare for the art show tomorrow. Hayden was a wreck trying to corral all the artists to make sure this show went off without a hitch. Mindy and I agreed to help them put it all together. The only problem being it was at the expense of spending my limited time with my girlfriend.

"So is your new boo coming?" Hayden asked with a grin across their face.

"Yes, she's coming. She's one of my subjects, too."

Hayden circled around the display we set up. "Flag girl?"

"Yeah."

"Oh, I see it. You made her look angelic."

"A goddess," I corrected.

Hayden threw Mindy a concerned look. Mindy shook

her head as she adjusted the painting on display. "Min, you didn't say he was in *love*, love."

I crossed my arms over my chest. "I'm not. We haven't been dating that long."

Mindy sauntered over to my display and rearranged two of the photos. I gritted my teeth that her placement was better. That's why she was my assistant.

"You don't even know the half of it," Mindy said to Hayden. "Lachlan even held off fucking her for a while."

Hayden shook their head, purple curls bouncing with the motion. "I don't believe it."

I frowned. "You two are annoying."

"He *is* in love," Hayden teased.

"He is!" Mindy agreed. "She makes the best damn coffee, too. I'm kinda warming up to small-town life. They got some hot bartenders in Drakesville."

I fixed her with a glare. "What bartenders?"

She laughed. "Not your brothers."

"Who?" I demanded.

She spun away, fixing another display. "Nobody you need to know. It's just fucking."

I rolled my eyes. I'd have to ask my brothers if they had the details.

Christ, I belonged in Drakesville with how quickly I became a gossip again. Small towns did it to you.

"Well, I can't wait to meet this hot barista," Hayden said.

"Coffee shop owner," I corrected. "And she's an artist too. She sells local paintings in the shop. You'll like her."

"Good, because your ex sucked!"

I sighed.

Didn't I know it? The ex who still couldn't stop harassing me. He had some sculptures in the show, and I wasn't looking forward to running into him. It was a big show, and I was hoping we could avoid him.

"He keeps asking about you," Hayden admitted.

"How so?" I asked.

"Asking if you're dating anyone new. How the business is going. Trying to get dirt, but I keep blowing him off."

I sighed.

"What did you ever see in him?" Mindy asked.

"I don't know. Can you both do me a favor this weekend? Make sure he stays away from Willow?"

They nodded.

A reminder pinged on my phone about dinner with Willow's parents tonight. After the uncomfortable conversations at dinner with my family, I was worried about meeting her parents. I knew she had questions about Henry that I didn't want to answer. It was driving an unnecessary wedge between us, but she thought I didn't notice. I'd been too busy this week to sit her down and tell her all of this. I had to get through the art show first, and then I could explain it all to her. She'd understand.

"I gotta jet," I told them.

"Good luck," Mindy said.

Hayden cocked their head, silently asking for an explanation.

I raked a hand through my hair. "Willow's parents want me over for dinner."

Hayden gave a low whistle. "That means it's serious, huh?"

"Does it?" I asked.

"Yes," Mindy answered for me. "Get out of here so you're not late."

"We're all set here. Go on, get," Hayden teased.

I shook my head at them and headed outside toward my

car. Once inside, I started the engine and headed home. I called Willow on the way.

"Hey, baby," she greeted.

The sound of her voice made my heart sing. This week had been jam-packed, and I hated disappointing her by not spending time with her.

"Hey, sweetness. I'm leaving the gallery now. Is that okay?"

"That's fine. I had my closer call out sick, so I'm closing the shop today. I already told my parents we'd be late."

At her words, I noticed the noise of the espresso machine and voices in the background. Relief washed through me that I wouldn't be late to meet her parents.

"Sorry."

"You wouldn't have been late, anyway. Please relax."

It wasn't that long ago that I was the one telling her to relax, and then my mom made it awkward by mentioning my ex and harping on us not wanting kids. My nerves at meeting her parents were justified.

"I remember being on the other side of this conversation last week."

She laughed. "I know. It'll be great. My dad will give you a plate of meat piled to the sky, and my mom will keep pouring you sangria. They want to meet the person who's taking up all my free time."

Why did it bother me she didn't say they wanted to meet the person she loved? It wasn't like we said those words to each other yet.

"Stop worrying," she reassured me. "Meet me in a few hours, and you'll see."

We hung up, and I spent the rest of the ride home doing exactly what she asked me not to.

I got home early enough that I had time to shower and

clean up my beard. It had been neglected this week and grew out too much to my liking. Looking a little too bushy, like Killian or Ronan's. I trimmed up my beard and smoothed down my hair, hoping it was presentable.

Walking into my bedroom, I opened my closet and tried to find the perfect outfit that told her parents I treated her right. God, what did that even mean?

I settled on a pair of my nicest jeans and a button-down. I then had to iron all the invisible wrinkles out. Willow called me while I was surveying myself in the mirror.

"Are you ready yet?" she teased.

"No," I admitted. "Can you come upstairs and tell me if I look okay?"

She hung up on me before answering, but a minute later, there was a knock on my door. I walked over to it and revealed her pretty face behind it. Her hair was in those beach waves, and she wore another floral dress. And damn, was she pretty without really trying.

I snaked my hands around her waist and pulled her toward me. It was true I was stressed about meeting her parents, but I also missed her this week. She didn't even flinch when I laid a long, lingering kiss on her lips. No, my good girl, let me lead her wherever I wanted, letting me devour her whole.

Pulling away, I grinned and wiped lipstick off her chin. "Hey, sweetness."

She squinted at me. "Did you make up an excuse so you could kiss me like that and leave me wanting?"

I laughed. "No. I really am freaking out about meeting your parents."

She spun out of my arms and circled around me. "It's fine. Black suits you. It's the mysterious artist about you."

"I don't want to be mysterious. I want your parents to like me."

"They will because I do. So, let's go."

Nerves clawed their way through my body, but I took her word for it. I grabbed my keys, and we left my apartment together and headed for my car. Willow gave me her parents' address, and I lifted an eyebrow. That was on the fancy side of town, but it didn't surprise me, knowing that Willow was a trust fund baby.

I put my keys into my ignition when her colorful nails caught my eye. They were in that trendy style of ombre colors, but this time, they matched the bi colors.

I grabbed her hand to inspect them again. "This is new."

"I got them done for the show tomorrow. You like?"

My horndog brain was thinking about watching those colors as she wrapped her hand around my favorite body part. Willow seemed to get where my thoughts went as she pulled her hands away and shook her head at me.

"Later," she promised.

Much later.

I pulled out of the parking spot in front of my storefront and headed to her parents' house. It was a brief ride, but I whistled at the sight of the Tudor-style home. I knew Willow came from money, but I didn't think I'd ever seen the evidence of that.

"It's not that big," she said, but her face told me even she didn't believe it.

I drove up the long drive and parked. We got out together, and Willow walked into the house just like I would have done at my parents' house. A part of me was surprised we weren't greeted by a butler. Her parents' house was nice and classy, but also felt lived in. I might have misjudged them at the sight of their square footage.

Willow led me to the sprawling backyard and the outdoor kitchen, where her dad had his massive grill already going. He was a portly, balding man whose face lit up when he spotted his daughter.

"Pumpkin!"

"Hey, Dad," Willow greeted, and then gestured to me. "I wanted you to meet my boyfriend, Lachlan Murphy. You know Mary Pat and Colin's son."

Her dad nodded at me. "Right. Colin's the only person I'll let look at my cars."

I nodded. My dad was priced fairly and one of the most beloved mechanics in town. He was good at what he did and had instilled that work ethic in me and my brothers.

I held out my hand to her dad. "Nice to meet you, Mr. Rivers."

He gave me a firm handshake that told me he was sizing me up. "Call me Bob."

"Bob. Right."

Bob let go of my hand, and he gestured to the grill. "You're not one of those vegans, son?"

Willow rolled her eyes. "Dad."

"Not me. Give me all the meat you got. I heard I might have a plate full of it."

He gave me a hearty laugh. "That's what I like to hear!"

Willow glided over to me and led me inside to the biggest kitchen I'd ever seen. My mom would have been in heaven. A slender woman stood mixing a pitcher of the sangria. Her dark hair was streaked with grey but pulled back into a slick bun. Her features mirrored Willow's, and I saw the beauty she passed down to her daughter.

"Hey, Mom. Wanna meet my boyfriend?"

Willow's mom snapped her head up at the sight of us,

and a smile played at the edge of her lips. "Well, it's about time. Lachlan, right?"

I nodded and put out my hand to her. "That's me. Nice to meet you, Mrs. Rivers."

Willow's mom raised an eyebrow at her. "So formal. Call me Abigail."

"Abigail. Right."

They were so intimidating that the insistence on calling them by their given names felt like a power play. Or maybe I was overthinking every single detail about tonight.

Abigail poured the sangria into glasses. "You like sangria?"

"Um... sure."

"He wants a beer," Willow told her.

I shot her a quick glare. Even if that was the truth, I still wanted to impress her mom.

Abigail laughed and spun around to open the fridge behind her. "Well, why didn't you say so? I have plenty of beer. But only the local stuff. Bob loves to support the community."

Willow beamed, knowing that also meant they supported her business.

Abigail handed me a Drakesville Lager and Willow a glass of sangria.

"Thanks. You know, Willow and I had our first date at the brewery."

Willow's face pinkened, but her mom gave me a bright smile. "Really? I love that."

"I also made him take a tour of all our restaurants," Willow added. "The Drakesville Tavern is a no."

Abigail wrinkled her nose. "I swear that place is a front. I prefer Sullivan's. Your brother Killian makes a mean cocktail."

"He does," Willow agreed.

Abigail handed Willow another glass while she carried the pitcher in two hands and led us into the backyard. She placed it on the table and then greeted Bob with a kiss. Willow scrunched up her face in disgust at the display of affection, but it was cute seeing her parents still in love.

We settled into seats at the patio table. I dropped my voice to a whisper. "How am I doing?"

"Fine. Relax."

Abigail sprinted to and fro between the kitchen and the backyard, bringing out the side dishes while ignoring my offers for help. Bob finished grilling, and he did indeed give me a plate of meat. On the table were burgers, steaks, grilled chicken, kebabs, green beans, mashed potatoes and a summer-style salad.

Willow groaned. "Dad, this is way too much food for the four of us."

Her mom waved her off. "Nonsense. We'll send you home with most of it."

As we settled in to eat and I took my first bite of burger, that's when I felt the interrogation begin.

Abigail gave a sharp eye to her daughter. "I'm glad to finally meet the person my daughter's spending all her free time with that she can't bother to have dinner with her parents."

Oof. Guilt trip was laced in that sentence. I was familiar with that move.

"Mom, I'm very busy running my business. So is Lachlan. That's not the only reason."

"Yes, Lachlan, how is your business going?" her dad cut in, saving me from his wife's cutting words.

"It's good. An adjustment from city life but…I like it. It feels like home."

"You have quite the portfolio," Abigail said. "I've been meaning to reach out to you for new headshots. The one I have for my firm is very dated."

I nodded. "I absolutely can do that. Need to check with my assistant on our schedule. Summer is our busy season."

She cocked her head. "Oh?"

"Weddings," I explained.

"Oh, right, you did Aspen's wedding," Bob interjected.

"Yes. Kai's an old friend, and I was happy to do it. Weddings are my biggest income driver, but I like to do all sorts of photography."

"He's amazing," Willow gushed.

I reached out and squeezed her hand under the table. Her praise filled my chest with warmth and pride.

"Well, we're glad our daughter found someone to love her right," Bob said and lifted his beer bottle in cheers.

My mouth dropped open, and the heat of the summer sun beat down on me. A glance at Willow's wide eyes told me dropping the 'L' word terrified her, too.

But I loved her. When I looked at her, warmth radiated off her, and her smile felt like home. She was everything I wanted in a partner. It wasn't this town that made me want to stay in this nosy small town. It was her. Confessing my love to her at her parents' house was not the time nor the place to spring that on her.

Instead, I lifted my beer bottle in response to her dad and toasted him back.

Abigail smiled. "We're so happy you came over. You're both so busy; I don't see how you find the time."

"We make the time," I explained.

"Sometimes I bring him lunch," Willow said with a grin.

"I love that," her mom said and paused dramatically.

"So, does this mean you're gonna change your mind about kids?"

Willow groaned. "Moooooom."

I shuttered. "Oh God no. I don't want kids either."

"Well, you're well matched with our girl," Bob said, shooting his wife a warning glance.

"Anyway!" Willow cut in. "What's new with you two?"

Her dad sighed and launched into complaining about a new incompetent CMO at his company, and then her mom filled us in on a high-profile case she'd just settled.

As we ate dinner, drank beer, and chatted with her parents about our weeks, my nerves fell away. Her parents were a lot like mine. Embarrassing, but they loved her, and that was all anyone could ever hope for.

While I drank my beer and watched the late afternoon sun shine down on Willow's chestnut curls, I knew more than anything that I had fallen hard for her. This sweet woman had captured my heart, and now I had to find the time to tell her.

Soon. After the opening night of the art show, when my stress levels finally went down. Then I'd tell my good girl how much I loved her.

CHAPTER TWENTY-TWO

WILLOW

I did a twirl for my cousin. "What do you think? Classy enough?"

My dress wasn't anything too fancy, merely a sleeveless black cocktail dress. Unlike my flowy floral dresses, the fit was tight and showed off my slender figure. Paired with my stilettos that Lachlan loved, the outfit made me feel sexy.

Aspen looked up from her perch on my bed. "It looks good. People aren't gonna be wearing ball gowns to an exhibit opening."

Well, I didn't think that either, but tonight was important to Lachlan, and I wanted to look the part. I even took off my crystal jewelry and wore the expensive tennis bracelet my mom gave me for Christmas to look classier.

"I want to look nice," I explained to my cousin.

"You look great. Lachlan will appreciate you supporting him tonight."

"Can you help with my hair? I want to curl it, and you're better at it."

She got off my bed and directed me toward my vanity chair. She helped curl my hair while I put the finishing touches on my makeup. Originally, I asked Mindy for assistance, but she was already in the city with Lachlan, putting on the final touches for the show. Thankfully, my cousin wanted to catch up and agreed to come over and help me pick out my outfit.

Aspen wrapped a strand of my hair around the curling iron. "So, things are getting serious with this one, huh?"

"I think so."

We met each other's parents, so that had to count for something. Although, we hadn't been dating for that long, especially for these feelings to come out of me so quickly. There was also that big issue that kept nagging at me — neither of us had said those three little words yet.

My heart told me I felt it. Every time it fluttered at the sound of his voice. It beat hard whenever he walked into my coffee shop and gave me that shy smile. Especially during those quiet moments while we lay in bed basking in the comfort of each other. My heart wanted to burst out of my chest when he kissed me. I was deeply and desperately in love with Lachlan Murphy, but I didn't know if he felt the same.

Aspen frowned at me and moved on to the next piece of my hair. "You either know or you don't."

I pursed my lips and blotted my mouth with a tissue, getting my lipstick the perfect shade. "I don't know if he feels like I do."

"And what's that?"

I sighed. She was prodding on purpose. "I think I love him."

"Again, you either know or you don't."

"Fine, you pain in the butt. I love him."

She curled a final section of my hair and ran her fingers through my curls, giving them the appearance of looking natural. "He loves you, too."

"You can't possibly know that."

"It's obvious. So, tell him already."

"What if he doesn't feel the same?"

"He does." She turned my head side-to-side so I could inspect her work. "Good?"

"Yes. Thanks."

"Good. Now get out of here and support your man. Then tell him you love him."

I wasn't sure about doing all that. I hugged her, and we walked downstairs together. She headed home while I waited a few more minutes for my rideshare to arrive.

During the ride to the city, I fidgeted with the bracelet around my wrist. I was nervous for Lachlan and how the photo of me would be perceived. But also excited to see what queer joy meant for our community. My emotions were a swirling mass of confusion inside me.

Once we arrived, I thanked the driver and made my way inside the art gallery. I'd been to exhibits at museums, but never anything like this. The idea of discovering new local artists to source for the shop excited me. Although, I had to remind myself this wasn't a networking event. I was here to support my partner first and foremost.

Upon entering the gallery, my instinct to dress nicely had been correct. I strolled through casually, glancing at the exhibits while searching for Lachlan. A waiter offered me a glass of champagne, which I took while I made my way through the maze of artwork.

I found the man in question standing in front of his photo display against a wall. I froze at the image of myself wrapped in the bi flag. I had seen the photo before, of course, but tonight, the intent hit me in the chest. Even before we started dating, Lachlan showed me how he saw me with his camera lens. He depicted me like a strong, bisexual goddess. I looked fierce and powerful. And I'd never love a photo of myself more than this one.

"Willow." Lachlan's deep voice pulled me from the display.

I turned to him, and the smile on his face felt like a warm hug. He looked good tonight, wearing black slacks and a silky black button-down fitted to his lean frame. He had the top button undone, teasing his dark chest hair. Damn, he was sexy as hell, and it made me want to rip off all those buttons.

Mindy stood next to him, sporting a hot pink body con dress and looking fabulous as ever. Beside her was a stranger with curly purple hair wearing a three-piece suit. On the lapel of their jacket, they had a pin that read 'they/them.' Oh, that must be Hayden.

Lachlan put an arm around my waist and gestured to me. "Hayden, this is Willow."

"Ah, the famous Willow. Nice to meet you."

I pointed at myself. "I'm famous?"

Hayden gestured at the photo of me on display. "You're flag girl."

I frowned.

Mindy laughed. "Get used to it, girl."

I turned to Hayden. "It's very nice to meet you. I'm excited to see all the artwork."

They eyed me up and down. "I can see what keeps Lachs in his boring small town now."

"Small town's not so bad," Mindy said.

Hayden groaned. "You can't leave me, too."

While they began to bicker, Lachlan steered me away from them. "Come on, let's check out the other artists."

He grabbed a glass of champagne from a nearby waiter and toured me around the room. Everything about the show screamed queer joy, and it made me hopeful for the future.

We had come so far in being accepted. Even when we were kids, it had been a big scandal when Lachlan came out. When anyone came out in our town. But Drakesville surprised me at how accepting our little town could be. There were still those who thought we were abominations, but tonight, I saw all the possibilities that one day, a new generation wouldn't have to endure that hate. I loved that.

We grabbed appetizers while we gazed at lesbian paintings and mixed media pieces. There was a display of sculptures, but for some reason, Lachlan guided me away from them. There were a couple of paintings I had my eye on, and I gave the artist my card to discuss displaying them in my store. All those sales went to the artist, though; I merely let them place them on my walls.

At one point, Lachlan got pulled into a conversation with one of his art school buddies, and I wandered off to the appetizer table. I grabbed a plate of quiches and another glass of champagne when a man approached me.

He had a head of beautiful silver hair styled to perfection, and he wore a pin-striped three-piece suit. He was the most beautiful man I'd ever seen and was the epitome of a 'silver fox.' But when my eyes trailed up to his, the sneer across his face had my hackles raised.

"You know you're temporary, right?" he asked.

"Excuse me?"

"Lachlan always comes back. You're just another replacement he's trying to use. He'll toss you aside and come back to me."

I clenched my teeth. I had a feeling I knew who this was. Why the heck didn't Lachlan mention his ex would be in attendance?

"I don't see how my relationship is any of your business," I told him firmly.

"He always comes back like a good little boy because he knows what's best for him. Some cute girl from his dumpy small town isn't gonna change that. He's mine and always will be."

"The city's overrated. And I can see why with assholes like you in it."

Okay, that was rude and so unlike me, but this guy was rude first.

"Just you wait. He'll realize no one can compare to me, and he'll come crawling back. I bet it took him a while to go out with you, huh? Lachlan will never get over me, no matter how hard he tries."

His words hit me hard, digging into my insecurities and reminding me how much I chased Lachlan. Was he right? It took Lachlan so long to get the hint, and then when we started dating, he held off on the sex because he said he wanted to get to know me first. But was that the real reason? Or was he only using me to get over his ex?

I wanted to believe it wasn't true, but this man's words confused my thoughts and reminded me that Lachlan never told me he loved me. What if he was still holding out for Henry? Maybe he ran away so much when I asked him out because he couldn't give me what I wanted. Was it possible I pushed him into a relationship too soon? He didn't want to talk about his ex, which I understood, but maybe it was because he wasn't over him.

I was at a loss for words, and Henry gave me an evil

smile. "Think about it, sweetheart. Lachlan belongs here with me. Not you. It's better you know that now."

He stomped off, leaving me to stew in my thoughts. I knew how I felt about Lachlan, and his photo of me told a different story than what this man was selling. But what if I only saw what I wanted to see? We needed to talk this through, but tonight wasn't the time for that.

I drank my champagne and plastered on a fake smile. Then, I searched for Lachlan. Later, I'd get the answers to my questions, but not now. Tonight, I was supporting my boyfriend. Just what any good girl would do. And I knew all about doing that.

CHAPTER TWENTY-THREE

LACHLAN

*A*fter getting lost in a conversation with one of my art school buddies, I realized my girl had disappeared. Panic ran through me because we had been so good at avoiding Henry all night. To the point I even had to steer her away from his sculptures. I exhaled a breath when I spotted her talking to Hayden.

I set my empty glass of champagne down on a waiter's tray and was about to head over to her when Henry stepped into my path. He looked great tonight. His suit was tailored perfectly to his amazing body, and his expensive haircut made him look angelic. But that smug look on his face reminded me of all the times we had this exact interaction.

"Lachlan. You've been avoiding me."

I shot him a death stare. "I thought I made it clear I want nothing to do with you."

He reached out to press a hand to my chest. "Come on, baby. We both know you belong with me. Quit playing in that small town and come back to the city."

I knocked his hand away. "Stop it. I love my small town and the people in it. And I don't love you. Not anymore."

"Come on, Lachlan. You know the cute small-town girl is beneath you."

If I was my brother Killian, I might have used my fists on him. Instead, I kept them balled at my sides. "Can't you take a fucking hint? We're done. Over. No more. I found someone who doesn't toy with me or play mind games. Someone whose smile lights up the room when she sees me. Someone I love with all my heart."

He scoffed. "She's just another way for you to try to replace me. You'll be back."

"No the fuck I will not. Do you want my brother to rock your shit again? Or do I have to do it my damn self? We're done, Henry. Leave me the fuck alone."

He bristled. "There's no need for such vulgarity."

"I love Willow, not you. Maybe I haven't loved you for a long time. I let you control me. Use me. Treat me like trash. Now, I found someone who treats me the way I deserve. And she will never be a replacement. She's the woman I love, body and soul. She's my muse. My reason for waking up in the morning. My light."

His face fell. "You're serious."

"Goodbye, Henry. Forever. I will never ever come back to you. My heart will always belong to Drakesville, Pennsylvania and that pretty brunette over there."

"Lachlan," he pleaded.

"You had your time for apologies. For changing. But you're not a good person. So have the night you deserve. I hope it's fucking terrible."

God, I needed a drink, but I was driving Willow home tonight after the opening, so I found a glass of water instead. Having said what I needed to say to my ex, the boulder that sat on my chest lifted. All those things I said about Willow were true, but I needed to tell her that. To admit to her how deeply and suddenly I had fallen in love with her. That she was the reason I wanted to keep my life in Drakesville. I don't know why it took me so long to realize that.

I was still friendly with most of my exes because sometimes relationships just didn't work out and that was okay. But Henry and I would never ever be friends again. I also never wanted to admit this to my other friends, but sometimes, he said I 'chose' by being with him, as if my bisexuality disappeared based on my partner. I had loved him for so long I let that slip, but none of my other partners had been like that. It was more proof that he was a dick.

Now to find the person I truly loved.

Willow wasn't with Hayden anymore, but they saw her with Mindy looking at Henry's sculptures. Great. She wasn't there when I checked, but I found them admiring some mixed media pieces.

She gave me a smile, but I noticed the strain on her face. "Hey, there you are."

I pulled her toward me and kissed the top of her head. "I'm sorry. I got busy talking shop."

Mindy shot me an annoyed look that I didn't understand.

Willow gave me that fake smile again. "No worries."

"What did you think of the show?" I asked.

"I loved it. I shamelessly networked to get some new pieces for the shop."

"That's great."

"She's got good options," Mindy interjected. "Some great painters and mixed media artists that would fit the vibe of the shop."

The artwork in her coffee shop was one of the things I

loved about it. It gave her shop a unique appeal instead of a boring corporate and clean look of other coffee shops.

I slid my hand down to grab Willow's, and we laced our fingers together. "Thank you for coming out for me tonight. It meant a lot."

This time, her smile was genuine. "Of course."

"You ready to go home?"

She yawned. "Yeah. I'm tired."

I turned to Mindy. "You staying at your apartment tonight?"

Mindy pursed her lips. "Of course, I am."

Alright, Min, keep your secrets. I'd get it out of her soon. "I'll see you tomorrow. We have the Olsen wedding in Princeton."

"I'm aware. All packed and ready to go bright and early. Don't get into too much trouble tonight."

Willow disconnected her hand from mine. "Gimme a minute. I drank too much champagne."

She went off in search of the bathroom. After she disappeared, Mindy crossed her arms over her chest and gave me an annoyed look.

"What?" I asked.

"Have you told her you love her yet?"

I rubbed the back of my neck. "No, but why is that your business?"

"You better get on with that before she slips away. She needs to hear it."

What the fuck was she talking about? But I couldn't ask her to explain because Willow glided back over to us. We waved goodbye to Mindy, who sauntered over to Hayden. I slid my hand into Willow's again, and we walked to my car together. Once we were on the road, a terse quiet filled my car. It set me on edge.

"Is everything okay?" I asked her, after we were halfway there.

"I'm tired."

But her voice sounded small and weak.

"Are you sure?"

"Yeah."

Hmm. I didn't like that. What was going on? She was an early bird, so maybe her excuse of tiredness was the truth, but my instincts nagged at me that I wasn't picking up on something big.

Silence filled my car again for the rest of the drive. There wasn't open parking on our street because of the time of night, so I went around the block a couple of times until I found a spot. That was one downside to living on the main street of town, but I'd lived in the city and was used to street parking.

We walked the block together, and I was surprised when she climbed the stairs to my apartment with me.

Once inside, I pressed her against my door and took her mouth. I kissed her slowly, savoring the taste of her lips on mine. She was eager in her response, molding herself to my body and sliding her tongue over mine. Her tiredness was long gone by the time I had her hiked up into my arms and carried her to my bed.

I laid her gently on the mattress, and her eyes shone with love. "Lachlan?"

"What's the matter, sweetness?"

She reached out and brushed a hand over my beard. "Nothing's the matter. Just missed you this week."

But her smile was still strained.

I turned my head and pressed a small kiss on her palm. "We don't have to have sex if you're too tired. Or if you don't feel like it at all."

She shook her head. "No, baby. I want slow tonight. No cameras. No breath play. No growly soft Dom demands. Just the two of us, skin-to-skin, becoming one."

"Whatever you need."

"Make slow love to me."

I should have told her then how much I loved her. Those words she needed to hear were on the tip of my tongue. She was practically begging for it with that request. But I wasn't clued in to what was going through her head, so instead, I took her mouth and did as she asked.

In the morning, I woke to the smell of coffee at my bedside table and my girlfriend smiling down at me. My early bird was already up and ready for the day — the price of owning and operating her own coffee shop.

"Hey, sleepyhead. Your alarm has gone off two times already," she said.

I bolted upright. "Shit."

She handed me my coffee. "Drink this first. You have time. Mindy said you're more than prepared. I had my staff put together breakfast for you to take for the ride."

"Oh. Thank you, sweetness. That's...you're the best."

I took a sip of my coffee and studied her. She must have walked over to her apartment this morning because she was already in her Drakesville Drip t-shirt and a pair of high-waisted shorts.

Gone was that strained smile from last night. Perhaps she really had been tired. But I kept thinking back to her wanting slow sex last night. Maybe that was all the energy she had time for. Yet there was a nagging at my heart that it was something else.

I drank my coffee and ran around my apartment, finding clean clothes. My equipment was already at the studio, ready to go, so I didn't have to worry about that.

I mentally went through my checklist for this wedding. The Olsens had been demanding and a pain in the ass, and I didn't think their marriage would last. But weddings helped me float, so I reminded myself that weddings were stressful for people.

Willow stood from my bed and followed me out of the apartment. Mindy was on the sidewalk waving a brown paper bag at me. "Let's go!"

"One minute." I turned toward Willow. "I'm getting in late tonight."

"See ya later, then."

That was not what a guy wanted to hear. It sounded like a dismissal. But one of the things I loved about Willow was how she didn't complain about my work schedule. I should be glad she was being so considerate, but something about her tone felt like we were in a fight I didn't know about.

"I can come over after?" I offered.

She waved me off. "I'll probably be asleep."

I tilted her chin up to me and laid a big kiss on her lips. She clutched at my button-down, pulling me closer like she was desperate to keep me here.

I cupped her face and slowly ended the kiss. "I'll see you later. We'll figure out our schedules."

"Okay."

Mindy glared at me, and I helped her load the car as quickly as I could. In the car, Mindy had another coffee in my cup holder, and I was grateful my girlfriend and my best friend had thought of everything.

I started the car, and then we were off.

"Did you tell that angel of yours that you're head over heels in love with her yet?" Mindy asked between bites of her burrito.

I shook my head. "Not yet. I need to find the right time. What did you mean last night when you said to tell her before she slips away?"

"Umm."

"Mindy," I growled out.

"Well...I saw her talking to Henry last night, and whatever he said to her made her upset. And then we saw you talking to him."

I slammed on the brakes. "WHAT THE FUCK!"

The person behind me beeped at me, and my tires squealed as I sped off, trying to focus on my driving again.

"She wouldn't tell me what he said, so you know it was bad."

"Did she know who he was?"

"Yeah. Because she asked if he was your ex but refused to say anything else."

Shit. There was something wrong last night, and I had been too oblivious to notice it. Yet again. What the fuck had he said to her?

A part of me wanted to get on the phone and ream him out, but that was what he wanted. To get a rise out of me. That's why he did it. Every time I tried to move on, he had to swoop in and ruin my chances. And then I went back to him when the loneliness crept in. It was his plan, but it wasn't going to happen this time.

"Why is he doing this?" I fumed. "I told him we're done. I basically told him to go fuck himself last night."

"And you should have! But now you need to tell the person you love that he doesn't matter to you and never will again. After this weekend, tell your girlfriend you love her and want to marry her."

"Whoa. No one's talking about marriage. That's way too soon."

She laughed. "Oh, hun. We both know that woman is the love of your life."

Was she?

Fuck, she was. Willow, the girl of my dreams, was now the woman who I woke up to every morning. The woman whose bright smile made everything right in the world.

"Maybe not today. Or even in a couple of years. But she's your other half. Now you gotta tell her. And soon, before whatever poison Henry fed her takes over."

CHAPTER TWENTY-FOUR

WILLOW

I didn't see Lachlan all weekend, which was normal when he was booked solid with weddings. It also gave me time to think about what his ex told me. Which was bad. Now my feelings were a conflicting storm in the pit of my stomach. How could I not think that I had pushed Lachlan into this relationship after that conversation? What if he did go back to his ex?

I didn't see him Monday or Tuesday either because Kelly called out sick, and I needed help managing the shop. I was also working through our plans for the town arts festival in the fall, so I practically fell into my bed each night. But I'd admit, a part of that was an excuse because I wasn't ready to have the important conversation I needed to with Lachlan.

On Wednesday, my cousin came into the shop right before we closed and asked for an herbal tea. I made her a green tea latte, but my curiosity was piqued. She was a double-shot espresso girlie, and she never drank tea.

I set her drink down and helped my staff clean up the shop. Aspen sat at the window drinking her tea, her foot tapping impatiently while she waited for me. After my employees had gone home and I finished counting the till, I plopped down in the seat across from her.

"Why are you here?" I asked.

She threw me a glare. "You haven't been answering my texts."

"I've been busy."

"That's not it. What's wrong with you?"

I sighed. Where did I even start?

She finished her tea and set it down. "Okay, we need a girl's night. Let's order takeout. I'm craving greasy food."

I cleaned up her trash and did one last double-check before closing up and heading to my apartment upstairs. We settled on ordering pizza and cheese fries from the pizza shop. Not unusual for our girls' nights in, but cheese fries were usually reserved for a special occasion.

"You want a drink?" I asked her while searching my fridge for something alcoholic.

"Only water."

I paused while I opened a bottle of wine and poured myself a glass. Now I knew something was up with her for sure. I poured her a glass of water and settled onto the couch next to her. Her hand rested on her stomach, and she stared blankly at my wall.

"Aspen, why did you come over?" I asked again.

"I have to tell you something, but when I walked into the shop, I saw the distressed look on your face and knew something was troubling you."

"Tell me your news first."

"I'm pregnant."

"Oh... are we excited about this?" I asked gingerly.

She pinched my leg. "Yes, I'm excited about this... although not expected."

"Mom-Mom was praying for a grandbaby at your wedding, so it's not that much of a surprise."

She laughed. "She was. I'm not that far along, and we calculated that it happened on our honeymoon."

"How's Kai handling it?"

Her face lit up. "Oh my God, he's so excited. We talked about having kids in the future, but this was a happy little accident."

I squeezed her into a tight hug. "I'm so happy for you."

"And you get to spoil my kid rotten as the fun, child-free aunt."

"I can't wait."

We were interrupted by the pizza being delivered, and I ran downstairs to retrieve it. Once inside, I grabbed plates and divided up our food. I couldn't control my laughter at how my cousin shoveled it in.

"This baby loves food that makes my face break out," she complained.

"Could be worse."

"Oh, it is. I'll throw this up later, but whatever."

I cringed. I never, ever wanted to be pregnant. Kid-free was the right choice for me. I was so glad Lachlan agreed with that.

I frowned at the sudden thought about him.

Aspen pointed a forkful of cheese fries at me. "Okay, good news out. Now tell me what's got you making that sad face? Did something happen with Lachlan?"

I shook my head. "No... it's... I don't know."

"What happened at the art show? Did you tell him you loved him, and it went poorly? Do I need to sic Kai on him? Or one of his brothers to knock some sense into him?"

Her questions were rapid-fire, and none of them were the crux of the problem.

"His ex got into my head."

"Which ex? Not anyone I know. Everyone he dated here is on good terms with him."

"No. The one that forced him to run home with his tail between his legs."

She frowned. "Okay, you got a lot of explaining to do."

I let out a frustrated breath and launched into repeating all the hurtful things Lachlan's ex had said to me. I didn't mention that Henry sent me messages via my social media channels to hammer in on his cruel words. I explained to my cousin that I hadn't seen Lachlan in a couple of days because I didn't know how to talk to him about it. Ever since his parents brought up his ex, he refused to talk about him, and that bugged me.

"You're not temporary," Aspen said firmly.

"How could you know that?"

"I've seen you two together walking in town hand in hand with two big goofy grins on your face. I see how your entire body lights up when you see him. Everyone in town talks about how cute you two are."

"But what if I'm only someone to pass the time with until he goes running back to that man?"

Aspen shook her head. "No. That's not what I see when Lachlan looks at you."

I took a gulp of my wine. I wasn't so sure about that. I loved the man so much it hurt, but the idea that he couldn't love me that way made my chest ache.

"Aspen..." I whispered. "I love him. I don't want to lose him. But what if I rushed into this? What if I forced him into something he wasn't ready for?"

"No way. You need to talk to him. Work it out like

adults instead of icing him out and stewing in your thoughts."

Damn my cousin for always calling me out when I did shit like that. I loved her but also hated her for it.

"You know I'm right," she prodded.

"I know."

I picked at a cheese fry and let my thoughts linger in my head. Talking it out with Lachlan was the right thing to do, but fear wrapped around my chest at the answers I'd get.

My phone vibrated against the coffee table, and I picked it up, seeing a text from Lachlan.

> LACHLAN: Hey, sweetness. I know work's busy for both of us. Are you free tonight? Or a lunch date tomorrow? Miss you!

Would he say that if I really were temporary for him?

Aspen nodded at my phone. "Is that your man trying to talk some sense into you?"

"Maybe."

"Let me get out of your hair, then."

I shook my head. "No. I need time."

She stood up. "Uh, no, cuz. You need to talk to your partner and have an adult conversation instead of being immature and avoiding him."

"Kelly called out all week. I needed to take care of the shop."

Her eyes cut into a glare at me. "That's bullshit. You have plenty of employees that could have picked up that slack. That's an excuse, and we both know it. Call your man and lay your cards on the table."

I lifted my feet on the couch and wrapped my arms around my knees. "I'm scared."

"I know, but that's what love is like. It's scary and

thrilling. But if you don't take the risk, if you don't tell that man what you're feeling, you might miss out on the best thing that ever happened to you."

She gave me a hug goodbye and left before I could protest.

I didn't answer Lachlan right away. Instead, I cleaned up my kitchen and put my dinner away. Feeling gross from being in my coffee uniform, I took a shower.

I still didn't respond to him when I changed into my pajamas. Or when I sat on my bed, slowly brushing out my hair and staring at my crystal shelf.

I hopped off the bed and went to my shelf, pulling off a rose quartz and rubbing it between my hands. The pretty rock didn't give me an insight that it could help with my relationship woes. Despite my cousin's urging, I wasn't sure tonight was the night to talk to Lachlan. I needed more space to think through what I was going to say. My heart said to bare myself to him, but my brain told me to pump the brakes. And I had no clue which part of me was correct.

I slumped against my bed and held the gem up to the light, urging it to give me a sign of what to do.

I loved Lachlan, and I had fallen deep for him, but he hadn't given me any sign that he felt the same way. I had to chase him so hard just for him to go on a date with me. It had Henry's words echoing in my head, reminding me of how aggressive I had to be for Lachlan to notice me.

I dropped the crystal onto my bed and picked up my phone, shooting off a response to Lachlan.

> ME: Let's talk tomorrow.

I threw my phone on the other side of the bed and ran my hands down my face.

You're just another replacement he's trying to use.
He'll toss you aside and come back to me.
What if all that was true?

My head and heart were waging war against each other, trying to get me to listen to one over the other. I needed to know where I stood with him. Even if it broke my heart in the end. It was better to find out now.

CHAPTER TWENTY-FIVE

LACHLAN

Since my art show, something had been off with Willow. That was a lie. The strain between us started when my mom mentioned my ex-boyfriend, and then I refused to talk about him. Perhaps that was a mistake. Her message to talk had my hackles raised, wondering what Henry said to her.

I rubbed a hand over my scruffy jaw while I waited for my food pick-up order. I asked her cousin what to do to get back into her good graces, and Aspen said to bring her favorite meal. And flowers. Remembering her eyes lighting up at the sight of a bouquet in her favorite color told me that was a good idea.

Brian eyed me from behind the bar at Sullivan's as he poured a beer for a customer. Killian was out on leave since Siobhan had the baby, so my oldest brother had been picking up the slack at the pub. "You look like you need a drink."

"Waiting for my food. I don't need it right now."

He delivered his customer's beer and came back around to face me. "What's going on?"

"Willow met Henry."

A scowl formed across Brian's face. "You're not going back to him, right? I thought things were going well with Willow."

I vigorously shook my head. "No. I'm not going back to him. Willow's who I want."

"Listen, kid, sometimes women need to know how we feel. You can't assume, okay? Don't let that douche nugget get in the way of another promising relationship."

I gritted my teeth. "That's why I'm bringing her food. Will you stay out of my love life?"

"You shouldn't have moved back here if you didn't want us all up in your business."

He left the bar for a second to go into the kitchen, and when he returned, he had my takeout order. "Here. Now go tell your woman you love her already."

"I'm going," I huffed out and high-tailed it out of there.

Truth was, I loved that my brothers gave a shit about me. Even if they were likely to put me in a headlock while telling me what to do about my relationship. Not everyone could be emotionally mature. Especially not them.

I left the pub, walking the couple of blocks to my storefront. The outer door of Willow's apartment was left open, and I trudged up the steps until I got to her front door. I knocked, and my heart ached when I saw the downtrodden look on her face. That wasn't what I wanted to see when I saw my girlfriend again for the first time in days.

I held up the takeout box. "I come with dinner. And flowers for the pretty lady."

Her eyes softened, and she took the flowers inside, immediately putting them in a vase while I brought in the food and set the bag on the counter. I found plates in her cabinet and transferred our food on them, then brought it over to her tiny kitchen table.

She looked down at her plate. "You know I love the shepherd's pie?"

I took out my burger. "No. I asked Aspen what to get."

"It's my favorite."

We ate in quiet silence, an uncomfortable tension wrapping around us. I didn't like it.

After we finished and I let her pick at my leftover fries, I took the plunge. "Are we in a fight that I don't know about?"

She gave a slow shake of her head but wouldn't look at me. "No."

"Then what's going on? Since my art show, I've felt this strain between us. Did I do something wrong?"

"No, I'm..."

"Sweetness, what is it?"

"I think we need to pump the brakes."

My heart sank to my stomach. "What?"

"Like go on a break," she explained.

"Why?"

She looked down at her hands in her lap. "I want to be with someone who loves me fully. I can't be the person you use to pass the time with before you go back to your ex."

Her words hit me like a freight train, letting me know exactly who put these thoughts into her head. "Did he try to tell you I'd go back to him?"

She lifted her head, and her shiny eyes cracked my heart in half. I was of half a mind to call up my brothers and let them have at Henry for hurting Willow.

"Yes," she whispered. "I don't want to be temporary."

"Tell me what he said."

She repeated all his nasty words back to me, and by the

time she finished, steam was practically coming out of my ears. Why couldn't he leave me alone? Why did he insist on destroying every good relationship I tried to have without him?

"I feel like I pushed you into this relationship," she admitted. "I pursued you relentlessly, and then when we finally went out, I was the one who pushed for us to be intimate first. I should have realized you weren't ready for a relationship. I don't want you to feel like you have to be with me when you really want to be with him."

Fuck me. He talked to her for, what, a few minutes? And he had her thinking every doubt under the sun about our relationship.

"I don't want to break up for good," she continued. "But I think it's in our best interest to take some time apart."

"Okay," I heard myself saying, but I wanted to scream at her to not listen to my ex. The words I needed to tell her were trapped in my throat.

"You should take some time to think about if this—me—is what you really want. Because I'm not going to be anyone's second choice."

"I... Okay. If that's what you think is best."

This wasn't what I wanted at all. The things I needed to tell her, my confession of love, were on the tip of my tongue. But I couldn't say them. Not when my girlfriend was showing me the door.

She gave me a sad smile. "Think about what you want, Lachlan. Then we can talk."

"Okay."

My voice was hollow, my emotions zapped out of me. I kept the words she needed to hear locked up tight.

I was in a fog as I walked out of her apartment and down the steps, but I found myself behind the wheel of my car. My instinct had me wanting to drive to the city and pull a Killian by punching my ex in the face. But I drove to Finn's house instead.

He didn't live that far away, having bought a ranch home near the school a few blocks away. I should have called or sent an SOS text to the group chat with my brothers, but Brian was working, and Killian was busy with a newborn. Ronan lived with our parents, and I didn't want Mom sticking her nose in this.

I parked on the street and noticed Ronan's truck was parked in front of mine. Good, I could talk to two brothers tonight.

My footsteps felt heavy as I walked up the drive and knocked on my brother's door.

Finn yanked the door open, his colossal body darkening the doorway. His brows knitted together. "What's wrong?"

"Willow broke up with me."

His eyes widened, and he led me inside.

Ronan sat on Finn's couch, and his face faltered when he saw me. "What happened?"

"Someone got dumped," Finn said with a shrug.

"I'll grab a beer," Ronan said and disappeared into the kitchen. He returned and handed me a beer while I slumped down on the couch.

Finn sat on the floor, gathering up the papers he had strewn about, and put his fiddle back in its case. "So, what happened?"

"Fucking Henry happened!"

"The fuck!" they exclaimed in unison.

I took a swig of my beer and then told them everything. About the strain between us when Mom brought up Henry and how he'd been harassing me. How she met him at my art show, and he told her she was only temporary and I'd always go back to him. Forcing her to ice me out these past couple days and when I finally saw her, she wanted us to go on a break. He had gotten into her head so badly, it made her doubt every single thing about our relationship. And I just agreed to the break. Like I always did when Henry undermined my happiness.

Finn took his seat in the armchair next to his couch. "He did the same shit he did to Trevor, huh?"

I nodded.

"And Samir," Ronan added.

"Katie."

"Amber."

"Hunter."

I groaned. "Can you not list off all my failed relationships?"

"No," Ronan said. "You need to understand that you keep making the same mistake."

"Oh, who was that cute blonde with the Star Wars tattoos?" Finn asked.

Ronan grinned. "Luke."

That joke had been the one that got me that first date with Luke the Star Wars fan. Damn, I had tried to move on, and Henry sabotaged each and every one of those relationships. Some of them had only lasted a few dates until he sunk his claws into them.

But those breakups didn't crush my heart like it did when Willow explained she wanted to be someone's first choice.

"So, what did Willow say exactly?" Ronan asked.

"That I needed to think about if I really wanted the relationship. She felt like she pushed me into it. Like I'm not ready," I explained.

Maybe that was why I didn't notice she kept asking me

out all those times. But that didn't mean she pushed me into a relationship I wasn't ready for.

"But she knows how you feel, right?" Ronan asked.

"Of course."

Finn narrowed his eyes. "Did you tell her how you feel?"

"No."

"So...your girlfriend told you she wanted to go on a break because she didn't think you were all in on the relationship, and you...didn't fight for her?" Finn asked. "Didn't even tell her you loved her to give her some reassurance?"

"What's fucking wrong with you?" Ronan asked.

I rubbed my scruffy jaw. "I don't know, okay? I couldn't get the words to come out."

Finn steepled his hands over his face. "Ronan, hit him for me."

I ducked out of the way before Ronan could give me a slap.

Ronan stared down into his beer bottle before speaking. "She has a point."

"What do you mean?" I asked.

"You let Henry ruin your chances of moving on. He gets into your partner's head, and you don't fight for them. Like you didn't fight for Willow tonight," he explained.

"That's true," Finn agreed.

Okay, fair point.

"So," Ronan began, weighing his words, "you need to do some reflection to figure out if you're serious about her."

"But—"

Ronan held up a hand. "No. Take an actual break from her. Be apart and figure out if this is what you want. Because if Willow's who your heart desires, you have to fight for her. And you haven't proven that to her by walking away tonight."

He had a lot of advice for someone who let his ex-wife take everything in the divorce. But his words rang true. I let Henry butt into my love life whenever I tried to move on, and I never stood up for those relationships. I let them slip through my fingers because it was easier to go back to what I knew.

"Do you want to be dragged around by the dick by Henry your whole life?" Finn asked.

I scrunched up my nose at his coarse words. "Of course not."

"Then Ro's right. Maybe this break will do you both some good."

Deep down, I knew they were right, that Willow was right to hit pause on our relationship, but my heart was about to burst from the pain. The anguish on her face tonight cut me to my core. I didn't want Henry back. Not by a long shot. But I needed to figure out what I really wanted. Willow deserved that.

CHAPTER TWENTY-SIX

WILLOW

I made a huge mistake. A big, awful, dumb mistake. And I knew that from the moment I watched Lachlan's forlorn figure walk out of my apartment. Maybe out of my life forever.

Why didn't I let him speak? Why did I let him walk out like that?

"Willow!" Matteo's yell snapped me out of my daze.

"Huh?" I asked and realized the drip coffee I was pouring was running over the cup. "Fuck, shit, bitch!"

Heat crept up my neck, knowing there were customers waiting for their coffee and there was no way they missed my slew of swears. That was not a good look for the owner of the shop.

I set the cup down and rushed over to the sink. Matteo took over, grabbing the customers their coffee. After inspecting my hand, I dashed off to my office to hide. Leaving Matteo in the lurch during a rush wasn't something a good boss did, but I hadn't been myself the past couple of weeks.

I paid bills and did inventory in the office while the hours ticked by. Then, I spent a long time scheduling our social media posts and futzing with the seasonal menu for fall and winter. I pulled a sales report to tell me what sold the most, but I also wanted to have an experimental item on the menu.

Matteo's shift ended, and Kelly took over while I pulled more resumes and called new candidates. Kelly told me last night she was pregnant again, and while I was happy for her and Jack, that meant I was back to the grind of filling out staffing. She promised she'd come back because she knew I was stressed about Siobhan leaving. The good news was that Siobhan told me she and Killian talked about it, and childcare while they both worked nights wasn't ideal. She'd be quitting the pub and returning to the coffee shop after her maternity leave. I felt guilty for being glad about that because Siobhan loved the pub.

I needed a stiff drink by the time I finished sifting through potential employees. My new hires had been the best out there, hence why they got the jobs and these other people didn't. I was in for some long hours soon. At least then, I'd stop thinking about Lachlan so much.

I played with the bracelets on my wrists, my brain replaying all my missteps by letting him go like that. I hadn't told him the worst part and the reason I couldn't get over what his ex said. After I blocked Henry from my personal social media accounts, he sent messages to the shop's accounts reiterating that Lachlan would get bored with me and go back to him. That might have been what pushed me over the edge.

I was still going through the paperwork when Kelly

appeared in the office doorway. "Hey, we're gonna shut down for the night. You okay?"

"Sure. Just looking for your replacement."

She frowned. "I'm coming back you know I love the shop. You can't get rid of me or Jack that easily."

I waved her off. "Head out. I'll lock up in a little."

"Willow, you sure you're okay? Matteo told me about your incident earlier."

I nodded. "Fine. Distracted by all the other stuff that needs to get done. All good."

She pursed her lips and turned to leave, but then she spun back around. "This doesn't have to do with the fact that a certain photographer hasn't been around in a while?"

I plastered on a fake smile that her narrowed-eyed expression told me she didn't buy for a second. "I'm fine. Don't worry about it."

"Willow."

"It's fine!"

She studied me for a second but then shook her head. "Okay, if you say so, boss."

I was plunged into silence at her departure, allowing me to finish the admin work I'd been putting off.

My phone buzzed, and I pulled it out, noticing a text from Mindy.

Dread tightened around my chest. It took her long enough.

MINDY: You have a lot of explaining to do.

I didn't reply.

Instead, I closed the shop and headed upstairs to my apartment. I opened my freezer, not having the energy to make anything, and pulled out a frozen meal. I popped it in the microwave and watched blankly as it spun around on the tray. When it was ready, I ate in front of my TV, staring at the black screen.

A couple of weeks ago, I sat Lachlan down on this couch and asked him to think about our relationship and if he really wanted me. Having not heard a peep from him since felt like the answer I had been looking for. His brothers had come around the shop a few times, but I hid in the back like a coward, not wanting to endure the wrath of one of the Murphy Brothers.

My phone buzzed again, and I rolled my eyes at the onslaught of texts from Mindy.

MINDY: Stop ignoring me!

MINDY: Okay, I warned you. Open up!

My eyebrows knitted together until my doorbell rang. Well, she had taken longer than I thought she would.

With a sigh, I dragged my feet to the front door and down the steps. Outside, Mindy was in all her pink glory, but her arms were crossed over her chest, and her gaze was like stone.

"Oh we're having a talk tonight for sure," she spat out.

She breezed past me, her high heels click-clacking against the steps as she climbed them to my front door. I hung my head and marched up the steps after her. In my apartment, she rifled through my cabinets, looking for a wine glass, the bottle already open, sitting out on the counter. I stared blankly at her making herself at home in my kitchen.

She held up a French manicured fingernail while she took a sip of wine. "Okay, I'm here to tell you one important thing."

"Okay."

"Whatever that fuckface told you at the art show was to fuck with your head. That's what Henry does. I'm not sure why he hasn't moved on to his next unfortunate partner, but he's made it his goal to destroy Lachlan. So, we're not gonna listen to a word he says, got it?"

Her raised eyebrow told me she meant business. I forgot how intimidating Mindy could be.

"Okay," I whispered.

"So we're gonna talk to Lachs and tell him you were confused and you don't want to break up."

I dropped myself into one of my kitchen chairs with a frustrated sigh.

Mindy downed the rest of her wine and settled into a chair across from me. "Go on. I'm waiting."

"It's not that simple," I began.

She arched a perfectly sculpted eyebrow. "So, explain it to me."

I blew out a breath. "I pushed him into this relationship. I'm temporary until Lachlan goes back to Henry."

She pointed a finger at me. "That's bullshit. Don't let that evil man get into your head. I know that's not what you think. Do you love Lachlan?"

"So much..." I whispered.

"Yeah, I thought so. So, here's what you're going to do. You have an adult conversation with your boyfriend. Doesn't have to be tonight, but it better be this week, or else I'm coming back here and forcing it. Do you understand?"

Her voice was commanding, and her face as cold as stone. Telling me if I didn't obey, the consequences would be dire.

"Okay."

"Okay?" she repeated. "Tell me you'll be an adult and talk to Lachlan?"

"Yes. I'll talk to him," I promised.

"Good."

She whirled out of my apartment as quick as she came, giving me whiplash. Mindy was a force to be reckoned with, and I appreciated it because she said what I needed to hear, even if I didn't like it.

I stared in her wake, trying to process what had happened. The much-needed drink was calling my name. I trudged over to the counter, found a clean wine glass, and poured myself a heavy helping. I chugged it down in an unladylike fashion, searching for that liquid courage. Then I poured another.

I slumped away to my bedroom, glass in hand, and sat against my headboard. The rose quartz crystal sat on my bedside table, and I grabbed it between my fingers, hoping the object could give me a sign of what to do. Pulling out my phone, I scrolled through the photos of me and Lachlan. Of all our adventures together since we became a couple. My heart sank to my stomach at how it physically ached to be without him.

I rubbed the crystal between my fingers again, and then I took the plunge and found his contact in my phone.

ME: Can we talk? I'd like to know where we stand.

CHAPTER TWENTY-SEVEN

LACHLAN

*A*fter two weeks of reflecting and torturing myself, I came to a conclusion: I wanted Willow more than I wanted anything in my life, and I needed to win her back.

I knew it that very first day when I woke up in a cold bed. And then when I couldn't bring myself to step into her coffee shop. Or how my heart ached when I thought about her. I let those morose thoughts marinate for a week until I realized what I needed to do.

I'd show her how I saw her from behind my lens by gathering all the photos I took of us while we were dating and putting them together in a photo album. My emotions would come out in my art like they always did. My brothers said it wasn't enough of a gesture, but Mindy sat down with me and helped pick the best selections.

I was sliding in the last photo and flipping through the pages when Mindy breezed through my office. There was determination on her face, alerting me to be afraid.

"What's with you?" I asked

"It's settled."

"What is?"

"Go talk to your girl. Because this sad puppy dog Lachlan has been terrible to work with."

Before I could ask what she meant, my phone vibrated on my desk. I shot her a suspicious look before opening my notifications.

My heart beat like a siren at seeing a text message from Willow.

> WILLOW: Can we talk? I'd like to know where we stand.

That did nothing to calm my anxiety. It wasn't a plea for me to come back, or I hate you and we're done for good. But it was a start.

> ME: Can I see you tonight?

> WILLOW: Okay.

Mindy came around to stand behind me, studying the photos. "These are great. You shoot her like she's the only woman in the world."

"She's the only person I want. I need her to know that."

"Good. Because you were so crabby at the wedding yesterday. That couple was so annoying, I don't think they noticed, but other clients will. So, none of that shit."

I frowned. Yeah, that was not good, but I'd rectify this soon. Once I had Willow back, I wouldn't feel like a black cloud was following me everywhere I went.

I closed the book and stood. "She wants to talk now."

A smug, satisfied smile spread across Mindy's face. "Good. Go get your girl."

"Lock up."

"On it, boss."

I left the studio and walked next door. The outer door to Willow's apartment was unlocked again, and I clomped up the staircase, each step feeling heavier than the last. My heart pounded in my chest, wondering if I'd leave tonight without the woman I loved back in my life.

I knocked on the door, and a few seconds passed before it creaked open, and Willow stood behind it. She was dressed comfy for the weather in a tank top and those cute high-waisted shorts. But what I noticed most was the sadness in her eyes.

"Sweetness," I breathed out.

"Hey, Lachlan. Come in."

She led me inside, and we sat on the couch together. The silence engulfed us, both of us too afraid to make the first move.

"Um…" she finally stuttered out.

"I don't want to break up. I never did."

"Not a breakup," she corrected. "A break to figure out what we both want."

I hugged the photo album to my chest. "I never wanted that, Willow. I want you."

"But I pushed you into this."

I shook my head. "I need to show you this."

"What's that?"

I carefully put it on her lap. "Look at it."

Her face was a mask of confusion as she slowly opened the photo album. Her eyes darted across the pages, and she took in all our adventures together. She poured through photos of our paint and sip projects, of our adventures through the taste of Drakesville, and at the fair when she looked ethereal against the fairy lights. I had mixed in some of the more subtle images from her boudoir shoot and then, finally, a photo of us at the art show that Mindy had taken. I had my arm around Willow, and she was staring up at me like I hung all the stars in the sky for her.

"Lachlan, why are you showing me this?"

I put my hand on top of hers. "I want to show you how I see you. How you're the only person I want. Not Henry. You."

"I'm not sure I understand."

"I need to tell you about my relationship with Henry. Then maybe you'll understand."

"Okay."

"I met Henry in college. He was much older and more sophisticated. Fashionable, too. He had his life together, owned his own gallery, and had connections," I began. "We started to date, but I didn't know he was still married. His husband told me I was just a boy toy for Henry, and I broke it off with him. Then after I graduated and started taking on wedding clients, he came back. He explained they divorced, and he was sorry to put me in the middle but would love to start fresh."

"Is he still married?" she asked.

"No. But then the cheating started. The first time I forgave him, and Mindy wanted to claw his eyes out."

She laughed. "That sounds about right."

"He said he changed, but it kept happening. He'd cheat. I'd forgive. Then he'd cheat again. We'd break up, and I'd find someone new, and he'd do what he did to you. I'd try to explain, but naturally, my new partner didn't want the drama. And I'd crawl back to him again. Rinse and repeat, over and over again. It's what he does. All the mind games. But I'm done. That's why I moved home. I needed a fresh start away from him so I could finally move on. Where he couldn't poison the next person against me."

Her face fell. "And I fell into his trap."

"Yes, but I've never fought for anyone else. I let those people slip through my fingers, and I crawled back to a man who was ugly on the inside."

"But not now?"

I cupped her face. "Now, I'm fighting for you. I should have told you that night that I didn't want to break up. That you were it for me. But my words got jumbled inside."

"But I'm still afraid I pushed you into this relationship."

"You did, but not in a bad way. You pushed me to put him behind me. To find someone who deserves my love. I'm done with Henry. I'm not letting him drive you away like he did everyone else."

"But—"

I lifted her chin and gazed into those honey-colored eyes. "Sweetness, please listen to me. I love you with all my heart. When I look into these pretty eyes, your love surrounds me. You're the person I want to wake up to every morning. The one whose smile makes every bad mood melt away."

"I love you, too," she admitted. "That's why what he said hurt. I don't know why I believed him."

"He's charismatic. He'll make you believe any lie he tells you. I wish I never dated him. I'm on good terms with all my other exes except for him."

She grinned. "Me too. Even Kacey."

I groaned. "But she sucks."

"I know. Didn't realize that until we broke up. But she was right that I spent too much time at my business and not enough with her. She didn't make the sacrifice feel worth it, but you do. I'll sacrifice all my sleep just to talk to you for five minutes."

"And so would I. You're it for me, sweet girl. And it took

me the time apart to realize how much I needed you. How you're my muse, my lover, and everything I've always wanted."

"I like being your muse. And I knew I made a mistake the moment you walked out of my door."

I caressed her cheek. "No more break, okay?"

She gave me a confident nod. "No more break. I can't stand being without you. These have been the worst couple of weeks of my life. I love you, too, Lachlan. I've been holding that in for so long because I didn't want to scare you away by telling you too soon."

"I should have told you I loved you sooner and warned you about my ex."

"Can we not talk about him anymore?"

I waggled my eyebrows at her. "Why you got some-where to be?"

"Yes. Beneath you."

"Oh you missed me or something?"

She brought my mouth to hers in a searing ardent kiss. A kiss of forgiveness and understanding. A kiss that told me how much she loved me.

"This is my favorite spot," Willow whispered into my chest as we lay together after several rounds of much-needed lovemaking.

I twirled her dark strands of hair around my finger. "I love you here. Right where you belong."

"Can I tell you something?"

"Mmmhmm."

"I love you."

I grinned and pulled her up to my mouth, giving her

another sweet kiss. "I love you, too. But I have to admit something to you."

"What's that, baby?"

I grinned. I still loved when she called me that. The only person who would ever call me that again if I had my way.

"I love Drakesville. I love this stupid gossipy town where everyone's up in each other's business. But you're the reason I want to stay. Your smiling face bringing me coffee every morning told me I belong here. Because it's not this town, that's home — it's you."

She said nothing but kissed me one more time until we were again making up for all the lost time between us.

Moving back home to Drakesville was the smartest thing I'd ever done. And I'd never regret it. Not when I had my girl at my side.

EPILOGUE

WILLOW

THE NEXT SUMMER

"What about this one?" Lachlan asked, showing me another new home listing on his laptop.

I sipped my coffee as he clicked through the photos of yet another home for sale.

I was so tired of looking at houses, but since he let his lease go a few months ago and moved into my place, we realized how cramped it was. My little place above my shop was great while it was only me living here, but we needed a bigger space for the two of us. The biggest challenge was letting go of my extremely short commute.

"We could put it on the list," I told him.

The house looked okay, but it was a little further out than I wanted.

He sipped on his iced coffee, and it made me smug that

I got him to drink anything other than boring hot black coffee. "How important is walkability for you?"

"Super. That's what I love about this place."

He sighed. "I'm exhausted from going to the laundromat. Or my parents. Or trading babysitting to use Killian's machines."

I frowned. "I know."

"It's only a five-minute drive."

I nodded, letting my thoughts murmur in my brain.

When Lachlan brought up finding a bigger place, I thought he meant a bigger apartment, but then he mentioned the idea of something more permanent. A place we could really settle down together. It both excited and scared me. Moving in together wasn't a big deal to me. I had moved in with so many partners over the years that it didn't phase me. But a house was a big step in commitment.

"Is this too big of a step for you?" he asked, rightfully guessing where my mind was at.

I shook my head.

With Killian and Siobhan getting married in the fall, we talked about if we wanted to get married someday. We did, but we weren't in a rush to do it. I wanted to spend my life with this man, but that scared me.

"You sure, sweetness?" he asked. "We could find a bigger apartment instead until you're ready for that."

"No. A house makes sense. And you're not getting rid of me that easily."

"Good. Because I'm not going anywhere. I'm fighting for you every day."

A smile tugged at my lips, reminding me of how much he fought for me every day. Lachlan was probably the most emotionally mature person I'd dated. The past year had been great. Sure, we had our difficulties like every couple, but we talked it through instead of yelling or giving each other the cold shoulder.

The best part? His ex finally took the hint and stopped bothering him. When he finally showed me all the messages he had put up with while we had been dating, it solidified everything for me. Lachlan would never ever, no way in hell, go back to that asshole. Not if I had anything to say about it.

I checked my phone. "What time do we need to be there?"

"Whenever. It's only a first birthday."

"But that's huge!"

He laughed. "For my brother and Siobhan, not Bean."

I laughed with him.

I hopped up from the bed and riffled through my closet. My hand stopped on an A-line maxi dress in an ombre-style. The colors weren't exactly a match for the bi flag, but close enough that I loved wearing it. I wore it to pride last month, and everyone got what I was doing with it.

I changed into it and put on my wedge heels. I settled at my vanity, doing my hair and makeup while Lachlan scrolled through home listings. It would take him like two seconds to throw on a pair of jeans and t-shirt. He was so boring sometimes, but I loved him.

I put the finishing touches on my mascara while he searched for our gifts, making sure we had everything.

"Is this for the baby?" he asked me, holding up what looked like a wrapped painting canvas.

Oh. I was planning on giving him that later.

"No. That's for you."

He raised an eyebrow at me. "For now?"

"Sure."

He tore the wrapping off the canvas, and his eyes widened at what he saw. "Oh...sweetness."

I grinned, looking at the moon phase painting he tried to buy from me last year. "We can put it above our bed."

"In the new house," he said.

"In the new house," I agreed.

He set the painting down and bent to cup my face. "I love it."

"I know."

He gave me a quick kiss but then darted away over to the dresser. I tilted my head, studying his action with curiosity. He took something out of his sock drawer and walked back over to me, his footsteps slow as molasses.

"What's going on?" I asked.

"It might be time to give this to you. Maybe it will help you understand why I want us to buy a house so bad."

He handed me a felt ring box. My eyes widened. Was this what I thought it was?

He went to his knees and opened the box for me, showing me a beautiful white gold ring with a round sapphire in the center and two tiny diamonds on each side. It was simple and elegant and absolutely perfect.

"It's my favorite color," I breathed.

"Mmmhmm. I know my lady looks good in blue," he said.

My heart launched into my throat. "Oh, Lachlan. Is this... are you..."

"Willow, I want to share a life with you. Forever if I get my way. I love your cozy apartment, but I want the house and the marriage. And maybe a dog, too."

"And a cat," I interjected.

A smile crooked against his mouth. "And a cat."

"Will you ask me already?"

He put a finger to my lips. "Be a good girl and be patient."

"I'm so patient, baby."

"You so are," he agreed. "Willow Rivers, will you make me the luckiest guy in all of Drakesville and marry me?"

I nodded, trying so hard to not let the tears fall and ruin my makeup. "Hell yes."

He laughed and slid the ring onto my finger. "God, can't wait to see how it shines when you wrap your hand around my cock."

I swatted at his chest. "You perv."

"You love it."

"Mmmhmm," I murmured and pulled him down for a kiss.

I had not been expecting an engagement today. But him pushing to buy a house made a lot more sense. This was a lot quicker than I was expecting, but when you knew, you knew. And I knew more than anything that Lachlan was my heart.

He wrenched away. "Stop kissing me like that, or we'll be late."

"Then let's be late."

He could only grin back at me.

I had to take another shower and redo my makeup by the time we were through, but it was so worth it while Lachlan and I were walking hand in hand to his brother's house. The sapphire on my hand sparkled under the warm summer sun and made the giddiness run through me. One day, he would be my spouse, and I loved thinking about that.

He guided me down a street before we got to his brother's house. We stopped in front of a white twin home with a FOR SALE COMING SOON sign on the lawn. And there was our realtor, Mary, standing in the driveway waving to us.

"We need to make a detour, remember?" Lachlan asked.

Uhh no? But we had gone on so many home tours and open houses, it didn't surprise me that I forgot.

I shot him a glance. "All these terrible homes are blending together."

He laughed. "This one will be good, I promise."

Like a lot of the homes in our town, it was a twin, which meant it shared a wall with another house. That wasn't a problem for me. But it had a driveway for multiple cars, which was something hard to find with this style.

Mary eyed my finger as we approached. "It looks like congratulations are in order."

I beamed. "Thank you."

The front porch was cute and the perfect place to have a cup of coffee in the morning. I already loved it. Mary led us inside, showing us the spacious living area that led into the dining room and kitchen. There was a mud room on the main level where the laundry was located.

"No more going to the laundromat," Lachlan said.

We looked outside first. There was a cute patio area with a fire pit and a decently sized fenced-in backyard.

"She loves it already," Lachlan told Mary.

"This could be what you're looking for."

She led us back inside, leading us up the steps. There were three bedrooms upstairs and a full bath. The bedrooms weren't that big, but that wasn't a big deal for me. We'd take the biggest one for us, turn one of them into our office, and the other would be a guest room.

It was perfect. It wasn't too big for the two of us, and maybe we could get that dog and cat we'd joked about.

Lachlan took my hand as we stood in the living room, surveying the house again. "What do you think?"

"I love it. Let's put an offer in."

"Finally," Mary said.

We had looked at so many houses that she was tired of us. We talked about details with her, and then we headed over to Killian's.

"How far was the walk?" I asked Lachlan.

He checked his watch. "I timed it. Six minutes."

That was perfect. The perfect distance to our shops while being tucked away in our own little haven.

I squeezed his hand. "I have a great feeling about this."

He squeezed back. "Me too."

"I love you. I'm so glad you moved home."

"Me too, sweetness. Now, are you ready to face my family? They're going to clock that ring immediately."

"They're my family, too."

He frowned. "Remember you love me, and you agreed to become a Murphy."

I laughed. "I am so ready. Lead me there."

ACKNOWLEDGMENTS

Book two in the Murphy Brothers is now complete and I hope you enjoyed it.

When I first started writing this series, I planned to write the order of books by the brothers' ages. After writing the first book and realizing how much Willow appeared, it just made more sense to tackle Lachlan and Willow's book next.

I'm especially proud that this book celebrates Queer Joy with another Bi4Bi couple. I really enjoy writing that and in the current political landscape of my country it feels like an act of rebellion right now.

Ronan and Freya are next and I'm really excited but nervous for you all to read their story. Stay tuned for more info about that one coming soon!

ALSO BY DANICA FLYNN

PHILADELPHIA BULLDOGS

Take The Shot

Score Her Heart

Against The Boards

The Chase

The Fake Out

Game On

Risky Play

MACGREGOR BROTHERS BREWING COMPANY

Accidentally In Love

Trapped In Love

Temporarily In Love

THE MURPHY BROTHERS

Protecting Her

ABOUT THE AUTHOR

Danica Flynn is a marketer by day, and a writer by nights and weekends. AKA she doesn't sleep! She is a rabid hockey fan of the Philadelphia Flyers. When not writing, she can be found hanging with her partner, playing video games, and reading a ton of books.

www.ingramcontent.com/pod-product-compliance
Lightning Source LLC
Chambersburg PA
CBHW052028240626
47153CB00006B/2007

* 9 7 8 1 9 5 7 4 9 4 1 8 0 *